KIDULT

KIDULT

KAREN McCAHON

BRAMMER
BOOKS

for my mum

1

THE HUMAN STALACTITE

There's a bang, like a bomb going off, followed by a scream. I was asleep, now I'm not, but I wouldn't say I'm awake. What time is it? I fumble for my phone – 4.07am. Maybe I was dreaming.

"HEEELP!"

Jesus Christ. No, that scream was real. It's Mum. What the hell's happened? Burglars? Must be burglars. I need a weapon. Where's a weapon? I flop out of bed and land in a heap of shoes and dirty clothes. I grope around for something sharp. Clink. Cereal bowl and spoon. A spoon? Nah, no one's scared of a spoon. Twang. Aha. My guitar. I could do a jab to the belly with the pointy end or whack 'em in the face with the other. I clutch it to my chest and tiptoe across the landing.

"Heeellp." That's no scream now, it's a whimper. Oh god, she's fading. Maybe she's been stabbed and now the life is oozing out of her. I'm way too freaked to open that door. What if they attack me? Maybe I should call the police. No, it'd take too long. If she's dying she needs help now.

I ease open the door, just a chink, and brace myself for whizzing bullets. With only the light from the streetlamp limping through the curtains, I can hardly see a thing. Ever so slowly my eyes adjust. I can make out a shadowy figure, like a freakishly tall man. Eh? His head's almost hitting the ceiling. My god there's a monster in there! Big deep breath Jess, calm yourself down. Look away; then look again. That's no monster, it's Mum. I flick on the light. And there she is, hanging from a hole in the ceiling like a human stalactite. Bits of paint and plaster cling to her polka-dot pyjamas and her hair is white with dust.

"I was in the loft," she whimpers. "My feet... I fell right through. Help me. My fingers are slipping."

Jeeez, she's gonna break her neck. What to do, what to do?

"Hurry, please."

Oh my god. OK, up to the loft, two rungs at a time. It's dark up here and there's no proper floor, just roof beams and orange insulation fluff. One foot wrong and I'll be dangling from the ceiling like a dusty chandelier.

I wobble my way towards her. Must NOT put a foot in that fluff. There she is, just ahead, but where am I supposed to stand? OK, one foot on a beam to the left, the other on a beam to the right. I reach through the hole.

"Give us your hands. Go on."

"No. I'll fall."

I grab her arms. "Wrap your fingers round my wrists."

"NO!"

"For god's sake Mum." She's not normally like this. "Just do it, or I'll go back to bed and leave you to it."

Whimpering, she grabs hold of me. I heave, but she's bloody heavy. How can someone so thin weigh so much? I can't do it. I can't get her up. My back's breaking and my fingers are slipping. I'm gonna drop her. Oh crap. I don't wanna kill my mum.

"WHAT THE...?"

Jeez! Who was that? I peer past Mum's dusty blonde head – and there in the doorway stands another blonde, all bug-eyed and bewildered. Ollie! When did he get back? My brother's been away for months at his summer job in the Highlands.

"Oh Ollie, thank god. I'm gonna drop her, help me!"

Ollie saunters into the room. He's in no hurry. His big blue eyes are rimmed with red, but he still looks disgustingly good. Why do I never look like that? I'm just a mongrel, me, lumbered with the worst bits of both parents, while he gets all the best. It should have been me that got the platinum waves. Hair that good is wasted on a boy. And those cheekbones, och don't get me started.

What's he doing now? Why's he sitting down? My feet are being cut in two by those ruddy roof beams and my back is about to snap, but oor Ollie is making himself comfy. Now he's laughing. Is he drunk? I bet he's been down the pub.

"WHAT'S SO FUNNY?"

He's laughing so much he can't answer. He's actually rolled onto his side clutching his stomach.

"Ollie, I need your help or else Mum's gonna..."

"...or else what, Jess?" he can still hardly speak, "or else she might break a toenail?"

Oh. He's right you know. Mum's only a few feet off the floor; she'll do less damage jumping down than getting hauled through a jaggy hole. I feel like an idiot. Trust him – he's such a know-it-all – but in my defence I was still asleep when I came to her rescue. Where the hell was he?

"Listen, Mum. If you let go of my hands Ollie will catch you."

But she's not having it. She's gripping on tighter, digging

her fingernails into my wrists. Why's she acting so helpless? My mum's not this quivering kitten. My mum's strong, capable, calm in a crisis. She's also supple from all the yoga she does, so why not just drop to the floor?

"Ollie! Just… grab her!"

Ollie wraps his arms round Mum's legs and succeeds in pulling her off me. But now he can't get his balance. With his arms round her knees and the rest of her towering above him, he's completely top heavy. He staggers backwards and forwards, like he's about to toss the caber. Then he makes a final bow-legged dash towards the bed where they both land in a grimy heap.

Well, I refuse to do the balance beam back to the loft ladder, my feet are louping enough already, so I lower myself down through the hole and yell on Ollie to catch me. He's in no mood. He has his arms folded all stubborn like. "You got yourself up there, Jessie-girl, you can damn well get yourself down."

So I launch myself at him – slicing through the air like a missile, splatting us onto the floor. "OW!" He elbows me off and wallops me in the arm. I wallop him back and we're kids again, tussling on the floor. But Mum is awfully quiet – she should be shouting by now. She's not hurt is she? I sit up and peep over the bed. There she is – curled in her duvet, sobbing in silence.

I scramble to my feet. "Mum! You OK? Have you broken something?" No answer. I get this lurching fear in the pit of my stomach. Why won't she speak? "Mum! What is it?"

"The ceiling." Her voice is all weird.

"You're upset about the ceiling? But it's only a ceiling. You're the one that always says, so long as everyone's safe…"

"It's not just a ceiling," she says. "It's everything. Everything's broken. There's a hole in me and it's just… it's black…"

"Oh."

Well, what do you say to that, eh? "Aw come on Mum, it's the middle of the night, you're tired. It'll seem much better in the morning. Let's go have a cup of tea."

She shakes her head and buries her face in her pillow. I hover for a bit but I can tell she's not for budging so Ollie and me trudge down to the kitchen together.

"What on earth was all that about?" I whisper, grabbing the kettle and giving it a shake.

"Mmmmm?" Ollie doesn't seem terribly interested. He's got his head in the fridge and is flinging out furry tomatoes. "Where's all the effing food?" he cries, as they drop with a squelch to the floor by his feet. I peer over his shoulder. Yep, the shelves are bare all right. He straightens up and glowers through puffy, beer soaked eyes. "Is this it? Is this all there is to eat?" I shrug; I don't have much of an appetite these days, but Ollie's desperate for some post-pub munchies. "Knew I should've got a kebab," he grumbles, nudging shut the door with his bum. He drops a festering cucumber on top of the toms and an icky, grey juice snakes across the lino. I step over it and switch on the kettle.

Ollie's at the Cornflakes now, shaking empty packs and wailing, "Where have they all gone?" Not that he actually waits for an answer, for he suddenly drops to his knees and begins scooping up dust bunnies from under the cupboard doors. I'm not joking. He springs up clutching a mound of grey fluff. "This place is like... totally minging."

"So? Who cares about a bit of dirt? Are you like the clean police or what?" Keep calm, Jess; don't get in a fight, not on his first night back.

"I just don't get it," he says for the umpteenth time. "This is like... filth."

"I thought students were supposed to like living in dirt."

"No Jess, students do not like living in dirt. We're forced to live in fleapits because we've no money, that's why it's always good to come home to a nice clean house."

I look round the kitchen through Ollie's eyes. Yeah he's right, it has got really rank. Grimy granite worktops and a crusty range cooker. Still, he's really starting to pee me off. "We've no time for cleaning," I hiss, blowing the bunnies out his hands. "Or cooking. Looking after Gran's been like a full time job. She wees everywhere, she wanders, she..." "Oh, yeah, sorry. Sorry. I forgot she'd moved in. Nightmare is it?" He has the cheek to look sheepish, while still scouring the corners for cobwebs.

"Nightmare? Nightmare?" I screech. "That like doesn't even..."

"Wait. Where is she?"

"Who?"

"Gran."

"Er, well upstairs asleep, I s'pose."

"Through that racket?"

Oh god, no. She must have escaped again. "Check her room Ollie, I'll..." But then the phone's ringing and there's no point checking her bed, for who calls in the night with good news?

We stare at the phone.

"Are you getting that?" snaps my bro.

"Why me?"

"You live here."

"Well, you're the oldest." Ha! Trump card! Ollie tuts, then snatches up the handset, giving the green button a bad-tempered jab.

"Hello? Oh..." his face has gone white. "Yes, Officer, she

does live here. Yeah... she's my gran." Oh jeez, the police, it must be bad. Is she dead? Has she been mugged? Ollie listens intently then his lips start to twitch. He looks like he's trying not to laugh. Surely not?

"What's happened?" I mouth, but he throws me a frown and turns away.

"Yes, Officer. Of course. We'll be right there." He hangs up.

"What? Is she all right?"

"Yes, she's fine..." Ollie starts to laugh, "but... you'll never believe this, Jess... she's... she's..."

"She's what? For Christ's sake spit it out."

"She's been caught shoplifting."

"Shoplifting? Where?"

"The 24-hour SPAR."

"And that's funny, why?"

"Well, cos she's 80 and she's nicking stuff and..." he shrugs, but he doesn't stop laughing.

I flounce from the kitchen and yell at the bottom of the stairs, "Muuum! We need to go fetch Gran. She's at the SPAR. It's like, urgent." No answer. So now I have to trudge all the way upstairs and still she hasn't moved. Not a muscle. She lies bundled under her duvet like a giant blue grub. "Mum, did you not hear me? You need to come now. Gran's at the SPAR, the police are with her."

Now I've dropped the police bomb, I expect an explosion of panic, but still she doesn't move. So I yank off the covers, but she stays curled on her side, completely rigid, like rigor mortis has set in. "C'mon, Mum," I groan. "You need to get some clothes on." I tug her arm and she comes to life a bit. Stands up, even opens her wardrobe door, but she doesn't get dressed, just plucks out a raincoat and fastens it over her pyjamas.

"Seriously? You're going out in your PJs? This isn't Possil, you can't do that!" She looks a right state – like an old lady herself. Her hair's grey with dust and her face is deathly pale.

Ollie appears. "You not washing that off Mum?"

If she hears she doesn't show it, for she simply walks downstairs as if in a trance. I yank on a pair of jeans and go stumbling after her, tripping out my trainers as I follow her out the door. "Mum! Wait up, we're coming too." She doesn't say a thing.

I manage to catch up and Ollie's not far behind. Then we amble down our road – Mum in the middle, me and Ollie linked on either side. I cannot believe my mum's out in her jammies. What if someone sees us? The suburbs of Scotland can be very judgemental, you know. I feel like I'm being watched. The bay windows of the sandstone villas bulge out at us like eyes. But it's five in the morning; the road's pretty much deserted, except for a few plump cats.

The SPAR's only round the corner so it isn't much of a walk but we can hear the commotion before we even get inside. The lassie that does the night shift there is a real skank. She's going mental – calling my wee granny all sorts, demanding she gets flung in jail.

The policeman just looks bemused. "So tell me again what she stole," he says, his eyes twinkling at us.

"I've already told ye ten times – two packets of Wotsits and a bottle of limeade."

"Uh-huh," says the policeman, pretending to jot it all down in his notebook. "That's very serious indeed."

"You're takin' the piss," screeches the lassie, "don't think ah don't know when someone's takin' the piss. But that's no the point is it? Theft is theft. And she battered me too. Look!" The girl rolls up her sleeve and points to some angry red welts just above her wrist.

"And when did she do that?" asks the policeman.

"Well, when ah tried tae grab the bag off her, she dug her fingers in tae ma arm and gave me a Chinese burn."

"Mmmm. I see. A Chinese burn," he says, still fake scribbling in his book. Gran's doing her best to look all frail and innocent, but don't let her fool you. She's been twisting my wrist all summer and it really bloody hurts. The policeman snaps shut his notebook and looks properly at Mum. "Are you okay, dear?" he says, his brown eyes crinkled with concern.

"Yes, I'm fine. I'm just… I'm just…" Mum trails off and the policeman raises his eyebrows at me.

"Is she all right?"

I shake my head. "We can't go on like this. It's too much. We're not getting any sleep. Mum… well, Mum's… look at her, she's worn out."

The policeman nods. "Oh I know all about looking after granny," he says. "My old nan had dementia and my mother was in bits. Has your Mum not got anyone to help?"

I shake my head, "Nah, my dad lives in Dubai," with an obnoxious bitch half his age, "and Mum's an only child. Gran's got sisters and stuff, but they live in Ireland."

The policeman looks all decisive. "Listen, tell you what, why don't I take these ladies down the station and ring social services, see if I can get a bit of help. Maybe some respite care?"

"NO!" cries Mum. "I'm not putting my mother in a home."

"No one's suggesting that. Just a wee break, that's all. Let you catch up on a bit of sleep then you get her back by the end of the week. What's there to lose, eh? Come on, the pair of you. We'll stop at the bakery on the way. What do you say?" Gran seems quite taken with the handsome officer; she's always had a thing for men in uniform. So with a wicked wee smile, she slips an arm through his.

"That's it?" cries the shop assistant. "She assaults me. And you feed her cake?"

"Watch it, hen," snaps the cop. "One day, that could be you. So show some compassion, eh?"

"As if," murmurs the girl, but she turns away to fiddle with the morning papers.

Well, Mum clearly doesn't have the strength to argue, so when the policeman opens the door she follows him to the squad car, though you can tell she isn't happy.

I call after her, "See you in a bit Mum, yeah?" But she doesn't even turn round.

Ollie, though, is looking a lot more cheerful. He's picked up a basket and is piling it high with hangover food – bacon, eggs, crusty rolls and milk. The skanky shop girl stares at him, chewing on her nails. When the basket's full he plonks it in front of her and she smirks like he's a right eejit.

"Yer havin' a laugh, right?"

"Eh?" Ollie looks puzzled, though I can tell where this is heading.

"You seriously think I'm serving you? After what that old bat did tae me? Sorry mate. You're barred. The lot of ye. So go on, scram." The girl picks up the basket and slams it down on her side of the counter, well out of Ollie's reach.

"But... but... you can't do that."

"Oh aye? Just watch me."

"I'll... I'll ..."

"Come on Ollie, just leave it." I grab his arm and bundle him out the shop. He doesn't protest; he's way too hungover for a full on argy-bargy. So hunched in defeat, we slope off home, bellies growling from the aroma of hot, crispy rolls.

* * *

After that, we both go back to bed for a bit and I manage to doze right through till lunchtime. When I get downstairs again, Ollie's already up, ransacking the cupboards for food.

"Mum back yet?"

"Nope." He's in a right grump.

I find some mouldy bread, scrape off the green bits and pop it in the toaster.

"Wanna bit?"

"No!" he snaps.

"Jeez. I was only asking. So... how long you back for?"

"A few days, then I'm off to Europe." Oh yeah. Ollie's going backpacking before uni starts back. Life of bloody Riley, eh? It's no time at all till I go back to school, he's got ages yet.

"No fair," I sulk. "Everyone's been abroad this summer except me. You should see all their pictures on Facebook. Amy went to Tuscany. She's got this awesome tan, but she also came back with a bit of a belly – too much pizza and ice-cream." Amy's my best mate. She only lives round the corner, so I've known her all my life.

"I didn't think Miss Vain did carbs."

"She's off them again now. Though I thought she looked quite nice with a bit of a tum, but you know how she is..."

"Oh..." We turn to stare at the back door. The handle rattles and Mum shuffles inside, no sign of Gran though.

"Where's Gran?" asks Ollie. "Is she okay?"

Mum ignores him and perches on a stool by the island in the centre of the kitchen. I pluck my toast from the toaster, pick up some jam and mosey over to join her. I sit down and open the jar, but then Mum does her best to put me off my grub. She keeps fumbling in her pocket and pulling out wads of toilet tissue, which she dumps beside my plate.

"Oi! Watch it. I don't need snot on my toast. Bad enough the mould..."

"What is it Mum, you lost something?" Ollie's hovering beside her all worried.

Oh hell, I know what she's looking for – Ollie's about to discover Mum's guilty secret. I push aside my plate and brace myself for fireworks.

"Got them!" Mum pulls out a pack of cigarettes with triumph. She slips one out and sparks it up; inhaling deeply before letting out a long, slow sigh of contentment.

"WHAT? Cigarettes! You're smoking! She's smoking." If Ollie were a cartoon character, his eyes would be out on stalks. I've no idea what that lad gets up to at uni, but it's clear that when he's home, he likes the house to be clean and his mum to be conventional. He turns on me. "Did you know about this? Why didn't you stop her?"

"How Ollie? She's 48 years old! What do you expect me to do?"

"I dunno... just... just... hide them!" Ollie lunges for her pocket, but I push him off.

"For god's sake, stop being ridiculous. So what if she's had a few puffs over the summer, it's been a very stressful time. She'll give up again soon, won't you Mum? She used to smoke at uni you know..."

"She'll damn well give up now." Ollie snatches the cigarette from her hand and throws it in the sink where it fizzles and dies in the tea stained water. Mum doesn't react. Just pulls out another and strikes an extra long match, the kind for lighting barbecues – she must have snaffled them from the camping box.

Ollie stares at her like she's from Planet Zorg.

"Did you have a nice night out dear?" she says and takes a deep drag, like she has no idea Ollie's in meltdown. Why's she so calm? Where's the tears at shipping Gran off to respite?

Ollie's thrown too. "What night out? Oh... yeah it was okay, but... where's Gran? Is she in a home?"

"No. She's in the hospital."

"The hospital? Why?"

Mum shrugs. "Urine infection or something. So did you go clubbing too, Jess?"

What? "I'm 15, Mum, I can't get into clubs! Anyway, I was here with you."

"Oh yes, so you were." And sucking on her fag, Mum stares off into space leaving me and our Ollie completely lost for words.

2

THE JAFFA CAKE DIET

Oh god. Ollie's going on and on at Mum. The state of the house, blah, blah, blah. Where's the food? Yak, yak, yak. He's completely doing my head in, but I don't think she's even listening. She looks completely zonked. Spaced out, stoned or something, though she's not the type to do drugs. He's telling her to go shopping – yeah like that's going to happen. Oh, wait a sec. She's actually picked up her bag. Are we gonna get a nice full fridge, groaning with goodies? Actually, Mum's never been much good at getting goodies. Mung beans and lettuce leaves are her idea of a treat. She's always been like this five-a-day fascist, force-feeding us smoothies that look like snot.

Not this summer right enough; she's hardly cooked a thing. Gran and me have been tucking into fish suppers, pot noodles, white toast – it's been brilliant. But Ollie's about to put a stop to that. Spoilsport.

Wow. Mum's actually got her shoes on. Fair play to Ollie, I haven't coaxed her out the house in weeks. Mind you, with her away, what's the bet he starts on me? Think I'll skedaddle for a bit of a snooze. So long sucka, go take a chill pill, for I am off to bed.

* * *

Ooof. How long have I been sleeping? What time is it? Three o'clock. Jeez, must have been up here for hours. And guess what I can hear? Yep, shouting. Ollie's yelling at Mum again, still at least it woke me up. I s'pose I'd better play peacemaker. I'm like the ruddy UN, I am.

"FAGS AND JAFFA CAKES! FAGS AND JAFFA CAKES!" Oh, this is his loudest rant yet. What's she done now?

I peek my head round the kitchen door and Ollie comes hurtling towards me waving a box of Jaffa Cakes.

"Two hours she was gone," he yells, "and what does she come back with, eh? Forty Silk Cut and a packet of Jaffa Cakes."

Yesss! Still no lentil muck. Ollie looks livid though, what's his problem? Jaffa Cakes are nice. "They're biscuits, Ollie, not dog turd. Stop making such a fuss."

"Jeez, Jess. You're as bad as she is! Look at the state of her. How could you let her get in such a state? Jaffa Cakes and fags, Jess, that's Mum's idea of a food shop! Don't you get how serious this is?"

"Fine. I'll go to the shops. What do you want?"

"I don't want anything from you, I want her," he jabs a quivering finger in Mum's direction, "to pull herself together. Do you hear me Mum? You need to get a grip!"

I kick him, right in the shin. How dare he? "You haven't been home for three months, Ollie Brody, what right have you to come marching in here, telling us we can't eat Jaffa Cakes?" I rip open the packet and cram one in my mouth.

"I've been working." He rubs his shin and wrestles the urge to boot me right back.

"Is that what you call it? What's wrong with getting a summer job here? Why d'ye have to go two hundred miles away?"

Ollie throws me a look of contempt. "Look at her, Jess, just look. She's not washing, she's not eating, she's barely even breathing. And you've just stood back and let it happen."

"Fuck off Ollie. Just fuck right off. We've had the summer from hell, me and Mum. So what if she's having a bit of a rest, she's entitled to one after all that stress with Gran."

"She's not resting. She's comatose. It's like invasion of the body snatchers. Where's the yoga, the beans, the new age relaxation shit? That's Mum. Not this chain-smoking, Jaffa cake buying robot. Has she even been working? Has she been doing her column?" Mum's a part-time journalist for the local rag.

"Course she's been working. Christ, she is here you know. Stop talking like she's not here. She's not a child." I turn to her. "You have been doing your column, right?"

She says nothing. Her face is completely blank. No tears, no fury – not a thing. Then she just picks up her car keys and opens the back door.

"Where you going?"

"The shops. We need beans."

I give Ollie this triumphant, told-you-so stare, but he doesn't look convinced.

"Beans, that's nice," he says. "So what you making Mum?"

What is it with him? Why's he trying to catch her out?

Mum shrugs, steps outside and quietly closes the door.

* * *

It's 7 o'clock. 7 o'clock and Mum's not back yet. That's four hours. Does it really take four hours to buy a tin of beans? I don't think so. Ollie's gone way too far this time. We were doing fine till he came back and now he's ruined everything. Where the hell can she be? I can't sit still.

But just look at him, lounging in front of the telly like he hasn't a care in the world. Well, I tell you this, he can bloody well go look for her. I grab the remote and punch the red button.

"Oi. What d'ye do that for?"

"Cos you need to get off your fat ass and go look for my mum. This is all your fault..."

Ollie sits up, sighing. "I'm worried too Jess, but what can I do? I don't have a car."

"Well... get on yer bike then."

He raises an eyebrow, but bends down to slip on his trainers. "Where do I even start?"

"Dunno. The tennis club?"

"Really? You think she's gone for a game of tennis?" "Yes... no, oh I don't know. Maybe she met up with a friend?"

Ollie nods. "Yeah. Maybe." Though neither of us believe it. "Look, I'll go in a mo, Jess, but sit down first, I want to talk to you."

I lower myself into Mum's armchair and he squeezes in beside me. I don't want to talk. I want him out there looking for her, but this is typical of him, wasting time when he could be doing something useful.

"I think she's ill, Jess, really ill."

I sigh and rest my head on his shoulder. I knew this was coming, though I don't think he's right. She's just stressed that's all, but now Gran's in hospital, Mum can get back to normal. Bleeuch, he's got B.O. "You pong," I say, squeezing my nose.

Ollie snorts, "Well, it is seriously warm for Scotland. You should get out there, Jess – go catch some rays. See how white you are, you're becoming a vampire." He holds a tanned arm against mine and I have to admit I'm pretty pasty.

"Actually, it goes with my new look – I'm going more grungy these days. Mainly because I can't be bothered ironing and Mum's given up doing the laundry. What do you think?"

I look up and Ollie manages a smile. "Yeah, I'd say grunge is more your thing. You're far too smart for Amy's airhead look."

"You mean far too fat."

"You're not fat, just normal. In fact…" He squints down at me. "You've got really thin Jess. Have you been eating?"

"Ssshh!"

"What?"

"I thought I heard something."

We both go quiet and sure enough there's the crunch of tyres on gravel.

"She's home?" We try to leap out the armchair, but with both of us in there we're sort of wedged stuck.

"Ooof. Jess, I take it back, your bum's like a beach ball."

"Shut it you. Just… twist round a bit. There." Free at last, we go stumbling into the kitchen just as Mum comes through the door, clutching a bright orange shopping bag. Well, that's good. There's definitely stuff in that bag, but she's looking a bit vacant.

"Oh thank god." Ollie engulfs her in a gangly man hug. But she doesn't hug back, just stands completely rigid like a kid braving a cuddle from a creepy uncle.

"Where've you been?" Ollie un-crushes her and scans her face.

"It was the ceiling."

"What was the ceiling?" Ollie looks puzzled and annoyed by the whole cryptic, weird vibe, but he's trying not to lose it again. So he takes the bag and peers inside. "You managed to get your beans then… oh… bleach. No food, only bleach. Why so much bleach?"

Something in her face scares me. It's gone from blank to shifty, as if we've sprung her doing something naughty.

"I couldn't do it," is all she says, as she trudges out the kitchen, handbag trailing behind her on the floor.

"COULDN'T DO WHAT?" Ollie screams after, but there's no reply.

"What? What is it? Ollie! You're scaring me. What's the matter?" Why does he keep staring at that bleach?

"I think she meant to drink it," he says, ever so quietly.

"NO! Don't be daft. Why would anyone drink bleach?"

Ollie looks at me like I'm an idiot. "Why d'ye think, Jess?"

"To…? No! Mum wouldn't do that. Would she?" Where's she gone? Disappeared back to her pit, no doubt, so I vault upstairs, tripping on the final step and grazing my knee on the rough rope carpet. She's already back in bed, rolled in her duvet in chrysalis mode. It doesn't even look like she's trying to sleep; she's just lying there staring into space.

"Mum! MUM!" She sighs and turns to face the wall. So I run to the other side of the bed and hunker down beside her, gripping her shoulders so she can't roll away. "Mum. Ollie says you were going to drink that bleach. Tell him it's not true. Go on. Tell him."

I point to Ollie who's appeared by my side. He looks scared, tearful, but also coiled with anger as if about to lunge. I know how he feels; I have this awful urge to shake her too.

"Go on. Tell him Mum," I plead.

"I couldn't do it," is all she says – so quietly that at first I don't hear. "I'm sorry. You'd be better off without me, but I couldn't even do that."

"Mum!" Is she really saying she meant to kill herself?

"Mum," I sob, "I love you. What were you doing with the bleach, Mum? Tell us. Please. Tell us it's for the toilet."

Mum closes her eyes like she's trying hard to concentrate. "One day you'll understand," she whispers. "One day you'll realise it would have been the right thing for everyone."

Ollie sinks down onto the bed, face in hands, shoulders heaving with sobs and I think, that's what I should be doing – that is a normal reaction. But what I feel is fury. I want to slap her. Hard. Like, really hard and scream in her face that she is a selfish, lazy woman who ought to get her ass out of bed and look after me like she's supposed to.

And know what else I feel? Embarrassment. Yeah, that's right. I mean why bleach for god's sake? What a stupid way to die. What the hell would we have told folk? Can you imagine? I've no idea what death by bleach is like, but I reckon it's all frothing at the mouth, bulging eyes and projectile vomit. Why not do a Sylvia Plath or a Virginia Woolf – elegant, dignified, CLEAN?

And if I'm honest, I'm terrified too, not just because I don't want to lose her, but because I'm scared she might have passed her madness onto me. It runs in families doesn't it? Will this be me in thirty years? A wreck of a woman, rotting in bed who finally departs by a bottle of Domestos? I couldn't put a kid of mine through that. I just couldn't. I'm never having children. Never.

3

CIGGIES AND CELEBRITIES

I couldn't sleep last night. For some strange reason I kept having nightmares. I had this one where Mum chased me down the road and I knew she was a Zombie and I'd have to chop her head off, but I couldn't bring myself to do it. I woke up more tired than when I went to bed. And completely freaked out too. Still, Amy's on her way round now. That should take my mind off things for a bit. We were supposed to be going into town for some retail therapy, but Ollie says he needs to go buy books for uni, so guess who's stuck on suicide watch.

Still, I'm glad I'll have Amy to keep me company. She's like the anti-suicide. All sort of chirpy and glossy and bursting with bubbles. Seriously, they should put her on prescription and lend her to depressives.

There's the doorbell, that'll be her now. I go skidding into the hall and fling open the front door. "Hey," I cry. I'm so pleased to see her.

God, she looks great. Just look at her – short dress, hair all sleek and nails manicured to perfection. I don't know how she can be bothered with the palaver. I find all that plucking and preening so boring, but Amy never goes out without make up on. She's brought a big pile of magazines, some monster bars of chocolate and a bunch of grapes. She's such a sweetie, but I'm still cranky, so I take one look at the grapes and say, "I'm not sick."

"I never said you were."

"So what's with the grapes?"

"I don't know. I just... thought they looked tasty. I can throw them away if you like."

"No, don't do that." Suddenly those little green pellets look really appealing. I can't remember the last time I had fresh fruit, so I grab a fistful and gobble them up.

"Can I come in?"

"Sorry," I splutter. "Come through. Just prepare yourself. Mum's got even weirder."

Amy raises a perfectly plucked eyebrow. She looks a bit apprehensive, but follows me into the kitchen. Mum's perched on a stool, still in her dressing gown, cigarette in hand.

Amy grabs me by the arm and we hover by the door. "Your Mum's smoking!" she whispers. She looks shocked, but also kinda awestruck. Amy's mum's this dumpy little woman, so she's always thought of mine as a bit... well, glam, I suppose.

"Ollie says she looks like a scrubber."

"Ollie's home?" she screeches. Amy has a thing for my brother. Still Mum doesn't look up.

"Yeah, Ollie's home. He went mental when he saw her smoking."

Amy stares at my mum. "I think she looks like a tragic heroine from an old weepy. Sort of like Marilyn Monroe, beautiful – but with this aching, sadness deep inside."

See that's Amy – all soppy and sweet. She's also got some serious rose-tinted specs cos looking at Mum I can't see a hint of Marilyn Monroe. To me she's more madwoman in the attic. And I tell you this, there's nothing glam about the way she smokes. I tell Amy to come look. She's starting to seem wary though, so I have to yank her by the hand.

"Hey Mum. Amy's here."

Mum looks up and manages a little smile, before returning to the task that requires all her concentration. This is how it goes. She takes one puff of a cigarette, stubs it out, strikes a match and lights it again. Then she takes another puff, stubs it out, re-lights it – you get the idea, over and over again, all day long. There's a massive pile of matches heaped in a cereal bowl. We don't have ashtrays in our house; we've never known someone who smokes before.

"What's she doing?" whispers Amy.

"I have absolutely no idea."

Amy looks scared and I don't want her to be. I want to hang onto that moment when she thought the whole smoking thing was cool, tragic and glamorous. So I slide a cigarette out of Mum's packet and put it in my mouth. It dangles there and Amy giggles.

"Give us a light Mum." I expect Mum to snatch the cigarette, break it in two and toss it in the bin. But she calmly picks up her matches and lights the damned thing. Oh my god – it is absolutely disgusting, like sucking on a gas pipe, only worse. Why would anyone do this? I'm about to chuck it in the sink, when I notice Amy's face; she thinks I look cool. Well, the cigarette might taste filthy, but I like looking edgy, so I'm gonna persevere. Big breath in. Oh man, my throat is on fire. I feel sick and my head's gone all swimmy. I take another drag and slide off my stool. Amy catches me and we clutch each other laughing.

"Can I have one?"

"Sure. Go ahead."

Amy's hand inches forward and slips a cigarette out the pack. Her eyes keep darting at Mum, like she's expecting a slap, but there's no reaction. So Amy lights up and starts puffing away like an old pro.

"Have you smoked before?" Now it's my turn to be shocked.

"Oh, you know. Only once or twice."

Well, it would seem Mum's resignation from parenting has its advantages. I fetch Amy's magazines from the hall and we sit for the rest of the morning, laughing at celebrities and puffing on ciggies (though I don't really inhale, far too painful). By the time Ollie gets back, the kitchen is a fug of smoke.

"For fffff.... sake! What is going on in here?" Ollie stands paralysed in the doorway, the August sun blazing in behind. I wince and turn away; we haven't actually opened the curtains, so the influx of light is blinding.

"I'm just doing what you said Ollie, keeping an eye on Mum. Plus, I've been taking an interest in her new hobby."

Amy giggles and Ollie glowers. So Amy crosses her legs and tries to look seductive. But sucking on a cigarette is not the way to win my brother. Oh no. Ollie dumps his bags on the floor and marches over, face like fizz.

"You pair disgust me. Look at you – two silly schoolgirls taking liberties with a loony. You make me sick. AND YOU!" He launches at Mum. "How could you? How could you sit there and let your little girl smoke? What the hell is Amy's mum going to say? What will Dad say?" He picks up the white and purple packet and pounds it with his fist. "Should I phone Dad now, mmmmh? Tell him all you're feeding us are these… these… cancer sticks?"

"NO! Ollie don't!" I can't bear the thought of Dad finding

out. "Don't phone Dad. Mum would hate it, you can't tell him, you just can't."

Ollie ignores me. "I don't understand, Mum. Help me understand! Tell me how to help you. What is it you're trying to prove? Eh? Do you want us to sink down with you? Is that it? If you're heading to the gutter, we're coming too? Answer me! For god's sake, say something!"

Ollie looks like he's about to lose it, so I grab his elbow and drag him across the room.

"I'm sorry Ollie," I'm sobbing now. "Just don't phone Dad."

He shakes me off. "Christ, Jess, is that all you care about? Getting in trouble with Dad? Stop being such a baby. Go on," he thrusts the crumpled pack at me. "Smoke till your lungs catch fire – be my guest. I don't care. Understand? All I care about is how to stop that woman who is supposed to be my mother, behaving like an imbecile."

"Okay, but can we sit down and discuss it calmly. Stop with all the shouting, please."

He's so busy glaring over my shoulder at Mum, that he doesn't even hear me. "Look at the state of you!" he yells across the kitchen. "Will you say something!"

"Do you know something Ollie? You're just like her. You don't listen either."

It's true. Part of the reason she riles him so much is because they're so alike. Perhaps he sees himself in her and it freaks him out big time.

"Er, I best be off." Amy's hovering by my side.

"Oh Amy, yes, sorry. I'll call you, okay?" She gives my arm a little squeeze then scuttles out the door. I stare after her, wishing I could walk out too, but oh no, I have to stop my brother throttling Mum for feeling suicidal.

"OLLIE! Sit down. On you go, over there." I shoo him with my hands. "That's right, now sit beside Mum." Ollie looks startled by my sudden briskness, but does as he's told. "Now, let me handle this, okay?" He nods.

"Right, Mum? Can you hear me?" I push my face in front of hers, but still she doesn't raise her eyes from the absorbing task of trainee pyromaniac. "MUM!" Now she has me shouting, but how else am I meant to get through?

"It was the ceiling." At last she speaks, but I'm still none the wiser.

"What you on about? Why do you keep banging on about the ceiling?"

"I could fix it if it wasn't for the ceiling, but it can't be fixed."

"What do you mean it can't be fixed? Of course it can be fixed. I'll Google a plasterer right now and..."

Finally Mum looks up and throws me a look of pure pity. "You have no idea."

"You're right I don't, so why don't you tell me!"

She leans in even closer and her breath is foul. I don't know when she last cleaned her teeth – maybe not for days or even weeks and that mingled with the smell of stale smoke is revolting. I try not to recoil.

"He's inside me now," she whispers and glances left and right, as if someone might overhear.

"WHO? I mean, who?" Don't start shouting Jessie, don't get hysterical.

Mum leans back on her stool and looks at me like I'm stupid. "Satan, of course."

"Satan?"

"Shhhh. He'll hear."

Oh. My. God. She is officially barking mad. A complete and utter nutter! How could this have happened? Ollie's face is sheet white; he gags and swallows as if about to be sick.

"Mum." I'm trying to sound as gentle as I can, when all I really want to do is grab her shoulders and shake some sense into her. "You are joking, right? You don't really believe the Devil's inside you?"

She shrugs and returns to her matches. No don't retreat, not yet. I try to remove the matches, but she grips hold of them like a life-ring.

"Mum! Just look at me for one more minute, please!" She glances up. "Mum. Listen. The Devil is not inside you. I swear."

"Oh Jess, but he is. He found me because I'm bad and now he lives in here." She thumps her chest.

"Ah, so you mean it like a metaphor. You feel guilty cos you've put Gran in hospital. It just feels like Satan's inside you, he's not actually there. Is that right?"

"Metaphor? Metaphor? The Devil's no metaphor, Jess! Don't you go making him angry..." She shakes her head. "If only I hadn't fallen through the ceiling."

The ceiling! What is it with that stupid ceiling? I've heard enough; I have to get out of here. I jump off my stool and it clatters to the floor, though I don't stop to pick it up, just race out to the garden.

"Here, Jessie. Suck on this."

I turn to see three giggly boys in swimming trunks scaling the garden fence and oh, crap, they're carrying massive NERF guns full of water.

"AAAGggghhh." Jets of freezing cold water slam into my stomach, then my face. "You little..." I begin to run, closely pursued by whooping, screaming monsters. "Tracy! Tracy," I yell to our neighbour. "Call them off would you!"

Tracy leans over the fence and laughs, "Aaaw, you know you love it Jessie. Go on boys. Soak her."

Well, yes, maybe last year it would have been funny.

I might have enjoyed getting chased round the garden, before stealing the guns and turning them on my tormentors. But not now.

"I'M NOT JOKING TRACY! For Christ's sake get your kids under control or I'll take those effing guns and snap them in two."

Tracy looks shocked. Okay, so that possibly came out a tad strong.

"Jeez, Jessie. Keep your hair on. What's with the attitude? BOYS! BOOOYS! STOOOOOP!"

Confused, my three little pals quit their squirting. "Why, Mum?"

"Because Jessie's got a strop on. Come on kids, back over the fence."

"But Muuuum!"

"No arguments; come on." Tracy flashes me a look of pure venom. "I have to say, Jessie, I'm very surprised."

Oh go for it, Tracy, tell me what a pig I am cos I don't feel bad enough already. But then I look at those three miserable faces and I feel awful; they look so hurt and bewildered. But what can I do? All I came out for was a bit of fresh air and here I am getting hassled again.

Well, the great outdoors isn't exactly working out. Time to go in, I think. Only now I get caught by old Mrs Clarke on the other side.

"Oh Jess dear. Jess! Is that you?"

I mean for god's sake. We really need a higher fence.

"Hello Mrs Clarke, yes it's me. How are you? How's the arthritis?"

"Oh can't complain dear, can't complain. I just wondered how your mother was. She usually pops in for a cuppa, but she hasn't been round for a few weeks now and last time I saw her she seemed... well, how would I put it? Um...

preoccupied."

Mrs Clarke is a sweet old lady, but she's also a spectacular gossip. One word from me about Mum's mental state and it'll spread round town faster than the flu.

"Thanks for asking, Mrs Clarke. But Mum's fine. She's had a lot of work on, that's all."

"Really dear? Because I haven't seen her newspaper column for a while now."

"Er, that's cos she's hitting the big time, Mrs Clarke. She's got a commission from a glossy magazine."

Mrs Clarke's face lights up. "Oh, how wonderful, dear. She must be ever so busy. What's the name of the magazine? I'll get myself a copy."

"Um, can't really remember, Mrs C. Something with a 'Woman' in the title. Let me think... Woman's Own – no, no, can't be that – Woman's Weekly? Nope, not that either. Tell you what, I'll ask Mum and let you know." I try to back away, but she isn't done.

"Yes, you do that dear and don't let her work too hard. She needs a break now and then. Send her round to me and I'll put the kettle on."

"I'll do that Mrs Clarke. Don't you worry!"

"And Jess..."

"Sorry, gotta dash. Bursting..."

I cross my legs and mime needing a wee then burst through the door, slamming it shut behind me. There. I have escaped the neighbours, but it's like getting banged back up in jail – my kitchen, a dark, smoky, cell. And there's Mum, still on her stool playing with matches. Ollie hasn't moved either. He's resting his face on the granite counter-top staring into space. Lethargy, it seems, is contagious.

4

MEN IN WHITE COATS

Well, Ollie's called Dad, which I was dead against. I don't want him knowing Mum's gone crazy, but I was also terrified Ollie would rat on me about the smoking, which is just bizarre because I don't ever see Dad, so what's he gonna do? I mean he's in Dubai now, married to his mid-life crisis – that twig-thin bimbo, Pippa. He's a walking cliché is my dad. Seriously, he drives around in a red convertible and hits the gym six times a week.

Anyway, Ollie called him and Dad said Mum got a bit depressed after she had me, but nothing too serious – just a bit weepy and tired. He said she was fine after a short course of happy pills and we should probably talk to her doctor. So I called the docs to see if they would send one out. The receptionist refused and said Mum could come in the following Thursday. So I got a bit stroppy and she got a bit snippy and said I would have to speak to the practice manager, which I did. The manager, though, was nice. Said Ollie should come in for a chat and now there's a psychiatrist at the door!

He's the tiniest man I have ever seen, can't be more than five feet tall. He has on a suit, but it looks really odd on him, like he's a little kid dressed in his dad's office clothes.

"I'm Dr Verma," he says, gazing up at me. "I'm a Consultant Psychiatrist and this," he gestures towards a fat hairy-faced woman, "is Gemma Corby. She's a Mental Health Officer, which is a social worker with specialist mental health training."

I smile at Gemma, but she just scowls and looks at her watch. Ignorant cow.

I let them in and he says he has to talk to Mum alone, so I position myself on the stairs so I can listen in. Ollie disappears outside. I think he's scared Mum'll hate him for setting a psychiatrist on her, but she doesn't seem bothered.

I press my face against the slats in the bannister; I can see into the living room, but I can't really hear. Dr Verma's perched on a footstool in front of Mum. He's asking questions, but I can tell he isn't getting much response. It's quite exciting this. Isn't that terrible? I'm upset, of course I am, it's just… it's all so dramatic, like an episode of Eastenders.

So I text Amy – "psychiatrist in my house!!!" And about half a second later she's on the phone.

"Jess! You okay? Oh my god! Why?"

"Well, Mum's gone a bit loopy, hasn't she?"

"OMG! Do you think they'll send her to Carthill?"

My stomach lurches and suddenly I feel sick. I don't know why it never occurred to me before, but it didn't even cross my mind that they'd actually lock her up. Carthill is our local mental hospital. I say local, but it's actually miles from anywhere. I think it was built in Victorian times, when they liked to keep their lunatics as far from town as possible. But everyone round here knows it. It's like the local bogeyman. When Ollie and me were tiny, we used to get really hyper and drive Mum round the bend. "QUIT FIGHTING,' she'd yell, "OR YE'LL HAVE ME CARTED OFF TO CARTHILL!" All the mums round here say stuff like that.

Anyway, I'm so upset I cut Amy off without even saying goodbye. My phone buzzes a few times but I ignore it. After a bit Dr Verma comes out and asks me to join him in the living room. I poke my head out the door to fetch Ollie. He hovers behind me as we wander inside; I swear he's trying to hide behind my back. Then he scuttles over to the window, as far from Mum as possible and stands, devouring his fingernails, miserable with guilt and worry. Since I didn't personally report Mum to the thought police, I feel able to kneel down beside her and try to take her hand. Irritated, she shrugs me off – don't come between Mum and her matches.

Dr Verma smiles at me then has to twist round to look at Ollie. I can see it will be difficult to talk to two parts of the room, so I get up and join Ollie by the window. Mum doesn't want me anyway.

"So," says Dr Verma, "I've had a chat with your mum and now I'd like to hear from you. What's been going on?" He glances at his notes. "Oliver, perhaps you can start, since you were the one to visit the GP."

Poor old Ollie – ratted out by the psychiatrist. He stands there staring at Mum, his mouth gaping, but I don't think she's even listening. Still, I better step in to save my brother – don't want them thinking he's lost it as well.

"Um, well Ollie's only really been back a few days. It's me that's been living with Mum."

"Oh Jessica, yes of course, do go on."

"Um, well we've been caring for my gran all summer. She's got dementia and she came to live with us and it's all been a bit of a nightmare. Then, a couple of days ago Gran went into hospital and now the doctors are saying Mum should put her in a home and I think Mum feels she's let Gran down. But I've said to her – I've said 'Mum, it's the right thing to do, cos when it comes down to it, it's either Gran or my exams'. I mean it. If Gran comes back to live with us, I don't think I'll get a single Higher. She keeps us up all night!" My eyes are welling up. For god's sake get it together, Jess; I am not about to blub in front of strangers. "Maybe it's my fault Mum's like this," I try to continue, but it comes out all quivery. "I don't mean to put pressure on her, but Gran really needs to be in a home."

Ollie slings an arm round my shoulder and squeezes. "Don't. It's not you Jessie," he says in a quiet voice. "That way madness lies, just look at Mum."

"Wise words, Oliver," Dr Verma smiles at him before turning back to me. "It sounds to me like you both did all you could to care for your gran. Neither you nor your mum has anything to feel guilty about. I think …"

"Er, sorry to interrupt, Dr Verma…." It's the hairy-faced social worker. "…but time's pressing on…"

"I'm sorry, are we keeping you?" Oops, that was me! And it sounded so sarcastic! I'm not normally that rude; it just sort of slipped out.

Hairy Face glares at me. "Dr Verma and I are extremely busy people. We have a huge workload and…"

Dr Verma raises a hand for quiet. "Thank you Gemma. I appreciate that you're busy, but kindly let me do my job."

Hoho. That showed her. I give her a smarmy little smirk and she purses her lips and looks away.

"So," says Dr Verma, "it all began with your gran going into hospital?"

I nod.

"Tell me about your mum since then."

I shrug.

"Well how, for example, has she been eating?"

"Oh, quite well." I know, I know, that's not entirely truthful, but Amy's got me so spooked about Carthill, I think it's best to downplay things a bit. Ollie though, thinks I'm being difficult.

"What you on about? She doesn't eat. At all. Nothing. I'm not sure she even drinks."

"Oh Ollie," I give this awful little laugh that sounds completely fake. "Yes, she's been off her food, but to imply she's not eating at all – well I'd say that's a bit of an exaggeration, don't you?"

Ollie looks like he might thump me. "No I bloody well do not. You know fine well I'm not exaggerating. What are you playing at?"

"Now, now," says Hairy Face, looking all officious and self-important. "Is she eating or not?" Her piggy little eyes dart between us searching for an answer. I shrug again and Ollie just glares.

Dr Verma leans towards Mum. "May I, Mrs Brody?" he says, gesturing towards her hand. These days Mum seems to move in slow motion, so although she's heard him and has deigned to cooperate, it takes absolutely ages for her to lift her arm and hold out her hand. Hairy Face is jiggling about, almost bursting with impatience. Dr Verma gently takes Mum's hand and pinches the skin on the back of her wrist. When he lets go, it doesn't just snap back into place – a little tent shaped bit remains standing up.

"You are dehydrated, Mrs Brody. When was the last time you had a drink?"

Mum ignores him and takes back her hand. She's been without matches for several minutes and is beginning to get agitated. Dr Verma turns to me.

"Your mum has not been eating 'quite well', has she?"

"Weeell, it depends what you mean by 'quite well.'"

Hairy Face wags her finger at me. "You've got to be honest with the doctor. This isn't a game …"

A game! How dare she! I hate her, I really do – with all her tutting and fidgeting and 'let's hurry things along'. I say as much and Hairy Face turns scarlet and Dr Verma asks her to step outside to let things cool. She skulks out the room absolutely fuming.

"Try to calm down," says Dr Verma, "this isn't helping. I understand that you're trying to protect your mum, Jessica, but she doesn't need protecting from me. It's herself she needs protecting from. If she no longer cares for her own basic needs, she'll become physically ill as well as mentally. Please, for her sake, answer my questions honestly."

"Okay," I squeak, feeling stupid and ashamed.

"So…" begins the doctor.

But before he has a chance to say another word, Mum blurts out, "IT WAS THE CEILING."

Jesus Christ, the fright we get. All of us jump, even Dr Verma.

"What was that, Mrs Brody?"

"It was the ceiling," says Mum again, though this time much quieter.

Puzzled, Dr Verma turns towards us huddled at the window.

"She wanders at night," explains Ollie. "It's like she's nocturnal. She hardly moves all day, but at night she prowls about. A few days ago she was up in the loft and she fell through the ceiling at four in the morning. Since then she's fixated on it and she's been much worse mentally."

"In what way?"

Ollie glances at me – he's tearing himself in two trying to decide what to do for the best. I gently shake my head and mouth, "No," but the eagle-eyed psychiatrist notices.

"There's something you feel you can't tell me?"

"Don't, Ollie."

Hairy Face is hovering by the door and decides to stick her beak in. "If it's all too much for Miss Brody, perhaps she should leave the room and let her brother handle things."

Honestly, that woman. I want to kill her, I really do. "What business is it of yours, eh? Why don't you just butt the hell out? If you social workers had given Mum an ounce of support in the first place, she might not be in this state. She was left to care for Gran without a single..."

Dr Verma jumps up and whispers something to Hairy Face, who makes a hissing noise through her teeth and once again flounces from the room.

"I'm sorry," says Dr Verma. "Please continue, Oliver."

Ollie's face is sheet white and sweaty. And for the first time something else occurs to me, something truly awful. If they do take Mum to Carthill, what happens to me?

Panicked now, I start to beg, "Please Ollie. Just leave it. Don't you see, they'll send Mum to Carthill. You can't do that to her, you just can't! I'll look after her here. I'll do better this time, I promise. I won't be silly anymore." I no longer care if Dr Verma hears or not, all I know is I have to stop Ollie splurging about the Devil. "Please Ollie. I'm begging you."

Ollie buries his face in his hands and stays there for a moment. When he looks up again, his eyes shine with tears, but his voice is strong and clear. "Mum is delusional," he says. "She thinks Satan is inside her. I'm not quite sure how it links to the whole ceiling thing, but it does. I think she may believe the Devil entered through that hole and I'm pretty sure her whole obsession with matches is also about him. She may be sparking them to appease him or to ward him off, I don't know which."

I sink down to the floor, tears streaming down my cheeks. Good one, Ollie, you've well and truly done it now; they'll take her away for sure. I'm sobbing so much that Hairy Face comes in and offers me a tissue. She looks at me kindly but I don't want her sympathy, so I ignore the tissue and continue to sniff, snot bubbling out both nostrils.

"Carthill's not so bad," she says, squatting down beside me like a sumo wrestler. "Your mum will be safe there and it's really quite nice inside."

"How would you know?" I mumble. "How the bloody hell would you know?"

"Because..." she takes a deep breath. "I was a patient there myself."

"Oh." Go figure.

"What age are you, Jess?"

"Seventeen," I lie.

Hairy Face nods and tries to stand up, but she isn't very agile and almost topples over. "You're a grown up now," she says, clutching hold of the windowsill, "not by much. But you're going to have to start acting like one, because your mum really needs you."

WHAT ABOUT ME? I want to scream. WHAT THE BLOODY HELL ABOUT ME?

* * *

Am I clever or what, telling the Hairy One I'm seventeen? At seventeen, I can stay home alone. I'll show her how mature I am. I get to my feet.

"Tea anyone?"

Verma and Hairy Face look at me strangely. Oh yes, I've got snot sliding down my chin. I wipe it away with the back of my hand. "So, milk? Sugar?"

"Um… just milk thanks."

I know they won't drink it, which is just as well, cos we have no milk, so I bustle into the kitchen and busy myself with glasses of squash and stale biscuits. Ollie comes through.

"You okay?"

I nod. "I told Hairy Face I was seventeen!"

"Why?"

"Because otherwise she'd shove me in a children's home. Duh!"

"Oh god, I hadn't thought of that. If Mum's put in hospital what do I do with you?"

"You don't have to do anything with me," I hiss. "I'll be fine. But shush, the Hairy One has ears you know." Placing the glasses of squash on a tray, I wander back through to the living room and arrange them on the coffee table in the middle of the room. Dr Verma is on the phone, hassling someone about a bed. Hairy Face is filling in a form, but I can tell she needs to talk to Verma to complete it. She's getting impatient again, glowering at the doctor, willing him to get off the phone. Eventually he hangs up and she pounces.

"Is this Compulsory or not?"

"I'm hoping Voluntary, but we'll see," he says and sits down again in front of Mum. "Mrs Brody. Mrs Brody! I am arranging for you to spend some time in hospital. Do you understand?"

Mum says nothing; she's totally focussed on far more pressing things. The box of matches and ashtray are both balanced on her lap and she's in the stubbing out phase of her cycle when Dr Verma picks up her matches and places them on the floor. Having successfully extinguished her cigarette, Mum reaches for the matches to relight it, but of course they aren't there. Finally her eyes leave her lap and swivel round the room.

"Mrs Brody. I will give you back your matches in just one moment, but first it is very important that you listen to me. Are you listening?"

Mum's eyes settle on his and she nods.

"I have arranged for an ambulance to come and collect you. It will take you to Carthill Hospital. Do you know where that is?"

"Yes, but I'm not going."

Ollie freezes in the doorway and I almost choke on my lukewarm squash. She sounded so normal then. That was my mum talking, not the weird automaton she's recently become.

"You do understand how ill you are, Mrs Brody? It is imperative that you begin treatment right away. And for depression this severe, it has to be as an in-patient."

Mum gives him a steely-eyed glare and for a second I catch a glimpse of the real Helen Brody. "I… am… NOT… repeat, NOT… going to hospital."

"In that case, Mrs Brody, you leave me no choice but to detain you under the Mental Health Act. You are an educated woman, you must know what that means."

Mum's beginning to look less sure of herself and her eyes are starting to stray, searching for the comfort of her matches. She spots them on the floor, but Dr Verma's too quick for her. He bends down and scoops them up before she even has a chance to stoop.

"I will give you the matches in just a second, Mrs Brody,

but first I want you to give me your full attention. If you enter Carthill as a voluntary patient you will be free to leave at any time. If Gemma and I admit you under a short-term detention certificate we can keep you there for twenty-eight days and you will have no say in the matter at all. In my opinion it's always best to come to Carthill voluntarily; that way you are an active participant in your own treatment. I look upon it as an important first step to recovery, don't you Gemma?"

Hairy Face nods. "Dr Verma's right, Mrs Brody. You don't want to be detained in hospital if you can avoid it. I've been there, and it isn't nice. Not that I wanted to leave once I started treatment, but it's always good to have the option. I'd have felt better about myself – more in control. Besides, think of your children – you don't want to be forced into an ambulance in front of them, do you?"

This strikes a chord. Mum looks at Ollie, then at me, and her eyes fill with tears. "My babies," she whispers, "I am so sorry …"

I start crying too, but I'm not sad, I'm actually kinda happy 'cos Mum sounds so normal. Maybe she doesn't need the hospital after all. She's coming back to us. She is!

But then she opens her mouth again. "I want to be a proper mum to both of you, but it's the ceiling. If only I hadn't fallen through that ceiling…"

Ollie and I groan at exactly the same moment.

After that things move pretty quickly. I prepare a bag, while Mum plays with her matches and Ollie paces round the house looking progressively more anxious. At one point, as I pass with an armful of toiletries, he grabs my arm and hisses, "We're doing the right thing, aren't we?" And although I'm not at all sure that we are, I nod anyway, cos I know how much he needs me to.

Back in the living room, I try to persuade Mum to put on some clothes. Her dressing gown is filthy and covered in little burn marks from all the matches she's been sparking. "Don't you think you would feel better with something fresh on? How about a nice, cool summer dress?" I hold up a floral number that she bought from Boden last year. She gives me a withering look, as if I'm the one that's mad. I suppose she's right, why get dressed up to go to a mental hospital? Still, there's always the neighbours to consider. "What if Mrs Clarke sees you in that state, eh? Think how she'll talk." Mum doesn't care.

"Well, at least let me comb your hair." She doesn't reply, so I take that as a yes and try to brush out bits of bedroom ceiling, but it's a tough job. Her hair is revolting, it can't have been washed in weeks and some parts are so tangled they're almost in dreads. I find myself crying again. How could I let her get in such a state? What sort of daughter doesn't notice when her mum stops washing and eating?

Then there's the rumble of a diesel engine. It grows louder, before drawing to a stop outside.

"The ambulance is here," says Dr Verma, quietly.

"Mum. Did you hear? Up you get." I grab both her wrists and tug her upright. She doesn't resist. Dr Verma places a hand under her elbow and gently steers her towards the front door. I hold my breath, I half expect her to shake him off and run away, but she doesn't. She just shuffles along like an obedient child. That is, until we get outside.

Two cheery looking paramedics have parked up on the kerb and are hoisting open the door of the ambulance. Both are a little overweight, one has a beard.

"Awright luv," says the bearded one, with a really strong Liverpool accent. "Oh. Wait a sec. What's that you got there then?" He steps in front of Mum and peers down at her hands. When he spots the matches, he shakes his head. "Sorry luv. Can't bring matches in an ambulance. Health and Safety, I'm afraid. We've got oxygen tanks in 'ere. Could all go ka boom." He throws his arms in the air then taps the matchbox. "You pass those along to the Doctor over there and he'll give em back when ye get to Carthill."

Mum looks at me uncertainly.

"Just do it," I hiss, glancing from left to right and over my shoulder. This is taking far too long. I want her in the ambulance and on her way in less than 30 seconds, certainly before any neighbours start sniffing around. That way if anyone spots the ambulance, I can just say it was her appendix. But now here we stand in a leafy suburb, with paramedics shouting about Carthill and Mum in her ratty dressing gown clinging to her matches. We are pure 10-carat gossip gold. Mrs Clarke's net curtains are already twitching.

Mum appears to think about it, but then says, "No," as I knew fine well she would. She crosses her arms, tucking the box safely under an oxter. I try to grab it, but she holds firm.

"For god's sake, Mum, just give me the bloody matches."

"No."

Aaaagh. Mrs Clarke is now hobbling down her drive and on the other side Tracy's front door is starting to open.

"Mum. I am begging you, give me the matches and get in the ambulance. You don't want the whole world to know you're going to Carthill, do you? Please, for my sake. Pretty please?" I press both my hands together as if in prayer. I would kneel at her feet if I thought it would make a difference.

"Oh Jess ..." Mum reaches out with her free hand and gently touches my cheek.

"Please, Mum?"

She nods slowly and digs the matches out from under her arm. I reach out to take them, but with a jerk she snatches them away again and hides them behind her back.

I'm starting to lose my temper. "What are you doing?"

"Is everything okay, dear?" Oh great. Mrs Clarke's materialised by my side, her face concerned, but her eyes also sparkling with excitement.

"Yes, Mrs Clarke, everything is fine. Please… could you just give us a moment? This is kind of… private."

She recoils. "Oh. Oh… I… I didn't mean to get in the way, dear. I was just looking out my window and I thought you might need some help."

"HELP? What possible…?" I stop myself. Granny bashing is not going to improve the situation; the damage is already done. Mrs Clarke is staring at Mum and it's clear from her expression that appendicitis will not be her diagnosis when recounting this story in the SPAR.

"Mum, just give me the box," I hiss again.

She leans towards me and whispers, "I'm sorry, Jess. But try to understand that I can't. I would if I could, but I can't."

Ollie throws a helpless look at the paramedic. "Can't she just take them if she swears not to use them in the ambulance?"

The paramedic with the beard shakes his head sympathetically. "No can do, I'm afraid. Can't take the risk."

The other paramedic decides to try a different tack. If Beardy is 'good cop' he'll try 'bad cop' to see if a firmer approach will work. "Come on now, Mrs Brody. You're upsetting your children and wasting our time. It's a short drive to the hospital and you can get your matches back as soon as you get there. So give them to me and get inside."

Mrs Clarke tugs my sleeve. "What's all this talk about matches?" she whispers. "Your mum doesn't smoke. So why does she need matches?" Her voice grows louder. "WHAT ON EARTH IS SHE DOING WITH MATCHES?"

"Eh?" puzzled, Ollie raises his eyebrows at me. "What's she shouting about?"

I'm confused myself, but then it clicks. "I think she's concerned that Mum's planning to burn down her house. Isn't that right, Mrs Clarke?"

"Well... no... not really... well, you can see my confusion, dear. Your mum doesn't smoke."

"So that makes her an arsonist?"

"I'll leave you to it, dear," and leaning heavily on her cane, she shuffles back up her path – not all the way though. Half way up she stoops to examine a rosebush, still well within earshot of the ambulance.

I turn my attention back to Mum who's now arguing with the paramedic. "... I'm not stupid," she's saying, "they won't give them back to me. I know they don't trust mad people with matches, so why are you lying? I've changed my mind. I'm not going."

Oh God, oh God, oh God, oh God.

Dr Verma steps forward. "We've already discussed this, Mrs Brody, how important it is to..."

Mum takes one look at him, knows she's about to get Sectioned and shoots off down the road. She doesn't get far before she stumbles out of her flip-flop slippers and falls. Spotting their opportunity, the paramedics lunge to grab her, but she's too fast for them. She jumps up, kicks away the slippers and goes racing off. She looks a bit like a superhero with her dressing gown billowing behind like a cape. The paramedics try to follow but they don't stand a chance. Mum's running like Satan's on her tail (which, let's face it, he probably is) and two plump paramedics aren't about to outrun her long slender legs. Red-faced and puffing, they quickly give up and come limping back to the ambulance to radio for the police. By the time the squad car screeches up, it feels like the whole neighbourhood's standing on the street, gossiping, texting, staring. Hairy Face places a protective arm round my shoulder and guides me back towards the house.

"Come on now. Inside. You don't need to be out here for this."

As we make our way up the path, I hear Tracy call from next door, "Jessie! Oi, Jess." I can't face her, so I keep my eyes on my feet. "JESS!"

Okaaay. I know Tracy, she isn't about to take the hint, so I look up and see tears are streaming down her face. "We're here, hen. Understand? Anything you need. We're here."

I nod, but can't speak, so Hairy Face thanks her brusquely and bundles me inside.

"Where's Ollie?"

"He wants to help look for your mum. But you need to sit yourself down, before you faint."

She's right. My head is swimming and I do feel a bit peculiar, so I stagger through to the living room and throw myself on the sofa. Hairy Face finds the remote control and turns on the TV. I think to myself, what a cheek, her wanting to watch telly at a time like this. But then she turns the volume up really loud and I understand – white noise to drown out any nastiness outside.

"So do they always run away?"

"Mmmmh?" She's immersed in emails on her phone.

"The lunatics. Do they always run away?" I'm having to shout over the din of Loose Women.

She looks up. "Actually we don't refer to people with mental health problems as lunatics these days; they don't tend to like it."

"Oh sorry." Oops. Touchy subject.

"That's all right. It's still a bit of a minefield the whole mental health lingo. But to answer your question, no, they don't always run away. Most people realise they need help and come in voluntarily."

"Really?" Who would do that?

She nods. "It's the ones like your mum who've lost touch with reality that tend to resist. I mean, think about it – if those matches are the only thing that stand between her and pure evil, it's perfectly logical that she won't let them go. It's a terrifying place to be." Her voice tails off and she sits for a moment lost in thought, perhaps recalling her own demons. "But rules are rules – you can't have matches in an ambulance and she's right, she won't be allowed them in hospital."

"So what will they do to her?" I whisper, shivering suddenly, despite the heat. "Will they put her in a strait-jacket?"

Hairy Face lets out a bark of laughter. "Oh dear me no! Where did you get that from? Straitjacket indeed!" She chuckles to herself and with a smile looks almost quite pretty. "No, straitjackets haven't been used in years. Your mum will be sedated, so don't worry, she'll be quite calm."

"Oh." I have a sudden vision of Mum being pinned down by the police while men in white coats jab her with a humongous needle of comedic proportions. How's that better than a straitjacket? Though I suppose she'll at least get to snooze.

Hairy's Blackberry rings and I just about jump out my skin. I could be doing with some sedation myself. She turns away and huddles over it, murmuring, "Yup... yup... uh-huh... well, we can do that at the hospital... no? Okay, I understand... yup... I'll let her know... okay... yup... see you there."

I'm properly shaking by the time she hangs up. Her face is grim.

"Well, they've found your mum and she's fine. So... um... I've got to go and finalise the paperwork as she's no longer a voluntary patient. You take care, eh?"

She stands up and slings her handbag over her shoulder. Is that it?

"But... but... where's the ambulance? I need to go with her!"

"No! Um... I mean... no. You cannot accompany her at this time."

"Why not? I can't let her go into Carthill on her own. Where is she?"

Hairy Face sighs. "Look Jess, your mum's going to be asleep for a while and they won't let you see her right now. So go get some rest and come up tomorrow, yeah?"

"NO! She's my mum and she needs me." I elbow past her and go stomping towards the front door, but as I'm rooting for my keys, Ollie comes in and I can tell by his face that I won't be going anywhere. Not today.

"Oh, Ollie. What is it? What happened?"

"Jess... not right now, okay?"

"But shouldn't we...?"

He shakes his head. "No. I'm going to have a bath." And slouched like an old man, he starts to climb the stairs.

Hairy Face places a hand on my shoulder. "Tomorrow, yeah?" and off she goes, leaving me standing in the hallway, bewildered and alone.

5

BEER AND BILE

The shakes are getting worse. Seriously, look how much my hand is jerking. Am I having a fit or something? I need to talk to Ollie, but he's still hiding out in the bathroom. I thought if I waited here with my head pressed to the door, I'd be ready to pounce as soon as he came out. But that was ages ago. He must be well wrinkly by now. Come on, Ollie, d'ye not know what I'm going through here? Oh, could that be…? Yes… the sound of water sloshing out the tub and the slop of wet feet on lino. Now the scrape of the bolt. "Ollie! I need to…"

"Jeeesus Jess!" He gets such a fright he almost loses his towel. "What the…? Can I at least get dressed?"

"Sure, but…"

He pulls the towel tight round his waist and marches into his room, slamming the door shut in my face. I wait. I wait some more then tap gently on the door but there's no reply. I mean how long does it take to pull on a pair of jeans? Sod it, so what if his arse is bare? It's nothing I've not seen before. I fling open the bedroom door and there he is, fully dressed, crossed legged on the bed playing some stupid game on his phone.

"You pig! You absolute rotten git! I've been waiting ages to talk to you."

"Not now," he groans. "I need to... I need... I need beer. OK? I'll just pop out. Then we'll talk, promise." He leaps off the bed and scoops up his wallet. I start to cry. "Oh, not the waterworks, Jess. Give us a break, for god's sake." Well, that kind of talk just makes me cry harder, doesn't it? He stands awkwardly, jingling the keys in his pocket. "I won't be long," he says eventually. "I promise. Cross my heart. Yeah?"

I nod, unable to speak. So he ruffles my hair and tells me to go warm some plates. He'll get us takeaway and a few yummy treats. Today, of all days, we deserve something nice.

After a bit he comes back with a poly bag stuffed with Chinese food, an enormous tub of ice cream and a six-pack of cheap, nasty lager from the SPAR. He opens a bottle for himself and while he's busy plopping noodles onto plates, I flip one open too. Foam spurts from the top and I have to be quick to get my mouth round it before it dribbles onto the floor. I've had wine before. Mum sometimes let me have a thimbleful on special occasions, but I've never had a beer. So I perch on a stool in the kitchen, bottle in hand and feel like a character from an American cop show. They always have a cold one at the end of a hard day.

Ollie turns to hand me my dinner. "Jess! Really? Beer?"

I glare at him. "Yes, I'm having a beer. So what? My mum's in a mental hospital and the whole world knows it. I think I deserve one, don't you?"

Ollie looks doubtful, but leaves it there. I can see the 'my mum's mental' card might prove fruitful for a while. I look down at my plate. "What on earth's that?"

"Mushroom foo yung," says Ollie, his mouth full of food.

"It looks disgusting. Like vomit."

"Well if you're not going to eat it, give it here. I'm starving." Ollie snatches my plate away and continues to shovel in chunks of greasy goo. I settle back and take another swig of beer. I have to say, it doesn't taste very nice – sort of metallic and bitter – but hey, it's far nicer than the smokes.

Ollie downs the rest of his beer and promptly opens another.

"So?" says I, "are you going to tell me what went on out there?'

Ollie groans. "And here I was just starting to feel human for the first time today."

"Sorry, but I need to know. I've been imagining all sorts of wild stuff, but my mind's probably making it far worse than it actually was. Right?"

Ollie looks away. After a while he says, "It was pretty bad, Jess."

"Oh." I take another swig of beer and feel my empty stomach start to churn.

"But I tell you this," Ollie suddenly grins. "Never, ever, get on the wrong side of Mum, OK?"

"Why?"

"Cos she is one scary lady. Whoa! Can that woman kick!"

"Really?" I sup some more beer and feel myself grinning too. "She gave them hell, did she?"

"God, yeah. There was this bizarre game of tag between her and the police and she was so fast, I swear she had them running round in circles. So they had to call for backup. Then there were more policemen plus the doctor and the paramedics – so in the end she was completely surrounded. But she still didn't give up without a fight, God no, she really let 'em have it."

"Where was this?"

Ollie's smile disappears and he begins to fidget in his seat. "Just... you know..." he shrugs.

"Ollie, where?"

He mumbles something, which I don't catch.

"I can't hear you Ollie, speak up."

"At the train station."

"WHERE?" I screech, hoping I haven't heard right.

"The train station, Jess. It happened at the train station. Okay? Mum clearly thought she would catch a train with her nightdress on and no money, so yes, she was at the train station."

"Oh Jesus Christ. Go on then, let me have it. Who was there?" Please say no one we know, please say it.

Ollie takes a deep breath. "There was a group of lads – a bit younger than you – hanging round the car park with skateboards. Gus Walters was one of them."

For a moment I'm mystified, the name doesn't ring a bell. "Gus... who...?" Then it clicks. "Oh, you have got to be joking! Not Hannah's brother?"

Ollie nods. "But maybe he didn't realise who Mum was..."

"Of course he realised who Mum was, cos you were standing there like a big neon sign, screaming this is Jess and Ollie's nutcase of a mother." I swallow the rest of the beer and open another. Ollie says nothing.

"So that's it then. My life is officially over."

"I'm sorry, Jess."

"God, what a mess." Hannah Walters is in my class at school. She's one of the Coven, which is my name for the three blonde bitches that persecute the plain girls in our year. Amy gets to be a sort of half-member of the Coven because she's so gorgeous and good with fashion, but she's far too nice to be terribly interested, so she sort of dips in and out when she feels like it. I am clearly not Coven material, but because I'm friends with Amy, they pretty much leave me alone. They toss the occasional catty comment about my clothes, but that's as far as it goes.

There's some girls in my class though, that the Coven completely torment. Fat Britney, for instance, she can't walk down a corridor without getting tripped up or spat on or stuff smeared in her hair. But it's not the Coven themselves that do it. Oh no, they don't get their hands dirty – they leave that to their minions. And it doesn't take much to whip the Coven worshippers into a frenzy of venom; those half-pretty girls are so eager not to become the victim that they'll torture any poor sucker that the Coven decrees.

"So I guess on the pecking order of popularity, I'm now lower down the food chain than Fat Britney."

Ollie gives a rueful grin. "Oh, Jess. I'm sorry. Maybe, they'll think it's cool?"

I snort. "Yeah right. Here, pass us your laptop." Ollie reaches behind and hands me the ancient, chunky Mac he inherited from Mum. I log onto Facebook and click on Hannah Walters' face. Yes, yes, don't judge me – I admit it; she's one of my Facebook friends. She asked to be, so what was I supposed to do? Refuse? In fact, she's even Facebook friends with Fat Britney. I think she does it to keep tabs on her victims, that way we can't plot a coup behind her back. Anyway, I open up her page and there on her News Feed is, "Epic drama! Unbelieeeevable!!!" Underneath there are all sorts of posts like, "Go on, spill," and "Do tell!" But Hannah's remaining tight lipped and mysterious. Vaguebooking. She's far too canny to post something public about Mum. But I bet her private message page is red hot with traffic.

I spin the computer round for Ollie to see.

"Ah. Well. Let them gossip now. By the time you go back to school, they'll be onto something else."

"Oh spare me, Ollie. That's the kinda thing Mum would say. You know fine well what it's like at school, so don't pretend this will just go away."

"Sorry. I know. It's going to be horrible."

"So what do I do?"

Ollie thinks for a bit. "I think you need to take your grunge look to a whole new level."

"Seriously? Fashion tips?"

He laughs. "Yes, if you like. See, girls like Hannah Walters prey on weakness, but the really weird kids creep them out, so they tend to give them a wide berth."

Actually he has a point. "Yes! You're right. No one goes near Meredith Baker!" She's the school Goth. "So do you think I should Goth it up?"

"Maybe. Or even just act hard. Remember, Gus saw your mother wallop several policemen. You could play up on that. Pretend you're a chip off the old block – mad, bad and dangerous to know."

"Yesss! I like it." I go to take a swig from my bottle and discover it's empty. "Oh. Where did that go?"

"In your belly. And before you ask, no, you cannot have another. You look half-cut as it is."

Yes, I am and it feels kinda nice. Sort of warm and fuzzy, though my tummy's far from happy. I haven't eaten all day and the beer seems to be burning a hole in my stomach. So I find a clean spoon and plunge it into the colossal tub of ice cream. "Mmmm. This is gooood. What flavour is it?" I look on the side. "Phish food. Yum."

"Hey, go easy. Leave some for me!" Ollie holds up a spoon, about to dig in too, but I nudge him aside.

"Nooo. Go away. It's all mine."

He sits back and crosses his arms, looking awfully smug. "You're going to spew, you do know that."

"Never." But actually, I am feeling a bit queasy. The beer, mingled with marshmallow, cream and chocolate is producing some pretty putrid gurgling sounds. I push the tub away. "I'm done. I need my bed."

Ollie looks at his watch. "It's only 8 o'clock."

I flap a pathetic hand in his direction, for I can't actually speak.

* * *

Well, I conked right out as soon as my head hit the pillow, but then I woke about midnight, with this stabbing pain in my stomach. Man, it was sore. I dragged myself through to the loo, half crawling like a commando. Then huddled over the toilet bowl, I retched a few times before the whole rotten lot came hurling out. Bile flavoured beer and bits of marshmallow, my puke was actually green. Yeeuch, it tasted revolting. After that I couldn't really sleep. I'd nod off, have these vivid dreams about Mum, wake up, then spend the next hour or so tossing and turning.

So now I'm absolutely exhausted. My head is thumping and I have this layer of fur on my tongue. Ollie though has strolled into the kitchen looking revoltingly fresh-faced. "Morning," he practically sings.

"Whatever," I grunt, glowering into my coffee.

"You ready?"

"I s'pose. What time's visiting?"

Ollie picks up my mug and takes a slurp. "Instant. Yuk. Um... they said we could go in anytime today. So let's just..." he falters, struggling for the right word.

"...get it over with?"

He grins. "Well, you said it, not me. Where's the car keys?"

"In that drawer, I think." I nod to the junk drawer where all the bits and bobs are kept.

"Got them," he says, shaking the keys. "So let's pimp this ride and go burn some rubber."

Yeah, right. Mum's got a Volvo.

Well, at first it feels like a nice trip out. I've been cooped up in the house for so long, that going anywhere in the car feels like a holiday. We stop for a fry up on the way and that's brilliant. Boy, does that black pudding sort out my stomach. But then 15 minutes into the drive, I say to Ollie, "How far is this place?"

And he says, "Another ten minutes, I think."

So that gets me thinking, how the heck am I supposed to get here when he goes off to Europe?

I've never been to Carthill Hospital before, never even passed it, cos it's not the sort of place you'd ever just stumble across. It lies at the end of this twisty, turny road that leads to nowhere but the hospital and the population en route consists entirely of sheep.

"Are you sure this is the way?"

"Yeah, I put the postcode in the TomTom."

After a bit there's a smattering of houses, then we turn a corner and before us looms this huge Gothic structure of dark, black stone. The front part of the building looks like a typical Victorian hospital – a couple of storeys high with curved bay windows. But it's flanked on either side by these enormous clock towers with battlements on top, which makes it look more gaol than hospital. Seriously, this place would make the perfect setting for a horror film. I have visions of some mad professor incanting lightning from one of those towers. I shiver, glad it's a sunny day, cos Carthill must be the creepiest place on earth in winter.

Ollie pulls into the driveway and that's when we spot the No Entry sign and electric fence. For a second I think Mum's being held behind that fence then I realise the hospital is derelict. The electric shocks are to keep vandals out, not to keep patients in.

"It's empty," says Ollie, looking bewildered.

"It says Carthill on the sign. When did it close down? They must have taken her somewhere else."

"No. They definitely said Carthill."

Freaked out, we stare at each other. Has Mum been kidnapped in some elaborate scam? Suddenly there's a loud rap on the car window and I scream. Honestly – at the top of my lungs. I turn to see a grinning security guard. I flick a button and the window whirs down.

"Ye lost?"

"Um, yeah, we were told to visit someone in Carthill. But here we are and it's..." I flap a hand towards the towering grey fence and broken windows.

"Dinnae look so worried, hen. They've no disappeared. This is the auld asylum; it's been closed fir a couple a years. Aw the patients are in the Annexe noo. Aboot half a mile doon the road on yer right."

"Oh thank you.

"Nae worries."

Ollie backs out the driveway and I lean out the window, staring back at the old asylum, completely transfixed by those towers. Why are they there? What's at the top? Surely in a hospital full of suicidal people, a winding staircase to a high exposed tower would seem like an invitation to leap. Though I suppose in days gone by all the patients would have been locked in their wards. Perhaps the towers were a warning – keep out, mad people about. One tower's white clock-face is still largely intact, though it's pitted with a few black holes. But the other has completely fallen out; leaving a gaping cavity like the building's lost an eye. Ah, maybe that's it. Visible for miles, these clocks would have loomed over the countryside like unblinking eyes, a constant reminder – step out of line and this is where you end up.

"Here it is," says Ollie, slowing in front of an NHS sign. We turn into a long wooded driveway and it's a relief when we get to the end and see a cluster of modern, single-storey buildings.

"Oh thank god," I say.

Ollie switches off the engine and smiles. "Yeah, the old place is freaky. D'ye think they actually locked folk in those towers?" He opens his door. "This is admissions; she'll be in here."

The small, squat, whitewashed building looks friendly enough, but what sort of horrors lurk in there? I've seen enough old movies to be properly scared of stepping foot inside a mental ward. My bum feels glued to the seat, so Ollie has to jog round and throw open my door. "Come on, move," he says, yanking me out.

The entrance is locked, so we press a bell and wait. After a few minutes they buzz us in, but there's no one in sight, so we hover about unsure where to go next. Eventually I spot a nurse striding down the corridor. I force my mouth into a grin, but as she gets closer I realise I know this person and I stupidly try to shield my face with one hand.

"Zat's Sam." I whisper to Ollie out the side of my mouth, trying not to move my lips.

"Whit?"

"Sam," I say it a bit louder this time, though still soft enough so that she won't overhear.

"Who's 'Ham'?"

Oh for god's sake. "Not Ham! Sam!" I snap just as she reaches us, so now I'm doubly embarrassed.

"Hi Jess," beams Sam and two lovely dimples appear on the cheeks of her friendly face. "I wondered if you would remember me."

"Course I do," I mutter, staring at my feet, "you had the bendiest legs in ballet class."

Sam giggles. "I still do."

Yes, okay – I used to go to dancing, but then so does every other lassie round here. Sam was one of the older ones in my class and I used to watch with envy as she'd pirouette en pointe, while I was stuck on tippy toes. She's got this really long brown hair, almost down to her bum, but today it's tied up in a bun.

"So…" she says. "Tough week, eh?"

I snort, "Yeah. You could say that."

"Well, you take a seat and I'll go fetch your mum. I know Dr Verma wants a word too."

Just then a little Indian man comes prancing over. He's taller than Dr Verma, though not by much. He's making these weird geometric shapes with his body. It's like a mixture of yoga and some arty farty contemporary dance routine. The three of us stare, intrigued by his contortions. He stands on one leg, the other held out at a perfect right angle, his arms coiling round each other like snakes.

"He's a psychiatrist," says Sam and I almost choke.

"What? Is he Mum's?"

"No," she laughs. "He's not practising. He's a patient."

"Really?" Ollie's bug-eyed. "How does a psychiatrist end up in a mental hospital?"

"Oh, we get all sorts in here. No one's immune to mental illness, you know. Not even psychiatrists. Anyway, have a seat. You, Pradip, come with me." She holds out an arm and the little man links his through hers as they go skipping off down the corridor.

Ollie turns to me and we both burst out laughing.

"Whoa!"

"I know!"

There are a couple of Formica tables on either side of the corridor. I pull out a brown, plastic chair and sit down.

"Do you know what this reminds me of?" says Ollie, looking round. I shake my head. "You know in American films, when they bring a prisoner through to see their visitor and the big guard growls, 'hands on table, no touching.' Well it looks just like this."

He's right. "I hope they don't bring her through in an orange jumpsuit..."

"Or wearing manacles..."

Ollie sits down and we both fall silent, staring at the ugly table. The place is as hot as a sauna and the smell of school dinners and hospital disinfectant is making me feel sick again. "I wish they'd hurry up."

Ollie gives me a nudge and I look up to see Mum stumbling down the corridor, leaning heavily on Sam. Tears sting my eyes and I have to focus on the table again to stop them overflowing.

"Here she is," says Sam, expertly pulling out a seat with her foot while using both hands to safely lower Mum into the chair. I glance at Mum's face then quickly look away again, but not fast enough, for it'll now be etched in my mind forever. She looks like Gran with dementia – old and vacant and slightly slack around the mouth. Her huge blue eyes are so swollen and heavy that they look like slits. And she can't sit straight either; she's pitching so much to one side that Sam has to kneel down beside her to give her something to lean on.

"I can't..." I scrape back my chair and jump up.

"Wait!" Sam jumps up too and Mum almost falls off the chair. Sam pushes her upright and keeps a protective hand on her shoulder, like she's supporting a massive rag doll.

"Don't go running off, Jess. Your mum's very sleepy, but it's temporary. I promise."

"That..." I yell, my voice thick with tears, "... is not my mum." Oh, what did I say that for? Sorry Mum. I take it back, I didn't mean it, honest. But I can't look at you, not like that.

They must have CCTV in the visiting area, because Dr Verma suddenly appears, slightly dishevelled and out of breath. "Ah. Jessica, Oliver, come with me." He nods at Sam then with a hand on my back, propels me along the corridor and into the safety of his office.

"Please." He pats a comfy blue chair and gestures for me to sit. I sink down into it and bury my face in my hands. Ollie perches on the arm beside me and tousles my hair. I swat his hand away. Is that supposed to make me feel better?

"You've had quite a shock," says Dr Verma, settling down behind his desk. "Your mum's on a lot of medication and it will take time for her body to adjust. But it will adjust and then she will start to improve. Here, please." He waves a box of Kleenex in front of me and I scoop out a handful. "And we have some positive news about her blood work. The results show multiple abnormalities..."

"WHAT?"

"Ah... excuse me, poor choice of words. I mean it is positive that we have identified those abnormalities, not that she has them. It gives us something to work on."

He sits back, clearly satisfied that all is now clear, but I'm still clueless.

"Er, what kind of abnormalities are we talking about?" ventures Ollie.

"Is she dying?" I screech.

"Oh, no. No, of course not." The doctor stares at Mum's file for some time then says, "Your mum has a hormone imbalance. Do you know what that means?"

I shrug, but I feel Ollie tense.

"It means," he goes on, "that she is going through the menopause. And that's not all. She also has an underactive thyroid and a significant vitamin B12 deficiency. On their own, all of these conditions cause depression. Put them together and add to that the stress of caring for your gran – well a major depressive episode was inevitable really."

"Is it... is it... serious?"

"Is what serious?"

"The thyroid thingy and B12."

"Oh no... no. These conditions cause very serious symptoms, but are relatively easy to treat. I'll get Sam to print off some handouts for you."

"But," says Ollie, looking confused, "if it's just depression why is she seeing stuff? I mean, if she imagines Satan's inside her, isn't that schizophrenia?"

"You're right, psychosis isn't normally a symptom of depression, but your mum certainly isn't schizophrenic, so please don't concern yourself with that. Sometimes a major depressive episode is accompanied by delusions and even hallucinations. We classify that as psychotic depression – that's what your mum has."

Ollie looks at me and smiles. He's obviously been worried that Mum's turning schizo and the diagnosis of depression is clearly a relief. I hadn't really thought about it, but yes, depression sounds much less serious than schizophrenia – even with a 'psychotic' strapped to the front.

"So you can cure her then?"

"One step at a time Jessica – for now we are treating the depression, the psychosis and the thyroid. She'll also be receiving regular shots of vitamin B12. So I'm very optimistic that your mum will improve. It may take some time though..."

"How much time we talking?" I'm desperate to know how long she'll be in hospital so I can figure out my living arrangements. Ollie's leaving for Europe in three days then I'm on my own, which is fine by me, but how long until somebody notices? I reckon I can get away with it for a couple of weeks by pretending Ollie's still there. I can pin his laundry outside – stuff like that. But then there's Dad to think of as well. What will I tell him? I become so caught up in these calculations that I completely lose track of what the doctor's saying, only tuning back in to hear him finish:

"...so you're probably looking at two to three months."

"Until she's better?"

"Until she's discharged. Then she may attend an outpatient facility for several months."

"You are joking, right? She can't stay in here for three months. No WAY!"

"Jess! Calm down," Ollie hisses.

"But... but... three months!"

Dr Verma looks at his watch. "I'm so sorry, but we're going to have to leave it there, I have another appointment I'm already late for. I'll get Sam to show you round. You'll see, Jessica, your mum will be quite comfortable here, even if it is for a few months."

It's not her I'm worried about, but I smile and nod all the same. Is it possible to pull off being home alone for that length of time?

Dr Verma takes us to find Sam. She's in the nurses' station, which is like this little greenhouse opposite the dayroom – windows all round to keep an eye on the inmates, I guess. The dayroom is full and the television blares noisily. I can see Mum slumped in an armchair in front of a cookery show, something she'd never do at home. Sam gives us the grand tour. She shows us Mum's room, which is painted a cheery yellow. I was worried she'd be stuck on a huge ward, so the little room for four is a big relief. Sam, though, squints at the ceiling and wrinkles her nose. "It's a bit shabby, I'm afraid." I glance up too and spot the spiderweb of cracks and peeling paint.

"We're moving in six months," explains Sam, "so it's not worth patching it up."

"Who's moving?"

"The hospital. All of it. Carthill will be no more. It's about time too. God, 2011, and here we still are treating patients like lepers – banished to the back of beyond. There's no excuse for it. But from February, our ward will be slap bang in the centre of Kilshaw, right in the heart of the community, exactly where it should be. And I'll be able to pop to the shops at lunchtime, grab myself a Costa on the way in – maybe even have a wee drink after work."

Centre of a community it might be, but not the centre of my community. Kilshaw's miles from us – would still mean taking three buses.

"Oh, Ann!" Sam's gaze slides to a woman in the bed next to Mum's. "You know you shouldn't be sleeping in the day. Come on, up you get now, before the doctor sees you." The woman yawns noisily and you can tell it takes a colossal effort to get herself upright and onto her feet.

"Seems cruel," I mutter.

"What does?" asks Sam and I think I might have

offended her, but when I glance at her face she just seems curious.

"Well, you know... dope them with medication, but don't let them sleep. That's torture, isn't it?"

Ollie sighs loudly and rolls his eyes. "For god's sake, Jess..."

Sam laughs. "It's okay, Ollie, I know what she means. But as my wee granny always says, sometimes you have to be cruel to be kind. They're not going to recover if we let them lie around all day. We have to establish a normal routine."

"That's what I've been saying!" says Ollie, and now it's my turn to roll my eyes. Know it all.

Ollie goes in to kiss Mum goodbye, but I don't. I know I should, but I really can't face her again today.

On the way home, Ollie and I do this massive food shop, then I scrub the cooker, get me an apron on and prepare us both a nutritionally balanced meal – veggie chilli from one of Mum's books, followed by fresh fruit salad and cream. This is the beginning of my stay home alone campaign.

"Mmmm. Good chilli," sprays Ollie, shovelling it in.

"Glad you like it," I say, primly spearing one stray pinto bean. "I have a varied culinary repertoire. I may spend tomorrow cooking for the freezer, so I have a selection of nutritious meals to hand... you know... for when you go away." Just casually drop it in there and wait for the reaction.

Ollie's fork freezes in front of his mouth. Rice and chilli slide off and he stares miserably down at his plate.

"I'm not going to Europe, Jess."

"What? Don't be daft! It's all paid for."

"How can I?"

"Look, put down the fork, I can't see your face. There. Now you listen to me, Ollie Brody, there's no point in us both being miserable. You saw her today; she didn't even know we were there. Go. Honestly. I'll visit every day. I swear."

"It's not that, Jess. How can I leave you on your own? You're only fifteen."

"Nope. Nuh-uh. No way. I'm not getting the blame for you missing out on your Europe trip. I'll be sixteen in four months time..."

"Five."

"Four and a half. But the point is I'm more mature than plenty of eighteen-year-olds. I can look after myself. And you know at my age, Grandpa was already in the army and Gran was working in an office. In those days, you could leave home at fifteen."

"Yeah, but there must be a reason why they raised it to sixteen."

"Look. In four months time, I can move out, leave school, have sex, smoke fags and get married. Is four months really going to make such a difference to my maturity? I'm the person now that I will be then. Besides, it's only illegal to leave a child on their own if it puts them at risk. I won't be at risk. Any problems and I've got Tracy next door and I'm sure I can spend some nights at Amy's."

Ollie picks up his fork again; he's looking a lot happier. "Really? You won't be scared?"

"I don't think so. Anyway, you go back to uni in a few weeks, so we can call it a trial run for then."

"I dunno. Maybe we should call Dad..."

"NO! I'd rather be put in care than live with Dad and poo-face Pippa. Remember that awful trip two years ago? It was disgusting – the way they were all over each other.

At it day and night they were. And Pippa made it very clear she didn't want us in the house. She'd completely ignore me if Dad wasn't about then turn on the charm when he was. I hate her. I really, really hate her."

"All right. Keep yer hair on. But he does need to know, doesn't he?"

"Why? Why does he have to know anything? He gave up that right when he fled the country to be with that bimbo. Mum would be so upset if you told him she was psychotic. Can you imagine the smirk on Pippa's face? Can you? Oh she'd just love that..."

Ollie drops his fork again. "Okaaaay! Give it a rest. I'll think about it. All right?"

Well, as he hasn't yet said "NO," that is completely fine by me.

6

NAKED HYSTERIA

He's going! He's really, really going! My brother might make out he's all mature and responsible, but really he's just a randy teenager. So he says I can stay on my own when he goes off to Europe. He won't phone Dad either, on the condition I go to Amy's at the first sign of trouble.

I guess you're wondering why I'm so keen to pack him off to Europe. Am I simply the best sister in the world? Nah. Truth is, it's all part of my game plan. See, if Ollie's miserable about missing his trip, there's no way he'll let me stay by myself when he goes back to uni. But if I give him a pass to go to Europe then he owes me. BIG TIME. And the precedent has been set. If I cope while he's on holiday, he can't then complain about me living on my own when uni starts back. There's no way he'll tell Dad either, cos then he'll have to 'fess up about the Europe trip. Cunning, eh?

I need to tell Amy, she'll be so psyched. I haven't spoken to her in days, and we usually talk all the time. Maybe she's in the huff cos I hung up on her when the psychiatrist was in. I'll take a walk round to hers rather than call. I don't want to explain the Mum situation over the phone anyway. Right, where's me shoes? I slip them on and open the door but as soon as I step outside my heart starts beating really fast. I don't want to meet any neighbours and Clarkey's curtains are already twitching, so I run back inside and slam the door shut.

"Olllieeee!"

"What?" I find him hunched over his rucksack, counting out boxer shorts. He leans back on his haunches, scratching his head. "I'll never fit it all in."

I snatch up the bundle of pants and burst out laughing. "Have you bought a pair of pants for every day you're away? You're seriously planning to go backpacking with twenty-eight pairs of pants?"

"What's wrong with that?"

"Ollie. You're meant to rough it when you go inter-railing. What else have you got?" I nudge him aside and stare down at the mountain of toiletries and oh, my god! "That's not twenty-eight pairs of socks is it?"

"NO!"

"How many then?"

"Fourteen," he mutters.

"Fourteen pairs of socks! It's August in the Med, Ollie, it's going to be boiling."

"Not everywhere. Some bits are just like Scotland and the evenings get chilly all over."

"You're such a girl, Ollie Brody, you really are. Honestly, I think you got my X chromosome and I got your Y."

He glares at me. "Precisely what was it you wanted?"

"Oh yes. I need you to give me a lift to Amy's."

"No. Don't be so lazy, she only lives two streets away."

"Oh go on Ollie, I don't want to bump into anyone. Pleeease?"

"No. Get lost, I'm busy."

"Pretty please and I'll help you pack when I get back."

He sighs loudly, but I can tell he's tempted. "And?"

"And what?"

"What else can you throw in?"

"Um... howz about I cook dinner again tonight?"

"Okay. Done."

So, sorry planet, but yes, we do use a car for a two-road journey. Amy lives in a BIG house, much bigger than ours. Her dad's Merc is in the driveway, but her mum's Audi isn't there. I wonder if she's gone out with her mum. I ask Ollie to wait and see, but he screeches off the second I step out the car. I ring the doorbell and Amy answers. Flawless as always, even first thing on a Sunday.

"Jess! What are you doing here?" Her eyes dart all over the place and she begins to blush. She knows then.

"Um, just came round for a catch up."

"Oh, how wonderful! It's so good to see you. Come on in." Okay so this is how I can expect folk to react. First response shiftiness, followed by embarrassment and last but not least, over the top enthusiasm.

"Please take a seat in the lounge. Can I get you a drink? Tea, coffee? Perhaps some juice?" Ah, formality and refreshments so she can scurry off to the kitchen and collect herself. Jeez, if this is how my best mate treats me, what chance do I stand with anyone else? I'm half tempted to be mean – to follow her into the kitchen, but I think, nah, let her make the tea.

Of course she takes ages, comes back clutching a tray groaning with tea and biscuits. And this is no Tetley dunked in a mug either. She's used a teapot and even put the milk in a jug. Oh dear, she is in a state.

"So, how's things?" she asks as she begins to pour. Then she flinches, cos out of habit she's asked the one question she really wants to avoid.

"Oh come on Amy, cut the crap. You know fine well how I've been. And actually come to think of it, if you knew what happened, why haven't you called?"

Amy's face crumples and she puts down the teapot. "Jess, I'm so sorry," she cries, "I've been in agony. Absolute agony. Mum said I should give you space. That you would phone when you were ready. And I didn't really know what to say…"

I'm not that interested in Amy's agony, but I desperately want to know what she's heard and who from.

"Yeah, you're in agony. I hear you. But where d'ye get the gossip? Facebook or neighbours?"

Amy's agony suddenly gets ten times worse. She's such a sweetie, she really is – torn between telling the truth and trying to shelter me. But I have to know, otherwise how will I protect myself?

"Um…"

"Tell me, Amy," I growl.

She squirms in her seat, folds her arms, unfolds them again, crosses her legs, uncrosses them. Finally, she screws up her face, opens her mouth to speak and then… nothing. Complete silence.

"Amy! Just spill."

Her mouth moves a couple of times, but still nothing comes out. I am really beginning to lose patience. I jump up. "Right, Amy, if you don't tell me this instant, we're no longer friends. Got it?"

She leaps up too. "Oh don't go storming off Jess. Here," she grabs my arm, "let's go up to my room."

I follow her upstairs to her fluffy pink bedroom, and she's right, I do feel a bit calmer up here. I mean, who can be angry in a room crammed with ponies and Build-a-Bears?

I pick up Harry Bear and give him a squeeze. In some ways Amy's so grown up with all her make-up and no carb diets, but step into her room and you'd think she was five years old.

"You really need to update this place before you start bringing boys back. It is seriously uncool."

Amy snorts. "I will be twenty-five before I'm allowed to bring a boy home and even then he'll be confined to the living room, so believe me there's no rush." I smile. Amy's dad is super protective of his princess.

"Anyway, where were we? Oh yes, you were about to spill."

"Fine." Amy snatches Harry Bear off me and hugs him to her chest. "Tracy told me. She wasn't gossiping though. All she said was your mum was in hospital, she didn't even say why..."

"Tracy? My neighbour Tracy? How were you speaking to her?"

"Er..." Amy buries her face in Harry's head and mumbles, "she came round and asked me to babysit."

"Babysit? BABYSIT! But I babysit Tracy's boys."

"I know..." wails Amy, "but she didn't like to ask, not when things were so difficult..."

"Traitor!"

Amy starts to cry. Good. Those are my boys. What right has she to look after them?

"So if Tracy didn't go into details, who did?"

"Jess, don't..." Tears rain down her face, smearing her cheeks with black mascara.

"I mean it Amy. Tell me now."

She knows I'm not going to give this up, so she nods and tries to speak, but she's having to gulp to get her words out. "There's... there's... there's stuff flying round Facebook."

"Hannah Walters?"

"Yeah, but she's no longer my Facebook friend, Jess. I've unfriended her. I've unfriended the lot of them."

And suddenly I'm crying too and we're hugging with Harry Bear squished between us. I'm so touched by her bravery. No one unfriends Hannah Walters and gets away with it. Amy's made herself Coven fodder for me and that takes a special kind of friend.

I sit back. "Amy, you've got to be her friend again. Just say you deleted her by accident. Or she's going to make your life hell."

"NO! That girl is ugly. She may look beautiful, but she's twisted and ugly inside. She said your mum was carted off in a straitjacket."

"Oh, that's just rubbish."

"And she said your mum punched a policeman in her nightdress!"

"Actually that bit's true."

Amy's eyes go wide then she giggles. "No way!"

"Yes, way." Then I'm giggling too. Am I like bi-polar or what? I've bounced from anger to jealousy, despair to laughter – all in the space of ten minutes. "But seriously, Amy, log on now and ask to be her friend again."

"Are you sure? It feels so disloyal."

"Sure, I'm sure. You can be my spy. An inside saboteur."

"Well, if you put it that way…" She picks up her pink netbook, but doesn't open it, just sits with it on her lap. "I don't know," she says, "I don't want to be her friend. I feel like a hypocrite."

"Stop dithering, girl. Look, give it here," I snatch the netbook and fling it open. Amy lunges to grab it back, but it's too late. I've already seen the message. What the…? That bitch. That fucking bitch, Walters. I'll bloody have her I will.

Amy winces as I read aloud in Hannah's squeaky voice,

"To all my BFFs, Meeting: Wednesday night at mine, 7 o'clock onwards. Agenda: Jess Brody's mum. For those who haven't heard, Jess's mum has been arrested and committed to Carthill for trying to set fire to a neighbour's house and assaulting several policeman. She was also caught exposing herself to children. And while our hearts go out to poor Jess, we must think about the safety of our community. What to do? Please forward any suggestions to me and I can add them to the agenda. See you Wednesday! XOXOXO"

Amy's crying again. "See? She's so horrible, how can I be her friend?"

I click on the Coven and make some friend requests on Amy's behalf. Then I lie back on a pillow and close my eyes. So old Clarkey's been gossiping, no surprises there. But who embellished the story, her or Hannah? Actually, probably Clarkey. I can see it now. A lonely old woman, suddenly the centre of attention, gets carried away. As everyone clamours to hear the gossip, she keeps on adding just a teensy bit more. In fact, all she had to say was, "I was scared my house would be set on fire," and Chinese Whispers would have done the rest.

But the bit about Mum exposing herself; where the heck has that come from? It makes her sound so sordid and twisted. I feel sick. I mean properly sick like I'm about to throw up. Okay, so Mum might have accidentally flashed some thigh when wrestling with the policemen, but she had knickers on under that nightdress and I know that for a fact. It's lies. All lies. Just horny teenage boys having a laugh, but it really isn't funny. We could be hounded out of town for this.

I sit up to find Amy's black-rimmed panda eyes boring

into me. I attempt a smile, but I can tell it's not convincing.

"I'm going to that meeting," I say.

"NO."

"I have to. Who else will defend my mum?"

"Me!"

"Oh, Amy, thanks, but you're not that great at public speaking are you?" Bless her; she even gets in a flap if she has to talk in class. "Besides, I think maybe you should keep your distance for a while. I don't want you getting dragged down with me."

"I'm coming with you, Jess – no arguments."

"Whatever, we'll decide later. OK? Right now, I need a makeover."

"Oooh." Amy's face lights up and she claps her hands together. Safe and familiar ground.

"Actually, don't get too excited, it's more of a makeunder. See, Ollie reckons I should grunge it up. Make myself intimidating, you know, like Meredith Baker. Then they won't torture me like they do poor Britney."

"They steer clear of Meredith cos she's a Grade A nutter! Oops sorry, I didn't mean..." Mortified at using the 'n' word, Amy slaps a hand over her mouth.

"Amy! You don't have to watch what you're saying with me. Meredith Baker is a nutter."

Amy winces. "No, it's not right. We should think more about the words we use. Meredith has a very challenging home environment, that's why she's the way she is."

"Really?" I don't know much about her. She's so sullen and prickly I always keep my distance. "What's wrong with her home life?"

"Well her Mum's a..." Amy slaps the hand across her mouth again. "I can't think of a PC word," she screeches, "my mind's gone completely blank."

"Are you searching for a word that isn't nutter?" I laugh.

Amy nods, her eyes wide.

"Try mental health problems, I think you're safe with that."

"Of course, of course! Mental health problems! Meredith's mum has mental health problems."

Ah, that explains a lot. "What sort of mental health problems?"

Amy shrugs. "I don't know. All I know is that her mum's been in Carthill. I think she might be a drug addict. But never mind Meredith Baker, what about this makeover! I'm thinking, grunge, but classy. None of that nineties stuff, more sort of Mary-Kate Olsen – smoky eyes, mussed up hair. Or what about Effy Stonem? She's scary, but hot."

"Whatever you think Amy, you are my guru." I stretch out my arms and bow down to her fashion greatness. She giggles.

"Oh, stop it you."

"Anyway, I have to go see Mum. Can you organise my outfit then?"

"No probs."

There's a beep outside. "That's Ollie."

"Give your mum my love," says Amy distractedly, but she's so engrossed in a grunge chic website that she barely looks up as I leave.

* * *

Ollie and I drive to Carthill in silence. It feels like I'm heading for a firing squad or something – seriously, the feeling of dread is that bad. Sam lets us in again and says Mum's in the dayroom. I expect to find her dozing in a chair, but then I see through the window that she's up at a table, deep in conversation with a grey haired woman. That's nice, she's made a friend and she's looking a lot more lively. I don't want to interrupt and yes, if I'm honest, I'm feeling a bit nosey, so I put a finger to my lips and signal for Ollie to follow.

"…but the Devil's in me…" I can hear Mum say as we tiptoe in. Then her companion pipes up,

"Aye, he is. That's why ye have tae embrace the Lord. Let the Lord in."

"How can I let the Lord in when I am consumed by the Devil? Surely I must expel the Devil first?" She has a point.

"Well ye'll get naewhere wae that attitude hen. Dae ye want him draggin' ye doon tae the firey pits o Hell?"

Mum looks terrified and I've heard enough.

"You," I jab a finger at the old crone, "leave my mum alone. Go on, get away." The woman sucks on her dentures and gives me a sour look, but gets up from the table all the same.

"We'll talk later," she mutters to Mum as she ambles on past, trying to act all nonchalant.

"You will not." I yell after her. "You are banned from speaking to my mother. Do you hear? Banned." I turn to Ollie, who's looking gormless and bewildered. "You stay here and guard Mum, I'm going to find Sam." So I stalk out the dayroom and rap on the door of the nurses' room. Sam beckons me inside.

She flashes me a dimply smile. "Your Mum's looking great, isn't she? I mean, compared to yesterday, you must be so pleased?"

"Um… yeah… but, that wee wummin she was sitting with…"

"Ah yes, wee Aggie…"

"Well, wee Aggie is spouting all sorts of claptrap and it's scaring Mum. When we walked in she was actually agreeing that Mum's got the Devil in her belly."

Sam sighs. "Yes it's a bit of a problem. See Aggie is the opposite of your mum. She thinks she's a vessel for the Lord..."

I'm intrigued. "Wait a minute, how's that a mental illness? Surely that's what the Clergy think. In fact, wouldn't it be nice to believe you've got God inside?"

Sam sighs again. "Sometimes it is, sometimes it isn't. See the Lord puts wee Aggie to the test. He asks her to do some dangerous things. Did you notice the burn marks on her face?"

I nod. The skin on one side is a shiny, mottled pink.

"Well that's from when the Lord asked Aggie to immerse herself in boiling water."

"Bloody Hell! And you're letting her speak to my mum! What if she decides to help Mum get the Devil out? Oh man, she might set her on fire."

"It's okay, calm down. Aggie doesn't hurt other people, only herself. Your mum's quite safe. The patients don't have access to anything sharp, pointy or flammable."

"Yes, but that's still not going to help Mum's mental state, is it? If Aggie keeps encouraging her psychosis. You need to separate them. Keep them apart."

"And how do we do that Jess? Your mum's a grown up. We can't tell her who she can and can't speak to."

I suppose, but it doesn't seem right, does it? I mean how can they cure Mum's delusions when that lunatic of a woman keeps telling her they're real? And speaking of lunatics here comes another. A young woman in her early twenties with an amazing figure and long dark hair has come running into the foyer between nurses' room and dayroom, tearing off her clothes and shouting, "HELP! HEEEEELP," at the top of her lungs. Sam rolls her eyes.

"What a day. I have to go."

"It all seemed so calm yesterday..."

"Full moon," she says and before I can ask if she's serious, she ushers me out the nurses' station and locks the door. By this time three other nurses have descended on the near-naked bundle of hysteria. So Sam walks off and comes back with a bed-sheet, which she tries to wrap round bare shoulders, but the woman is having none of it. Oh no, this one's determined to disrobe. She spits, screeches, hits, and kicks and I don't know what to do. I feel like a Peeping Tom, just standing here watching. But how am I meant to get to the dayroom? Oh wait – bit of a lull now – so just let me sidle on past to re-join my brother. Haha, look at his face! Talk about red as beetroot! Squirming with embarrassment, he's desperately trying to avert his eyes, but it's difficult not to glance up each time the hot naked lady yells a new obscenity. It's like trying to drive past a car wreck without having a squiz – damn near impossible.

"So," says I, trying to change the subject, "how have you been, Mum?"

"I would be a helluva lot better if that drama queen out there would just shut her mouth. All night she was at it. Oh, woe is me! Like some cheesy Chekov actress."

Ollie and I smile at each other. This is the most lucid thing Mum has said in days.

Mum catches my smile. "It's not funny! How am I supposed to sleep?"

"Oh it's not that Mum, it's just nice to hear you speak, that's all." I glance out the window to see the hot naked drama queen being huckled off down the corridor. I have to say, I kinda agree with Mum. There's something not quite convincing about the woman's histrionics, as if she's playing at being 'crazy' rather than genuinely losing control. Surely no one would fake mental illness, but perhaps when you've reached rock bottom, there's something quite liberating about it. If folk think you're mad anyway, what's to stop you getting your kit off in public?

Mum stands up. "Come on, let's get away from that bloody TV."

We follow her down the corridor and into her room, but there's no peace to be had there either. The partitions between rooms must be paper-thin, for the banshee wails of the drama queen next door aren't exactly muffled. In fact it sounds like she's having histrionics in the bed next to Mum's.

"All night she kept it up," says Mum, arms folded, face indignant.

It isn't pleasant, I'll give you that, but at least it's giving Mum a bit of a shake, sparking some normal emotions. She pats the bed next to her and I sit down. She nuzzles into my neck and puts her arm around my waist. Wow, I'm getting a cuddle. When was the last time I got one of those? What's she saying? "Bring us some matches, would you?" she whispers, like she's asking for cocaine. Oh I see, I'm not getting love, she's just trying to score.

"NO! No matches for you." Christ, imagine if wee Aggie got her hands on them – the whole place would be up in flames. "No Mum. No matches. You don't need them."

But actually she does. For whatever drug has been keeping her calm is clearly wearing off. She's now wringing her hands like she's rubbing in soap and her knee's jiggling with agitation. She looks at me so pleadingly and with such obvious desperation, that if I had matches on me, they'd be hers.

Okay, enough's enough. I don't want to be there when she loses it, so I tug on Ollie's sleeve and murmur, "Let's go." He looks at his watch and makes a face.

"We only just got here."

"I know. But..." I nod my head in Mum's direction. She's up and pacing about.

"Um. Mum. We're thinking of heading off, but we can hang around a bit longer if you like?" Ollie bellows it extra slow, like he's speaking to a toddler with hearing difficulties. Mum doesn't reply. She's lost again to her demons. Ollie's eyes shine ominously.

"Why you so upset?"

"Och, I dunno," he says, pressing away tears with the heels of his hands. "It's just when you get a glimpse of the real her and then she goes back to this. It makes it harder somehow. Well it does for me."

"But she's been brilliant today. If you think what she was like yesterday."

"Yeah. You're right. It's just, I go away the day after tomorrow and I'd like... well, I'd like..."

"Like her to be all better so you don't need to feel guilty?"

"Precisely," he grins. "Which is far too much to hope for, I know. So come on. Let's blow this joint. It's completely doing my head in."

7

PSYCHO

Today's the day. Hannah's meeting. And I've hardly slept a wink. As soon as I drifted off last night, my heart started racing like I was on a treadmill, which kept jolting me awake. Typical isn't it? The very day I need to be on the ball and here I am with a heid like mince.

I'm still going to that meeting though and I need to plan what to wear. So I've told Ollie he'll have to visit Mum on his ownsome. Look at him. His face is pure sulk but he can hardly complain, given he's jetting off to Europe tomorrow. I've not told him about the meeting though. I don't want to risk him cancelling his trip, so I've just said I'm entitled to a day off, which is fair enough, don't you think?

Right, as soon as he leaves, I'll text Amy to come round with my new grunge wardrobe. But he keeps faffing about. What's he playing at? "Are you going today or what?"

"Yes! I'm going!" I tell you, if looks could kill! Still, he's flounced out the door now, and as if by magic here comes Amy, plodding up the driveway bogged down by bags. I step out to help and she hands me a make-up bag about as big as Ollie's rucksack.

87

"Is this your normal make-up bag?" I ask, marvelling at its size.

"Yes, why? What's wrong with it?"

"Um nothing, it's nice, just... very big."

"Is it?" She sounds surprised. "Why, how big is yours?"

"I don't have one."

"What d'ye mean you don't have one? Where do you keep your make-up?"

"I only have a couple of lipsticks and a powder puff."

"Oh, Jess!" she shakes her head, as if I'm a truly hopeless case. "What are we going to do with you?" We walk inside and she points to a seat in the dining room. "Sit."

I do as I'm told and she stands behind the chair and yanks a comb through my hair. "OW!" She's really rough. To take my mind off the pain I ask to have a look through the massive bag of make-up.

"Sure." She picks it off the floor and bangs it down in front of me.

"You know, you're quite scary when you do makeovers," I say.

"It's a serious business."

"Okaaay." I begin to rummage. "Wow! How many mascaras have you got in here? They all look exactly the same."

"Well they're not." She sounds indignant. "Look, that one you're holding is a daytime mascara. It gives a natural look. I have several of those in different shades – black, very black, blackest-black, brown, medium brown and so on. Then that one there gives more definition, though it isn't too racy so you could still get away with wearing it to school. But this one," she plucks a thick, yellow tube from the bag, "this makes your eyelashes look enormous. Then there's your waterproofs, your volumisers, your..."

"All right! All right! I get it." Afraid she's about to start on lipstick, I push the bag to one side. "Anywaaaay, my plan for tonight is this. I'm going to drink some beer before I go, not much, just a few mouthfuls so you can smell it on my breath, then I'll turn up smoking a ciggie. When Hannah answers the door, I'm going to lean in close like this," I beckon for Amy to bend down. She does and I press my face right up to hers and pretend to blow out smoke. She stumbles backwards in disgust. "See! Effective isn't it! And as I blow smoke in her face, I'll growl something like, 'havin a pow-wow without me luv? Ah don't think so. Step aside.' Then I'll barge past her and break up the meeting. What do you think?"

Amy looks worried. "Um. I'm not too sure about the whole beer and fags thing, Jess. What if her mum sees? Won't you get in trouble?"

"Isn't that the whole idea?"

"Weeell, no, not really. Surely the idea of going grunge is to keep out of trouble, not to cause it. What does Ollie think?"

"Um, I haven't actually told him."

"That you're going to the meeting?"

"That there's a meeting taking place."

Amy tugs my head back by the hair. "JESS! You have to tell him." Her upside down face looms over mine.

"Ow. You're a really mean makeover lady. Give me back my head."

"No. Not until you see sense. You have to tell Ollie about the meeting."

"NO!"

Amy lets go of the hair and I rub my neck. She sits down. "Why not? I don't understand."

So then I have to tell her how Mum might be gone for

months and how I don't want to live in Dubai with Dad and Pippa Poo-Face. "So you see how important it is for Ollie to go on this trip," I finish, expecting another lecture about staying out of trouble.

But Amy isn't listening. Her face is rapt and suddenly she exclaims, "You've got an empty!" she clutches my arm with excitement. "A house with no parents! We can watch horror films, have boys over – have a party! Oooh Jess, this is so exciting."

"Hang on a sec, Amy, no one would come to my party. I'm a social outcast, remember?"

"Oh Jess, you're aiming too low. We'll make new friends. More mature ones. Oh, oh, I've got it!" She's so excited, her feet begin to move like she's jogging in her chair. "We'll get ourselves all glam, head into town and bag ourselves a couple of students. Yeah? We can bring them back here."

Mmmm. Student totty. That does sound interesting; the boys at school are all so spotty and immature. "I like your thinking, Amy, but no parties. I can't upset the neighbours or risk the police turning up."

"I hear you. Just a few friends over for drinks. Or... oh, I know, a dinner party."

For god's sake. "Yeah, okay, Amy, whatever. You have a think. Just... can we get on with the makeover as well?"

"Oh, yes, yes," and she delves an arm into her bag of magic and half an hour later, ta dah! I look like a moon-faced, mousy-haired Frances Bean Cobain. I stare in the mirror that Amy holds up.

"I dunno Amy, you've done a really good job, but I've never worn this much make up before. D'ye really think I need that much black around my eyes? And what's that stuff on my cheeks? I'm not sure about that at all." I turn my head to get a side-on view.

"It highlights your cheekbones..."

"But I don't have any cheekbones, I'm too well fed for heroin chic."

"It works," Amy hisses through gritted teeth. "Now put on the clothes."

She thrusts the bundle onto my lap and I squeeze myself into a frayed denim mini. Then I slip on an oversized check shirt and start to button it up to the collar, but Amy slaps my hand away with a loud tut and undoes most of the buttons. She drapes a clunky silver cross round my neck and fastens a studded strip of black leather to my wrist. Then all that's left is the ripped black tights and chunky boots. "There. Come look." She grabs my hand and pulls me through to the full-length mirror in the hall.

"So?" she says, giving my mussed up hair a final fluff.

"Actually it kinda works. I like it." If I squint through half-closed eyes, the outline of grunge looks really quite convincing. Wait. What's that noise? Oh Christ, a key in the lock. Ollie's back! I duck behind Amy.

"What are you doing?" she tries to shake me off, but I crouch down behind her and peek through a crack by her elbow.

Ollie comes in and blinks, bewildered. "Jess? I can see your feet you know. Why are you hiding behind Amy?"

"Um..."

Amy thrusts her hands on her hips, which means I have to scooch down even lower to avoid being seen. "She's frightened you'll take the mick," says Amy, "but you wouldn't dare, Ollie Brody, would you?" Wow, makeover Amy is really quite menacing. She tries to step aside so Ollie can have a neb, but I cling to the back of her skirt like a toddler.

"Take the mick out of what?" He darts round the side of Amy, but I'm too quick for him and I begin to crawl through her legs. But she's too fast for me, and before I can make it through she presses her knees into my sides and sits down on my back with a thump.

"Ow. You big fat..." My arms buckle and I nosedive into the carpet.

"Jeez Jess, if you can't even let Ollie see you, what chance do you have tonight?"

"Tonight? What's happening tonight?"

"Gerrroff," I mumble into the carpet. Amy slips off sideways and I scramble to my feet, desperate to get to Ollie before Amy splurges about the meeting. "We've been invited to a party! Isn't that right, Amy?"

"Em... yeah..."

But Ollie has other things on his mind. He stares at me with eyes full of mischief and a mouth twitching like he's gulping down a gut full of laughter. "Whoa!" he erupts, "Who's gone mental with the war paint?" So I look like a clown, huh? I lick my fingers and start to rub my face. Amy grabs my wrists, her face like thunder.

"Don't you dare, Jess Brody. And as for you," she spins round and glares at Ollie, "you think it's cool to laugh at your little sister? To destroy her confidence, make her feel self-conscious? If she gets an eating disorder it'll be entirely your fault."

Ollie raises his hands in surrender. "Sorry. Sorry. I'm an idiot, forgive me Jess! You look great, honest, you do. It's just a bit of a shock, that's all."

Deflated, I slink through to the living room and throw myself on the sofa. Ollie follows, his face now anxious and miserable. "I mean it Jess, you look amazing. Really grown up. Just ignore what I said. I'm a moron."

"Yes you are... d'you mean it though? You really think I look good?"

"Yes! I wouldn't lie, not about this. If you looked like a dork I'd tell you. I mean – I wouldn't want you making me look bad."

Satisfied her work is done, Amy heaves her massive bag of make-up onto her shoulder and heads off home. Before she goes, I make her promise not to come tonight. She says she won't, but she doesn't sound entirely convincing.

"Right, I'm off out for beers," says Ollie. "Don't wait up. It could get messy."

"Oh. OK." I don't want to be on my own, though I suppose with Ollie out the way I won't have to dodge awkward questions about the "party." But I'm sooo nervous. Maybe I'll just open that beer now, have a couple of swigs so it smells on my breath. Mmmmm. Yum. Tastes nicer today, it's so icy cold I can hardly taste the bitterness. Actually, it's going down rather too well. I've almost finished that bottle. Ah well, Ollie's away tomorrow so he won't be needing his carry out. He'll never notice if I open the last one too. And while I'm at it, what about a ciggie? There's some of Mum's left in the kitchen drawer. I dig them out and spark one up, but yeuuuuch, they taste no better. I stub it out – I'll save those till I get to Hannah's door.

Right, what time is it? 6 o'clock. Maybe I'll amble over. It won't take an hour to get to Hannah's, but it's doing my head in just sitting here. I can walk mega slow.

Okay, got my keys, got the cigs, off I go. One foot in front of the other. Actually, I'm a bit wobbly after that beer. I can't actually walk in a straight line. Oh, Morris Road, I'm here already and it's only twenty past. And there's one of the Coven – Chloe Brown no less. Oh god if she spots me the whole thing's ruined. She's walking right past.

Aaaaagh. I look down at my feet and she doesn't even clock me. Wow, it's like I'm in disguise. Right, I'll just walk up and down for a bit, keep an eye on who's arriving. Oh but wait, that woman in the house opposite keeps darting to her window to stare at me. Oops, must look like I'm casing the joint. Best go in before the neighbour calls the police. So what if I'm bit early? The last thing we need is another Brody woman being bundled in a squad car.

I knock on the door, cigarette in hand and Hannah's mum answers. What's she doing here? I didn't think she'd be home. I don't know why, I just presumed Hannah would be hiding all this from her parents. Right, don't panic Jess, don't run away.

Hannah's mum is a right snotty cow. She stares at me like I'm dog vomit.

"Yes?" she barks with a posh Radio 4 twang.

"I'm here to see Hannah," I take a deep, long drag on my fag and prop a nonchalant shoulder against the wall.

"Well, you can put that filthy thing out for a start," she jabs an angry finger at my cigarette.

I can't stop myself, I snap up straight, mumble, "Yes, Mrs Walters," drop the fag on the step and grind it out with the toe of my boot. What a rebel, eh?

"Who did you say you were?"

"Er…I didn't. But Hannah will want to see me."

She looks at me like, 'yeah right,' but she leans inside and yells,

"HANNAH. Someone to see you."

"Just send her in!"

"No, come to the door!"

"Why?"

"Because… because… she's smoking a cigarette."

"WHAT!" Hannah appears in the hall. "Meredith Baker,

you are not welcome... oh..." She stops dead about a metre from the door and stares. "You're not Meredith! You're... Jess?"

"Yep." Now how's this going to work? I can't exactly barge past her mother.

"Um... how nice to see you," she says. Yeah, right. "But what are you doing here? We were just... um..." Hannah's frowning face suddenly breaks into a smile as she stares past my shoulder. "Oh hello!" she says and I turn to see a middle aged woman and her two daughters, come grinning up the drive.

"Lucinda!" beams Hannah's mum, "do come inside. Help yourself to a glass of wine and I'll be with you in a minute." I guess they must be neighbours because I don't recognise them from school, but why's the mum going in as well? I stand aside to let them past then I go to follow, but no sooner have they crossed the threshold than Hannah's mum bars the door with her arm.

She turns to Hannah. "So? Who is this?"

Hannah's squirming. If she'd answered the door it would have all gone to plan, but this is turning into a disaster.

"It's Jess, Mum, you know..."

Hannah's mum looks at me and it is clear that, no, she does not know.

"Jess who?"

Hannah's dressed for a cocktail party, she's teamed up a little black dress with killer high heels and her sleek blonde hair is teased into an elaborate do. (Seriously, high heels indoors? Who does that?) But her bronze mask is beginning to slip. She keeps sucking on her bottom lip, smearing lipstick onto her teeth, which leaves one lip bare, while the other's still a deep, glossy pink. Worse than that, beads of sweat are bubbling up on her brow. "Jess Brody, Mum!"

"OOOH! Brody!" The penny finally drops. Hannah's mum's mouth gapes open and the arm that barred my way drops to her side. I take advantage to squeeze on past and walk briskly down to the end of the hall. The previous guests disappeared into a door on the right, so that's where I'm heading. I keep expecting Hannah or her mum to rugby tackle me and turf me outside, but when I turn to look, they're both still at the front door, heads together in frantic conversation. So I smooth down my skirt, which is in danger of turning pornographic and step through the door.

Hannah's massive living room is buzzing with people, not just Hannah's friends but their parents too. Half the neighbourhood is here and sitting on a pouffe in the centre of a huddle is old Mrs Clarke, clutching a sherry. Most folk are deep in conversation, so no one's noticed my grand entrance, well, no one except Fat Britney who stands alone, scouring the room for someone to talk to. She's spotted me, and her face has gone crimson. Yeah, Britney – go ahead and squirm, for that's the end of any sympathy you'll ever get from me! Unsure what to do, I find a quiet corner and sit on the floor. I'll wait for the meeting to start and then butt in.

"...it's the children I feel sorry for," I can hear old Clarkey above the din. She's half-deaf, so she always shouts. "First their dad leaves them...what's that?" Someone's asked a question that I don't catch. Clarkey listens intently then continues, "No. I don't think she was mad back then. No he swanned off with a hussy half his age. Lives abroad now and never visits the children. Poor mites. They have no one. No one." She shakes her head sorrowfully and her audience erupts with questions.

I feel like springing up and slinging that sherry in her face. Mum told her these things in confidence and now she's using them as cabaret. This is my life she's broadcasting, not some titillating titbit from Hello magazine. And Mum didn't tell her those things because she wanted to. Oh no, she used to visit old Clarkey because she felt sorry for her. Clarkey would moan about her arthritis and pump Mum for gossip; it used to drive Mum up the wall.

"...I heard screams in the night." She's off again. "There was one night I almost called the police, I've no idea what was going on..." I can't take much more of this, but thankfully Hannah's mum appears in the doorway and signals for quiet. Her face is flushed; it's one thing having a meeting behind my back, but to do so in front of me will require a whole new set of tactics.

"Em. Thank you everyone for coming. It's lovely to see such a strong turnout. It shows what a close-knit community we are, when we can come together at this difficult time to offer the Brody family our full and heartfelt support."

I almost burst out laughing at the stunned look on some folk's faces. A murmur goes round the room.

"I thought..." some brave soul begins, but Mrs Walters' hand shoots up for quiet.

"And isn't it wonderful," she says, turning to look at me, "that Jess Brody can join us this evening." Then she begins to clap. Honestly, half the room joins in and suddenly I'm getting a round of applause. This is turning into the most surreal night ever.

"...that's not Jess Brody," bellows Mrs Clarke, squinting through her bifocals, but nobody pays any attention.

"So… um… shall we make a start? Now, because Jess is here, perhaps we should just tear up this agenda and let her take the lead. Don't you think?" Mrs Walters theatrically rips her agenda in two and I spot Hannah anxiously scooping up bits of stray paper from coffee tables and chairs. I think about asking to take a look, but then I figure, nah, whatever's on there is bound to upset me.

"So, Jess, stand up, stand up!"

Oh my god, she's expecting me to address the room. Even just standing is proving problematic. How do you get off the floor in a minuscule mini skirt without flashing your pants? I manoeuvre myself onto all fours (lucky there's no one behind) and from there make it to my feet with dignity intact. Phew! I'm over hurdle number one, but now what to say?

"… um… Jess dear, what are you wearing? What's happened to you?" The moment I see old Mrs Clarke's disgusted face, I know the grunge look's been a mistake. It might have worked if it was just the girls. But with the adults here too, my best bet would have been to go for respectable. Judging by the pursed lips and scowls of my audience, I've lost their support before I've even opened my mouth. So how am I to play it? Come across like prickly Goth, Meredith Baker, so I don't get bullied at school? Or play down the grunge to suck up to those adults that might make Mum's life a misery. Well, it's a no-brainer, isn't it?

"… ah… um… I'm just trying out a new look, Mrs Clarke, bit of a giggle really." Out of the corner of my eye I see Amy enter the room and as she tiptoes over towards a chair she gives me a cheery smile and a double thumbs up. Okay, so I know I told her not to come, but man am I glad she ignored me. "Um… so… um I'll probably go back to my old clothes after this." The Coven are whispering behind their hands. Hannah's looking a lot more sure of herself and I know all my stuttering is about to win me a full on drubbing at school. Forget the clothes and get it together, Jess. Regain the upper hand.

"Um... yes, so I read about this meeting on Facebook." Hannah glares at Amy. "Um... yeah and there were mistakes on there. Things that weren't true. So I thought I had to come and speak for my mum. She's not dangerous, she wasn't arrested and she didn't try to set anyone's house on fire. And as for the other... stuff... well, that's just lies. Nasty, nasty lies."

Mrs Walters folds her arms and suddenly looks rather confrontational. She's a stocky woman, with a helmet of plastic looking, blonde hair – a bit like a Pit Bull in a wig. "Now hold on a minute, Jess, my Gus was there. You weren't." Oh dear, shouldn't have called her darling boy a liar. "Gus saw your mum resisting arrest. And well, to be frank, he saw the other stuff too."

"Mum wasn't arrested! She was being sectioned. Why would she be arrested? Gus was wrong about that and he was wrong about the other stuff..."

"Excuse me for interrupting," a tall man at the back speaks up, "but I'm rather losing the thread here. What other stuff?"

Oh my god I want to die.

"Er... well," begins Mrs Walters, "Gus saw Mrs Brody, exposing herself." Her face has turned scarlet again and she suddenly seems engrossed in plucking imaginary bits of fluff off her spotless white top.

"THAT IS A LIE!" I'm in danger of losing it. "Your Gus is thirteen years old. Have any idea what boys that age think about all day? Well I do – sex, breasts and other lady bits. My mum is hot. She's a babe with a brilliant figure.

And I bet Gus and his mates were really excited to glimpse a bit of leg. But that's it. As far as it goes. Get him in here, go on. If he's going to slander my mother then he'd better have a bloody good story."

"I will do no such thing, he's been put through enough already..."

"So you're willing to tell the whole town my mum's a perv on the strength of your son's mucky mind. Tell you what. Let's get our diaries out and arrange another meeting. I'll get the police to attend – the ones that were there that day. Let's see what they say about Gus's version of events." Oh I am good, I am on a roll. Mrs Walters' face blanches from deep red to sheet white.

"Well, that aside..." she blusters, "your mum did try to burn down a neighbour's house."

"Really?" I turn to Old Clarkey, who knocks back her sherry in one noisy gulp, "and which neighbour's house did she try to burn down?" As if I don't know.

"Jess dear, I didn't say she tried to burn down my house, I was just worried that she might..."

Mrs Walters looks horrified. "EXCUUUSE ME, Mrs Clarke! That is not what you said at all."

Suddenly everyone is talking at once. A few people even walk out. Walters and Clarkey both look like idiots. Ha! They'll be kicked off the Neighbourhood Watch, frozen out of community barbecues. Double ha! But suddenly old Clarkey screeches, "WOULD YOU PLEASE LET ME TALK?"

A shocked hush descends on the room. "I never said that Jess's mum tried to burn down my house, it was you lot that said it." She stares round accusingly. "All I said was I got worried when the paramedics tried to get a box of matches off of her and she refused to let them go. Who wouldn't be? She didn't have any cigarettes, all she wanted was matches."

A hundred wary eyes swivel my way and I feel this awful lurch in the pit of my stomach.

"So?" says Walters, looking even more like a terrier now she's locked her jaws onto me. Her whole social standing is at stake and she's not going down without a fight. My winning streak is about to backfire.

"What do you mean?" I challenge, stalling for time.

"Why did your mum refuse to give up the matches?"

Walters is making it sound so weird and incriminating that I begin to babble, "Um…I know it sounds a bit odd, but Mum was holding the matches as a sort of security blanket. They made her feel safe."

"Why on earth would holding matches make her feel safe unless she was planning to use them?" Old Ma Walters is loving this, playing at Advocate for the room.

"No, that's not it at all, she…"

"Well what did she do with the matches to make her feel…" and here she makes an inverted comma sign with her fingers, "SAFE?"

"I dunno, she just sort of sparked them…"

"That doesn't make any sense. How would sparking matches make her feel safe?" God, she's relentless and she's right too – sparking matches doesn't make sense. I don't know what to say, I'm so flustered by her interrogation.

"Um… well, see, Mum was a bit psychotic and she…"

"Psychotic?" Walters leaps on the word with triumph, as if it proves everything. "Psychotic, sounds dangerous to me."

God, the woman's thick. "Psychotic doesn't mean Psycho," I cry, miming the famous shower scene by plunging an imaginary knife through the air. "It just means she's lost touch with reality." I have to shout that last bit because the whole room is in uproar. Oh no, what have I done? I look at Amy for help, but she has her face in her hands and doesn't see.

"…is your mum schizophrenic?" someone yells repeatedly over the racket.

"NO! She's not and even if she was that doesn't make her dangerous. She just thinks the Devil's in her and she tries to keep him happy by sparking matches."

The whole room goes silent.

"Devil worship?" squeaks a lone voice.

Oh no. What am I doing? All at once, questions are being sprayed like bullets. So many voices that I can't make sense of a single one – except some woman to my right who keeps saying over and over again, "I don't understand… who did she say got stabbed?" The whole room surges forwards – slavering hounds, closing for the kill. I'm crying now, ultra volume mascara slithering down my cheeks like two fat slugs on a lettuce. I feel like screaming and suddenly there's a high-pitched shriek and I wonder for a second if it's me, but no, everyone's turning to stare at Amy. She grins goofily, unsure what to do, but glad to have distracted them if only for a moment. And then a second saviour steps forward, this time the tall man from the back of the room. He pushes his way through the crowd and places a protective arm round my shoulder.

"STEP ASIDE PLEASE," he barks like a drill sergeant. "COME ON MOVE. That's right. Out the way." Sobered by his authority, most people slink back, some shamefaced, struggling to understand how on earth they got so carried away. Only Ma Walters refuses to move, feet planted firmly in front of the living room door.

"I think it's time you called this meeting to a close, don't you?" says my protector.

Ma Walters' hard little eyes, glitter in defiance. "People have a right to know," she hisses. "It's all very well being a bleeding heart liberal until someone in the community gets killed."

The man stoops down and stares her straight in the face. Speaking very slowly he says, "End this now or I call the police."

"Oh yes, on what grounds?"

My man reaches in his pocket and pulls out a warrant card, which he flourishes in front of her nose. "Oh we can start with incitement to violence. But my colleagues can get most creative..."

My god, he's a policeman! Ma Walters sputters something incoherent and flees. My lanky friend laughs, "Man, that felt good!" Who'd have thought it, eh? Saved by the polis! The oddest end to the weirdest day ever.

8

MARTIANS

So what do you think of my neighbours? They nice or what? Know something: the minute Mum's well enough I think we should get the hell out of here. Live somewhere less stuck up. I like the idea of the city – a great big melting pot of freaks. Then we won't stand out. I HATE it here. I hate the way my life has become public property. All those snooty faced in-breds judging my family; what gives them the right? They love it though, sucking up the drama like their own personal soap opera.

Anyway, rant over.

Ollie's gone. He was up and away at the crack of dawn. I said goodbye so bravely then sat on the living room windowsill, bawling my eyes out as he disappeared down the road.

I know, I know, I've only got myself to blame. But that meeting's changed everything. Staying alone doesn't seem like such an adventure any more, it feels bloody scary. In fact, if Ollie hadn't taken off so early I might've changed my mind and begged him to stay. But too late. I'm on my own and I have to deal with it.

To make matters worse, the lovely weather's decided

to break. The pewter sky makes it seem so dark and of course the house is still filthy cos Ollie didn't help clean even though he said he would. I feel proper low.

Then there's my first trip to the hospital on public transport. Jeez those Victorians did a real fine job of sticking that place in the arse end of nowhere. First it takes twenty-minutes to get from our house to the train station. I don't want to be seen, so I pull on a baseball cap and scurry the whole way, head bowed like Victoria Beckham fleeing the paps.

Then when I finally get to the station I find the train only runs every two hours. Two hours! So I spend a really miserable hour-and-a-half, crouched in a corner of the waiting room, hoping no one spots me. The train takes fifty minutes to get to Carthill, stopping at every bloody station imaginable. Then at the other end, it's a fifteen-minute walk from the deserted station to the hospital and it's all uphill. I have to walk past the old asylum as well and now the weather's broken the place feels so dreich and creepy. And windy too! It's not windy back home, but because Carthill's actually on a hill, it seems to be blowing a gale.

Anyway, I'm here at last – all sweaty and out of breath, cheeks stinging from the wind. And now Sam's not even on shift, it's her day off, which is like fine for her but I could've done with a friendly face. It's a male nurse that answers the door. Mmmmm. Not bad. What's his name? I stare at his badge. Arthur! Seriously, who's called Arthur these days?

"She's in her room," says Arthur and I just nod. I'm feeling far too grumpy for flirting.

Mum's sitting by her bed just staring into space. It's weird seeing her look so vacant. My mum always had a book in her hand or a Sudoku puzzle or something, she would never just sit like this.

Ann in the next bed's got a visitor too, who looks up and smiles at me. "Hi," she says, "I'm Denise, Ann's daughter."

"Oh. Yeah. Hi."

"I'm so glad your mum's here," she whispers across the bed. "It's so nice for Mum to have someone that's… you know… familiar…"

I get what she means. See, her mum, Ann, is a retired teacher, educated and respectable. She's in Carthill because she fell apart when her husband died. She comes across as sad and quiet, but ultimately quite normal. Whereas some of the other patients have these bizarre quirks and curious tics. The ones in for drug or alcohol related psychosis, I find really scary. Other patients, like this wee guy Paul, have some sort of learning difficulty, but no real obvious mental illness. Paul's a sweetheart, but he looks really grubby. So I can see why Ann and Mum have been given beds beside each other.

Mum's quite calm today, a bit dopey perhaps; I think they might have upped her drugs again. She asks where Ollie is and my heart starts beating really fast. "He's gone to Europe," I say.

"Oh," is all she says. I have this big speech planned about how I'm staying with Amy, but Mum doesn't even ask who's looking after me and I feel like crying. It's like she doesn't care anymore. Ever since the spring all she's thought about is Gran and herself. And now she's so wrapped up in her own little world she's forgotten to be my mother. In fact, I feel like her mum. I have to do her washing, bring her treats, nag her to brush her teeth. There's no one looking out for me and I'm feeling proper sorry for myself.

When she's done sorting her mum's locker, Denise comes round to perch by me on the end of my mum's bed. It turns out Denise is a teacher too. In her thirties, she's still really pretty.

"Your mum's doing well," she says, nodding at her. Mum's rifling through her toiletry bag, probably still on the hunt for matches.

"Yeah. I s'pose."

Denise looks at her own mum who sits staring into space. "Mine's been in two months now and there's no real improvement. She's having ECT next week."

"REALLY! They still do that?" I thought ECT was outlawed like straitjackets and creepy asylums. If you've seen One Flew Over the Cuckoo's Nest, you'll know the bit where Jack Nicholson gets his brain blasted by 200 volts of electricity – ECT does not look nice.

"Yes, they still do it," says Denise. "In fact, Mum's had it before."

"NO!"

Denise sighs. "Yeah, it helped her a lot, actually. She's had a few major depressions over the years and the only thing that's brought her out again is ECT. But she's lost some memories along the way and that's really sad."

"God, I hope it doesn't come to that with my mum."

Denise pats my hand. "I don't think it will. Your mum's responding to treatment. She might have a long way to go, but she's still responding."

"I s'pose."

"You okay?"

"Yes. Well, no actually. It's just..." I drop my voice to a whisper, though Mum shows no interest in what we're saying. "Mum doesn't seem to love me anymore." I feel my eyes fill with tears and my chin start to wobble and I am absolutely affronted. I've only just met this woman and here I am dribbling with emotion.

"Oh Jess. It is Jess, isn't it?" I nod. "See, Jess, the thing about depression, is that it's so introspective and all consuming that it shuts out everything else. Your mum has no room in her head right now for anything but her own pain and obsessions. I know. My mum's the same and it's really tough on me and I'm thirty-three, so I can't imagine how you must feel. What age are you? Seventeen? Eighteen?"

"I'm seventeen," I say loudly, hoping Mum might respond to that, but she doesn't.

"You poor thing, you need a mum at that age."

"I do," I wail. "I really, really do." Oh dear, a little bit of sympathy and the floodgates spring open. "I just want my mum back."

"Oh Jess." Denise puts her arms round me and suddenly I find myself clinging to a complete stranger. "It will be okay, you'll get your mum back, you'll see."

"Will I?" I lean back and sniff. "Do you really think so? Cos I don't see how. It's as if my mum's gone and all that remains is this shell that looks a bit like her, but actually in many ways doesn't. It's like aliens stole the real Helen Brody and left behind this really dodgy fake."

"Yeah, well those Martians must have a thing for middle aged women, cos they've nicked my mum too."

I snort, picturing little green men drooling over mousy Ann and my greasy haired mum. "But you really think so, you think I'll get her back?" Poor Denise, how the hell's she meant to know, she's not a psychiatrist. But still, she tries to reassure me without filling me with false hope.

"I think so, yes, just... she might not be exactly the same as before."

How? I want to ask. What will be different? Which

parts stay with the Martians? But I know the person I really have to ask is Dr Verma and I won't ever dare cos I'm completely petrified of the answer.

Anyway, after visiting, the long trek home. I don't get in till gone six and I can't be bothered cooking; doesn't seem much point just for me. So dinner is a bowl of cornflakes and four chocolate digestives in front of the telly. Well, there's naff all on so I think, I know, I'll download a film on Apple TV. A little treat, I deserve it. Then I think woo hoo, I'm here on my own, I can download an eighteen. What can I watch that Mum and Ollie would freak at? Well Amy was so excited about horror films the other day that I think, yeah let's go for horror. I've seen the Scream films and they're a bit lame, so I google 'scariest horror film ever'. Apparently it's The Exorcist, a really old film from 1973. So I get it on download, grab my duvet and snuggle up on the sofa. OH MY GOD!!!! It is way beyond scary. I mean, really, you cannot imagine this sweet little girl getting possessed by the Devil. The things she says! I turn it off ten times, then turn it back on again so I can get to the happy bit at the end. I manage to see it through, but renting a horror film on my first night alone is a really BIG mistake.

I finally go to bed about midnight, but I'm way too scared to turn off the lights, which stops me getting to sleep. I lie tossing and turning for ages then I get up and wander into Mum's room. Don't ask me why. I think I just want some company. But when I sit down on her bed, I remember the hole in the ceiling. I look up and it suddenly seems really sinister – like a dark chasm to another dimension. That totally freaks me out cos I get to thinking that maybe the Devil did enter through that hole and possessed my mum like he did the girl in the Exorcist. Well, there's no chance of sleep after that, is there?

9

NOEL BLOODY EDMONDS

Bills, bills, bills. They're mounting up. Mum hasn't opened her mail in months and since she's been away I've just been scooping letters off the doormat and plonking them on the table at the bottom of the stairs. But now the heap's so high it wobbles every time I walk past.

Maybe today's the day to tackle it. Take my mind off that stupid film. OK. I'll sweep the lot onto this tray and take them into the dining room to sift through at the table. Oh man, it's gonna take more than one trip.

Right. The real junky ones can go straight in the recycling. There. That feels therapeutic. Now I can arrange the rest into piles. The tallest stack by far is from British Gas – I can tell because the logo's stamped on the envelope. I get this scary pounding in my chest. Why is British Gas sending us so many letters? Are they about to cut off our supply? I rip open the most recent one and yes, turns out we haven't paid a bill in months and they've referred us to a collection agency. I'm not entirely sure what that means. Big burly men breaking down the door and snatching the TV? And will they cut off the gas? Jeez if they do, that means no cooker, no heating, no hot water.

We owe six hundred odd quid and I have no idea how to get hold of the money. Ollie withdrew three hundred from Mum's account when she went into hospital and I've been using that for food and train fares. But I hadn't even thought about paying the bills.

I go through to Mum's office – a tiny little box room at the front of the house, barely big enough for a grey metal filing cabinet, Ikea desk and faux leather chair. I don't normally go in there; in fact I can't remember the last time I did. Mum's fiercely protective of her workspace and always keeps it obsessively neat – well, she used to. As soon as I open the door, I'm blown back by the stink. The waste paper bin is overflowing with rotten apple cores and inky-black banana skins. On the desk, mouldy coffee cups jostle for space with piles of paper and scrunched up tissues. I pinch my nose and squeeze myself onto her chair, then with my free hand I jerk open the drawers in her desk. Nothing much to see, just pens, elastic bands, that sort of thing. So I swivel the chair round and start on the filing cabinet. In the bottom drawer I spot a hanging file, marked bank statements. I pull it out and inside is a cute little ring binder, with each month's bank statement filed neatly inside. Only the statements stop dead at January this year. Where are the rest?

I need both hands to rummage through the piles of paper on the desk, so I have to release my nose. "Yeuch." The smell! God knows what is lurking at the bottom of that bin, but I am in no fit state to tackle it. Aha. Unopened bank statements, strewn between half-finished newspaper columns and by the looks of it more British Gas bills. I open the statements and file them. Her password is at the back of the folder so I log onto her online current account. There's hardly anything in there, less than £500.

And there's no sign of any money coming in either; the newspaper hasn't paid her in months. That's when I really start to panic. If I can't pay the gas bill, what chance do I have if anything else plops through the door? What about the mortgage? Electric? Mobile phones? I have a bit of a tantrum and boot over the bin, which spews all sorts of blue, furry food onto the cream carpet. I leave it there, take a deep breath and force myself to calm down.

Looking again at the account, it isn't as bad as it could have been. She's got direct debits set up for electric and phone, so those are up to date. But there's no sign of any mortgage payments. Christ almighty, is the house about to be repossessed? I race back through to the dining room and rip open the remaining letters, but there's nothing about a mortgage. And actually, come to think of it, I seem to recall that Dad pays the mortgage as part of the divorce settlement. So the only immediate catastrophe is the gas arrears. I phone the number at the top of the bill and give them my sob story about Mum being in hospital. They're brilliant. They promise to call off the debt collectors and let us pay it off a little at a time. I transfer £200 online and they say they'll send a direct debit form for Mum to sign.

I feel quite good after this, really mature and in control. So I reward myself with a big mug of tea and two choccie biccies, but then I start to panic again. I have about eighty quid left in the kitchen drawer. There's three hundred in Mum's account, but I can't touch that because it has to cover direct debits and I'm not sure if it'll even last one month, let alone two. I am destitute, completely and utterly screwed.

So I make my way up to Carthill, clutching a fistful of bills and Mum's little book of bank statements. She's sitting in her room, staring into space, so I sit down beside her and pull out the file. She takes one look and goes mental.

"NOOOoooo."

Seriously, she leaps off the bed and runs out the room. I'm so stunned, I just sit there frozen, but then I snatch up that file and go stomping off after her. She's in the dayroom, apparently engrossed in Deal or No Deal.

"Mum." I stand right in front of her so she can't see the telly. She cranes her neck to the left to look around me, so I step over that way. She moves her head to the right, so I slide across there. You get the gist? We could go on like this all afternoon, except the daytime telly addicts are getting restless.

"Haw Hen! Sit doon or git oot the road. Ah cannae see a thing."

"MOOOVE, WOULD YE!"

I smile sweetly. "So sorry, I'll be out your way just as soon as my mum stands up. Come on Mum, people can't see the telly."

"No. I'm watching this."

"Mum, I have walked miles in the wind and sat for fifty minutes on the world's slowest train. At least have the decency to come talk to me."

"No."

God, she is stubborn and I am raging. No, I am way beyond raging. I am absolutely apoplectic. I grab her wrist and try to pull her up, but she clings to the chair with her other hand. And the Deal or No Deal aficionados are beginning to lose the plot.

"GIT OOT THE WAY! NURSE, NURSE, SHE'LL NO GIT OOT THE WAY AN A CANNAE HEAR NOEL EDMONDS."

"Go read a book," I snap but that doesn't go down well at all. Wee Aggie is first by my side, eager to settle a score.

"Ah could tell you were trouble," she hisses. "Git oot the way."

"Or what?"

"Ye'll rot in Hell."

"I'm already in Hell, Aggie, it disnae get worse than this."

"Yer possessed like yer mother."

"No Aggie, not me. Noel Edmonds is. Look at him, can't you see he's the Devil in disguise?" Aggie looks doubtfully at the TV though I can tell she sees the sense in this. But then a tall well-dressed man comes striding up, scowling at me.

"You should be ashamed of yourself," he says. "Psychosis is no joke. You think it's funny to laugh at sick people?"

"NO, I do not think it's funny and I tell you what else isn't funny – having to mop up the mess you 'sick' people create. Oh it's so easy for you, isn't it? Hiding out here watching daytime telly while other folk cook your food, pay your bills, wash your clothes. Life of bloody Riley. Your poor families, what you put them through, but you don't give a crap do you? You're pathetic. The lot of you. Pathetic."

Okay, so maybe not my finest moment, but to be fair some of the patients seem quite perked up by a bit of a barney. Others, though, are really upset.

"Now just you hold on a minute, Missy..."

"NURSE! NURSE..."

"What is it, what's going on?"

"WHO IS SHE? Get her out of here. Get her OUT!"

People are crowding round now, some jostling me, others pointing fingers in my face. Some woman turns the telly up full volume and parks her bum in front of it, adding to the general din. Mum just sits there, pretending not to see a thing and I think that does it. She doesn't even care that I'm about to get lynched; she's gonna let them rip me to pieces. So I bend down and scream in her face, "I HATE YOU. DO YOU HEAR? YOU ARE DEAD TO ME. DEAD. YOU ARE NO LONGER MY MOTHER." If there's a flicker of emotion I don't get to see it, because I'm being dragged away by two burly nurses and suddenly I feel scared. I've lost control. Am I about to get sectioned too?

Turns out not. I don't suppose they can section everyone that has a bit of a paddy. They lead me to the nurses' station, where Sam's waiting, hands on hips.

"Jess, what on earth's got into you?"

"She deserves it, they all deserve it. Bloody parasites the lot of them. Lounging in here at taxpayers' expense while the rest of us..."

"Jess! Have you been reading the Daily Mail?"

"NO! I..." Oh of course, she's taking the mick and yes, I suppose I do sound like a blue rinsed fascist.

"You can't go sounding off in there, Jess, it's not fair on them and it's not fair on the staff either. Some of these people are really sensitive and it might take days to get them calm again."

"OK Sam, I'm sorry, it's just... Mum makes me want to scream. She won't talk to me. There's no money in the bank and I don't know what to do. She's left everything in such a mess and I can't begin to sort it out if she won't help me."

Sam pulls out a chair. "Here, have a seat."

I collapse onto one of those office wheely chairs and it goes sliding across the room. Sam laughs. "Be careful. The floors are far too shiny, it's like a skating rink."

I laugh too. "Hours of fun though on a boring nightshift."

"I wouldn't go that far," sighs Sam. "Nothing about this

place is fun. So go on, what's up?"

"Mum. What else? I can't believe her. I tried to talk to her about the bills and she ran away. Honest to God, she bolted out the room then sat there bewitched by Noel Bloody Edmonds. We're about to go bankrupt and she's watching a stupid quiz show!"

"Your mum can't cope with bills right now, Jess."

"And I can? What am I meant to do? Where am I s'posed to find the money? I need to know if there's another bank account. I need to ask her." I jump up, ready to stalk back through to the dayroom, but Sam springs in front of me and slowly shakes her head.

"I can't let you go upsetting the patients again, Jess."

"But I need to know!"

"Now is not the time."

"When is? Once the house gets repossessed and I'm out on my ear?"

"Look, sit down. I'll make us a cup of tea."

Reluctantly, I drop my bum back down, while Sam boils a kettle and slops milk into mugs. She dunks in a teabag, scoops it straight out and chucks it in the bin by her side.

"Sugar?"

"What? Um... no thanks. Milk's fine."

"Here, get this down you, nothing that a hot cup of tea won't cure."

"Thanks." I take the chipped blue mug and stare at the steaming milky liquid. Yuk. Dishwater, as my gran would say.

Sam sits down and takes a sip of scalding tea. She winces, puts down the mug and wiggles a mouse to wake her computer. "Come closer, I want to show you something."

I skid across on my wheely chair. "What?"

"I'm going to take you through all the things that are

wrong with your mum, then when I'm done, you tell me if she's pathetic."

So we spend the next twenty minutes trawling through websites on B12 deficiency, thyroid problems and the menopause. We read harrowing accounts of women struggling to cope with just one of these conditions. I mean truly awful stuff – despair, suicide, divorce, yet my poor mum has all three.

"So you see," says Sam, "her body's been so lacking in the vitamins and hormones it needs to function that it's essentially been shutting down. It's actually impressive she managed to soldier on as long as she did."

"Okay, I get it." I do. I really do. Poor Mum must have been struggling for months – years even, without so much as a word of complaint. "But that doesn't help me does it? What do we do for money?"

Sam pulls a face. "I don't know much about that side of things I'm afraid. I think there's advice lines you can call; I'll get you a number. Who knows, maybe you're entitled to some benefits? What age are you now Jess?"

"Fif... um... seventeen."

"Oh really," she sounds surprised. "I thought you were younger than that."

"Nah, just a really bad dancer. That's why I got held back with the little ones."

She gives my knee a friendly swat. "Shuuut up. You were great. Really graceful."

I wasn't, but it's nice of her to say so. "Anyway, thanks. You've been brilliant. Again."

"Och, it's no trouble. I know how hard it is for you. And where's that brother of yours? Why's he not here supporting you?"

"Um... he's gone off for a wee break with his pals." Sam's

eyebrows shoot up. "No. It's fine. Honestly, he needs it. He's a bit too like Mum is our Ollie."

"And your dad?"

"Dubai."

"Whoa, you're really on your ownsome, aren't you?"

There's something about sympathy that makes my eyes leak. I have to bite my thumb to stop myself howling.

"You get yourself home," says Sam. "Treat yourself to a big bar of chocolate."

I nod, then I'm escorted off the premises – in the nicest possible way, but they make it quite clear I won't be allowed to see Mum again today.

* * *

Well, after all that I could do with some company so I text Amy and ask her over. She comes bounding round after dinner, psyched about a night with no parents.

"So," she says, stretching out on the couch, feet up on the coffee table, "it must be nice. No one to nag you, do what you want…"

"Yeah, Amy it's a right ruddy party…"

She slaps a hand over her mouth. "Oh sorry. Sorry, Jess, I keep putting my foot in it, don't I? But you know what I mean. My parents are so full on. Do this, do that – Mum's so obsessed with housework I swear she's obsessive compulsive."

I grin. "Yeah, she is a bit. She does my head in when she hovers about with her coasters."

"I know. And try putting a magazine down or your feet up on the chair. It's impossible to get comfy in our house. This…" she says, sweeping an arm round my tip of a living room, "is a room that says chillax. I love it. And Dad! Don't get me started on him; he's made me have maths lessons all summer. I mean, who does maths in the holidays?"

"Well at least they care, Amy."

"Yeah. I just wish they'd back off a bit. You know?" Amy's indignant gaze demands a response, so I nod, but I don't know, not really. My dad doesn't give a crap and my mum; well she's never been the most mumsy mum. I know she loves me – or at least I think she did, but I've never been the centre of her world, not the way Amy is. How does it feel to be mummy's little princess? Judging by Amy's sulky face it definitely has its downsides, but it must be nice too, surely, to be that loved?

Amy raises an eyebrow. "What you staring at? You look well weird."

Embarrassed, I glance away. "Ach, nothing. Just thinking about mums – how different mine is to yours."

"God, give me yours any day!"

"How can you say that? She's in a bloody mental hospital!"

"Precisely," grins Amy. "So you get room to breathe and a break from all the nagging."

Nagging? My mum doesn't nag. Why not? Is there something wrong with her or something wrong with me? Why doesn't she hassle me to do my homework? Or make me do maths in the holidays? I've never brought a boy home, but when I do, will she even bother if I take him upstairs?

"What is it Jess?"

I flap a dismissive hand. "Nuthin."

Amy slides her feet off the table and snaps up straight. "Nothing, my ass. You've got a right face on. What is it? Has something happened to your mum?"

"No. Well, not really. It's just... when I think about your mum and then I think about mine... they're very different, aren't they? Mine's not like other mums..."

"Too right she's not," huffs Amy, banging her legs back up on the table, "your mum's cool – a proper laid back parent. She gives you freedom to make your own choices and that, my friend," she wags a finger at me, "will make you a rounded human being, ready for life in the real world. Christ, I don't even know how to boil an egg. Mum never lets me near the cooker cos she says I make a mess."

Is that really it? Just Mum's parenting style? I shrug. "I dunno, Amy. To you she might seem cool, but to me, well sometimes I think she's just a bit cold."

"JESS! How can you say that! Your mum's ill right now, that's all. She'll be back to her old self soon enough."

I nod and try a smile, but can't seem to conjure one. "So, how 'bout we download a comedy? I could do with a laugh."

"NO. Not comedy. Horror!"

"Oh no. No horror. I watched The Exorcist last night. You heard of it?" Amy shakes her head. "Well it's the scariest horror film ever. I swear I didn't sleep a wink..."

"No way!"

"I'm serious. It's horrible. I can't do that again tonight."

"Oh go on, Jess. It can't be that bad. And it won't be as scary second time around. Please? I'm not even allowed to watch fifteens at home. I've never seen anything scary. Please, please, please, please, please..."

Oh for god's sake, who can resist Amy's doe-eyed pleas? "Fine. Watch it if you want to, but there's no way I'm going through that again. I'll read a book."

Amy grabs my hand and gives it a squeeze. "You're a star, Jess. I'll just watch a teeny bit, then we'll download something funny. I'll give you a shout when I'm done."

I get up, but pause by the door. "You sure about this, Amy? It's really, really scary."

"Stop fussing, I'll be fine. How scary can a film get?"

"Okey-doke. But don't say I didn't warn ya." I leave her hunting for the remote control and trudge up to my room. I sink down on the bed and spark up my Kindle, but I barely manage a page before my eyes start to droop. Next thing I know I'm being juddered awake by the thump, thump, thump of someone pounding up the stairs. I roll off the bed and am just reaching for my trusty guitar shield when Amy bursts through the bedroom door, her face bloated with tears.

"Jess! Jess! Oh my God, Jess, it was horrible."

"Wh...? What was?" I slur groggily. "What time is it?"

"I don't know, but it's dark out and I can't go home like this. I need daylight. Daddy will have to pick me up."

"NO! You need to pull yourself together, Amy. I can't have your dad round here or he'll know Ollie's away..."

"I can't go out there, Jess, not on my own."

"Fine. I'll walk you home, but not till you stop snivelling."

"No, I need my dad."

"Well you can't bloody have him."

Jeez I could do without this. I rummage for my phone, which has worked its way under my pillow. I fish it out and squint at the screen – quarter to ten. Amy has to be home in fifteen minutes or her parents will freak. I grab her clammy hand and she grips my arm with the other one. "C'mon." She clings on so tight as we clump downstairs that I almost lose my balance.

"Amy! You're gonna push me over, give us some space would you..." As soon as we get to the bottom, I prise off her fingers and nudge her in front of the hall mirror. "Right, what's the damage?" Under the glare of the overhead light, the full horror of Amy's blotchy skin and swollen eyes become clear.

"Christ, Amy. How long have you been crying for?"

She sniffs. "I dunno."

In fact she's been crying so long, not a trace of make-up remains on her miserable face. What to do? There's no hiding she's been sobbing for hours.

"Aaah. I've got it! A weepy. You've not been watching a horror; you've been watching a weepy. Quick. Name a sad film."

We stare blankly at each other. Nothing springs to mind. So I shoot through to Mum's computer and type in 'saddest film scene ever'. Up pops an article from Time magazine. "It says here that the death scene from The Champ is the saddest movie scene of all time. It's been scientifically proven."

"Never heard of it," mumbles Amy, through a mouthful of hair.

"Stop chewing your hair, you'll get a furball in your stomach!" She spits it out and starts gnawing a knuckle instead. I look back at the screen. "It's another old one. 1979. Oh but look, it's on Youtube. Right, this is the film you've been watching, ok? The Champ, not The Exorcist. Got it?"

She nods, I press play and a little blonde cherub appears on screen. He's leaning over this man – a boxer – lying on a table, injured from a fight. Blonde cherub says, "The Champ always pulls through." The boxer nods, "That's right," he says. Then he dies. Just like that. "Chaaamp," wails our little blonde moppet, "Nooooo. Wake up. Wake up champ," and he drapes the Champ's lifeless arm round his shoulder.

Well, I've had an emotional few days, so it wasn't going to take much, was it? I feel my eyes start to burn and I try to blink back tears, but you know what? Sod it, if I can't have a good old howl in my own house, where can I? So I let them spill over and once I start I can't stop. "That is sooo sad," I sob. Amy looks at the computer screen then back at me, unmoved and slightly puzzled.

"What's wrong with you?" I wail. "Are you dead inside?"

"Um. No," says Amy, briefly removing knuckle from mouth. "I'm just waiting for the boy to vomit ectoplasm or something."

Ah, of course, impossible to bungee between genres. You can't switch straight from horror to weepy and expect to feel the pain. Never mind, at least we have our story straight. I look at my watch. 9.57. We'd better get going.

"C'mon Amy, grab your stuff. We're going to have to leg it back to yours."

Reluctantly, she picks up her bag and I push her out the back door. She clings to me, shivering, even though the night is warm and calm.

"Can't we just phone my dad, Jess, please? I'm way too freaked out to walk home."

"NO. And we're not walking either, we've no time. Come on. Run!" I grab her hand and haul her along, while she whimpers and stumbles behind me. By the time we get to her front door, we're both out of breath and sweaty.

"God, we need to get fit," I gasp, hands on knees, mouth hanging open. "C'mon you. Get that key out." But she doesn't even get a chance, for the front door's suddenly flung open and there stands Amy's mum, demanding to know where the hell she's been. I look at my watch again, six minutes past ten. God, her parents are intense.

"Sorry, sorry. My fault," I say, stepping into the hall. "We got engrossed in this film and lost track of time."

Mrs Duncan doesn't seem to hear. She's staring at

Amy, her eyes wide, her bottom lip trembling. "Amy!" she screeches. "What's happened? You've been attacked? Oh my God. JIM! Jiiimmm! Get down here, something's happened to Amy!"

Amy's dad comes thundering down the stairs, his managerial belly bouncing beneath his tie.

"AMY?" His face turns red, even his shiny, bald head goes a bit puce. "Amy! Talk to me. Who did this? Who did this to you? I'll kill them..." He barges past onto the front step and his head swivels from side to side, searching for Amy's attacker. I grab the back of his shirt and tug hard; finally he seems to notice me.

"Jess? What...?"

"Nothing's happened to Amy," I say. "We were watching a weepy, that's all. Then we both got a bit emotional talking about Mum and lost track of time. She's not that late." I point at my watch.

"So why's she so sweaty and scared looking?"

I'll never let that girl watch another horror film, EVER. She looks like a victim of torture, standing there petrified, hair plastered to her forehead and panting like she's run all the way from Guantanemo Bay.

"Um... well, we watched this film, where the dad died and then we got to talking about my mum and um... Amy got so scared and upset that she might one day lose you ..."

Oh well played, Jess. You absolute genius. Amy's parents seem to melt.

"Oh my baby," coos her mum. "Oh my poor, poor baby. Come here." She opens her arms wide and Amy falls into them, sobbing. "We're not going anywhere, my love. I promise. Not for a very, very long time..."

Amy's dad gets this really soppy look on his face then he too joins in the hug, encircling his wife and daughter in his big, beefy, bear embrace. For a moment I'm so filled with longing I can't move, then I tiptoe out the door and leave them to it.

10

CLUBBING

I'm trying for a lie in, only my stupid phone keeps pinging. Go away, I need to sleep. I bury my head under the pillow, but it does nothing to muffle the incoming texts. So I slide out of bed and stagger over to my desk. I snatch up the phone and glare at the screen. It's Amy. Six text messages. Six? It's barely even light out.

Text 1: 'CALL ME. GREAT NEWS!!!'

Text 2: 'CALL ME NOW!!!!'

TEXT 3: 'GET YR LAZY ASS OUT OF BED JESS AND PHONE ME NOW.'

Has she won the lottery or what? Fine, I'll call. She picks right up.

"Jess. Jess. Listen..."

"I am..."

"Sssh. No talking, just listen. Guess what?"

"What?"

"Sssh. I said no talking."

"But you..."

"Ssshh..."

Fine.

"Listen Jess, thanks for last night. Mum and Dad – well,

we had such a good talk and we... well, we all feel so sorry for you. So Mum suggested I stay at yours tonight. Can you believe it? She says you could do with some girly company. Result eh?"

"Um... yeah, that's nice. Should be fun."

"No Jess. You don't get it. I'm not talking sleepover in a onesie here. Don't you remember our plan?" She drops her voice, "Clubbing? Yeah? Students? Remember?"

Oh, yes. That plan. "I dunno, Amy. I'm tired, it's chucking it down and... it seems like a lot of hassle."

"What you talking about? Hassle! It's exciting, fun – just what we need."

"We won't get into a club..."

"Course we will. You in your grunge gear, you look about twenty."

"But they all ask for ID."

"So? What's the worst that can happen? We get a knockback. Then we go to the pictures instead. Still be fun. What's wrong? I thought you'd be well up for it."

"Amy, you thought the Exorcist was a good idea. Remember? I just could do without the drama... like your parents calling to check up on you and finding no one here."

Silence. "Fair point," she says eventually. "Look I'll make sure they don't come sniffing around. You be ready for six. I'll do your make up when I get there. Later babe." And she hangs up.

So it's not like I have a choice, but what exactly am I meant to go clubbing with? I have £80 in the drawer. That's it. The sum total of my living expenses for the next three months. Maybe I should call back and cancel. Ach, no, sod it – who needs food anyway?

Well, before my night out I thought I ought to visit mother. So I trail all the way up to Carthill, but I shouldn't have bothered. I'm still so angry I can barely even look at her. What a complete waste of time. I've only been here five minutes, but I think I'll just go. What's the point, eh?

"Right, Mum, I'm off." I stand up. If she begs me to stay I will. But she just nods and stares down at her hands; she can't even look at me.

So I stride over to the nurses' station and ask Sam to let me out.

"Gosh, that was quick," she says.

"Yep." I'm in no mood for chitchat.

"Oh. OK," she says, though it clearly isn't. Two tiny words, loaded with meaning – what kind of daughter abandons her mother after five lousy minutes?

So we walk down the corridor in silence and I can tell Sam keeps glancing at my face, but I don't look back or smile or anything. I'm in such a rotten mood. Seriously, this is like PMS on steroids.

We get to the door and Sam's hand hovers over the keypad but then drops to her side. "Is this about yesterday?"

"Nope. Can you just do the code and let me out?"

"In a sec. Why don't we have a talk first?"

"No thanks. I just want out of this place. It gives me the heebie-jeebies."

"Okay, we could talk tomorrow then?"

I shrug and Sam punches in the door code, but then doesn't actually shift to let me past. "She needs you, Jess. You know that, don't you?"

"If you say so, Sam. Can I go now?" Christ, she's really starting to wind me up. Look at her – all do-gooding dimples and understanding eyes. What the hell does she know? Mum doesn't need me. She doesn't give a shit about anyone but herself.

Still Sam doesn't move. Right, that's it. I will barge on past. Ooof. We might both be thin, but it's still a squeeze. I feel like slapping her, I really do. Something sharp digs into my arm, so I give it a yank. Is that her ID badge? I tuck it up my sleeve.

Well, I'm free at last, but I hover for a sec, expecting an outstretched hand and an angry demand for the badge. But Sam doesn't say anything. Just gives me this wounded look and quietly shuts the door.

Oh. My. God. Did I really just do that? I've never stolen anything in my life before. Never. Not because I'm a goody-two-shoes; I've just always been too scared. I start walking really fast, then at the bottom of the drive, I stop to shake the card from the sleeve of my denim jacket. Look at it. Grainy photo under the NHS logo. That could easily pass for me. I've got ID. Woo hoo! I can get into any club I like.

As I stroll on towards the train station though, I start getting really nervy. What if Sam calls the police? Will she figure it's me that's taken it? And what if she gets in trouble? Can you get sacked for losing an NHS badge? Maybe I should just turn round and hand the bloody thing back. But then I remember the look on Sam's face – I've disappointed her enough already. I can't take any more of that today.

I obsess all the way home. I half expect the police to be surrounding the station as my train pulls in, but of course they're not. Even if Sam did report me, they've got better things to do than hang round a train station waiting on me. No, they're far more likely to turn up at my house, then what'll happen? Will I get a warning? Maybe I'll be sent straight to jail, or whatever they call the place they send teenagers. Oh, for goodness sake Jess, get a grip. You can just say it was an accident. Fell in your bag as you were squeezing past.

Amy's already on the doorstep as I turn into my street. She's flicking through a magazine, using the massive bag of make-up as footstool. I run up and show her the ID card, spouting my fears while scanning for men in uniform. She doesn't hear the bad stuff though. Just starts dancing round the garden, hugging the ID card to her chest.

"Wow! This is awesome, Jess," she cries, squinting at the picture. "It could pass for either one of us." She bounces up and down screeching, "EEEEEEKK. We're going clubbing, EEEEEEK."

"Sssh. For god's sake." I haul her inside then allow myself to smile. Sometimes Amy's good for me. If I were here on my own I know I'd dissolve in a heap of sweaty paranoia. But with Amy, it suddenly feels like fun.

We get ourselves ready and phone for a taxi. Amy's raided her piggy bank and is feeling rather flush. I tell her I'm skint and she says she'll pay for everything, which is a load off, I can tell you. We think about going to one of the city centre clubs but you get some really raj types there – you hear about fights and stuff all the time. We reckon students might be safer. If they're all as soppy as our Ollie there won't be trouble at the Student Union, so that's where we decide on. Only being fifteen and stupid, we don't realise you need a student card to get in. Duh!

We arrive at the entrance to the Union and I hold up Sam's NHS card and this bored looking guy says, "Aye, but where's your student card?" And I say, "eh?" and he says, "your… student… card?" like I'm dumb. Well, I'm all for turning round and heading straight home but Amy's super quick. She flashes him her most dazzling smile and purrs, "We're just off a loooong shift. Came straight from the hospital and forgot them. You're not actually going to send us all the way home to fetch them are you?" She cocks her head to one side and looks him straight in the eye. The bored guy on the door suddenly looks a lot less bored. Clearly smitten, he waves us straight through.

We make a beeline for the disabled toilet so we can shriek and jump and act our age without being noticed. "You were amazing, Amy. Oh my god, my heart is beating so fast. Feel it."

"Mine too! But we're in, Jess. We're really, really in. What should we order at the bar? What do students drink? Do you think we might get off with someone? Oooooh. I'm so nervous."

Amy's bound to pull. She has this amazing figure, which she's poured into the teeniest, tiniest dress. She looks great, but also slightly slutty. I'm a bit worried about the kind of guy she might pull. And we're dressed so differently. I'm Gothing it up, so we aren't going to be attracting the same sort of bloke. I don't want to get separated, so I stop with the squealing and say, "Let's not drink too much, eh? Just enough to take the edge off. And we gotta stick together. Okay? Don't disappear with anyone. Deal?"

"Yeah. Yeah, 'course." Amy's nodding away but I can tell she's not paying the slightest bit of attention. This is her first taste of freedom and she is about to go wild. I want to do some more planning but she pushes me out the toilet door and tugs me towards the bar where we have to fight our way over a heaving dance floor and elbow folk aside to get served. It's so hot, I can hardly breathe and my nose is pressed against someone's smelly pit. But Amy's face glows with happiness. "Two Bacardi and limes," she yells over the din of thumping music. The barman looks confused so she has to yell it again and he's smirking slightly as he goes off to make the drinks. I don't blame him. Who drinks Bacardi and lime? But Amy clearly thinks it the height of sophistication. She downs the first one before she even gets her change and immediately orders another. I can see how things are shaping up, so I drag her from the bar before she can do more damage. We find a corner and stand there, staring at the dance floor, sipping our drinks.

It doesn't take long for Amy to get hit on. This slimy looking guy in an open necked shirt and chinos comes up and asks her to dance. She grins – way too eager – and almost skips off onto the dance floor. You can tell he thinks his luck is in. I try to keep an eye on them, but they go bobbing into the throng and that's the last I see of her for ages.

I feel like a right Jessie No Mates. This isn't my kind of music at all. I've never been a big fan of pop and recently all the bands I like are either odd or old, or a bit of both. So I try to look like I'm digging the tunes by nodding my head and doing the occasional jiggle, but I can tell I just look lame.

Oh no, there's a guy looking at me. He has the most beautiful wavy brown hair that skims the nape of his neck – not too long – Jim Morrison sort of length. He has on these tight black jeans and I can make out the muscles in his legs. Why do I find skinny legs in black jeans so sexy? His lips are full and his eyes big and blue and he's wearing a Nirvana t-shirt.

He can't be interested in me. He must be transfixed by my uncool dance tics; I feel like a complete idiot. Look down at your boots Jess, don't you dare stare. But my eyes seem to have a will of their own. They swivel straight back up and oh my god, he's still looking over. He smiles and it's such a nice smile. Not mocking at all. Oh no, I'm gawping aren't I? With my mouth hanging open too. He looks really uncomfortable now. Oh crap, I didn't smile back. He smiled at me, but I didn't smile back. Go on Jess, smile. How hard can it be? It's not coming naturally, but I think I've managed to paste on a grin. I bet it looks really fake and creepy, but I can't seem to adjust my mouth into any position that feels normal. He'll run now for sure. NO! He's walking towards me. Aaaaagh. What do I do?

I have no idea what to say, but he seems fairly chilled. "You been dumped too?" he asks. An innocent question, but with the music so loud he has to lean in close to my ear. His breath on my face sends goosebumps slithering all the way down my back. Talk about erotic!

"Yeah," I smile, this time leaning in close to him. "My pal's gone off with some sleazy bloke and now I'm stuck here on my own."

He grins. "Ah the age old story. Girl meets boy. Girl dumps friend."

"Yeah."

There's an awkward silence till he says, "So you don't look like you're into hip hop..."

"Nor do you!"

Then we both laugh, "MATES!" at exactly the same time.

"It's quieter out there," he says, nodding towards the corridor.

"Oh. OK," I reply, trying hard to play it cool. But I follow like an eager puppy as he ambles out to find a quiet spot to talk.

His name is Tom and he's a second year English student. He asks what year I'm in and I flash the NHS card. "Well,

Sam," he says, "I've never kissed a nurse before…" And next thing we're snogging. It is just… no, I can't even begin to put it into words. See, I've only ever snogged three boys before. Once when I was twelve with a nerd called Alex cos I needed to get the first kiss over with. It was a disaster. Our teeth kept clashing then he told everyone I kissed like a vampire. I steered clear of boys for a long time after that. Then I had two more half-hearted snogs at the school disco, but I was just going through the motions. Locking mouths with some guy I didn't even fancy made me feel queasy and faintly ridiculous.

But this… this isn't on the same planet… or even the same universe. It feels like every part of me is melting into him. My tummy keeps doing this funny little jump like I'm on a rollercoaster and for a second I wonder if I might be about to puke. But for the most part all I can think of is my mouth on his and how good it feels to be held and how wonderful he smells. We kiss for so long my chin starts to burn from the scratch of his stubble. Better take a break.

Reluctantly I prise myself off him and mumble, "I need the loo."

He groans, "Noo. Don't go," and pretends to lock me in his arms.

"I have to, or it might get messy."

He sticks out his bottom lip. "Fine. I'll nip to the bar. But don't go disappearing. Promise?"

"Promise."

Well, I float to the toilet, a humongous grin pinned from ear to ear. It soon fades when I catch myself in the mirror. All that snogging has scraped off the makeup round my mouth, leaving the top half of my face Goth white, while the bottom half is a fiery red and coming up with hundreds of angry pimples. Christ, I've just found the man of my dreams and turns out I'm allergic to him. Deflated, I slink back out, but I now feel so self-conscious under the glare of the corridor light that I can't look him in the eye. I go all silly and shy – hiding my face behind my hair. He hands me a beer and I take a sip but I'm not in the mood.

"I think I need to find my friend," I say. "I didn't like the look of the guy she went off with."

"Oh." Tom sounds hurt, like I'm giving him the brush off, which isn't it at all; I just want to go somewhere dark where he can't see my stupid spotty face.

"We could… go back inside… you could help me find her?"

"Yeah? Yeah… okay."

I feel much better in the dark of the disco. We muck about, pretending to dance like rappers. I even shake my booty like one of those half-naked girls from MTV. I'm having so much fun that I forget all about trying to find Amy, until I spot her weaving off the dance floor. Sleazy guy has his arm round her waist; it doesn't look romantic though, more like he's holding her up.

"Oh, there's Amy," I yell at Tom, pointing towards them.

"Seriously?" his face is grim.

"What?"

"That guy she's with…" Tom shakes his head. "Has she known him long?"

"Nah. They just met tonight."

"Oh. That's bad, Sam. He's a complete scumbag." And suddenly I feel sick. Really, really sick. Not just because Amy looks completely wasted, but because Tom called me Sam again and I realise it isn't Jess he's into. He isn't going to want some fifteen-year-old schoolgirl. He's psyched about kissing a nurse.

"You okay?" He looks so concerned, his big blue eyes gazing into mine that I feel myself choke up. It's so unfair. I've had this tantalising taste of what it feels like to be the centre of someone's world and now it's all going to be ripped away. "Don't worry," he says, mistaking my selfishness for anguish about my friend. "I'll help you get her home." But his kindness is just making things worse, cos now I want to scream and shout at the injustice of it all. I want him more than I've ever wanted anything, why the hell can't I have him?

Well, Sleazeball comes over and passes me my friend. She can barely stand and her head is lolling about like she has no neck control.

"How much has she had to drink?" I scream. Sleazeball just shrugs and a smirk dances round the corners of his mouth. I can't hold Amy, so I lower her to the ground where she slumps over, her sleek brown hair mopping beer spills off the floor. I straighten up and glare at Sleazeball, but Tom is already in there.

"What have you given her Chris?"

The Chris bloke shrugs so Tom jabs him in the chest. "I repeat. What did you give her?"

Chris shrugs again but then says, "She might have dropped an 'E'... maybe..."

Tom turns to me. "Has she done 'E' before?"

I can't think straight. 'E'. What the hell is 'E'? Oh god no. Not Ecstasy; that kills people doesn't it?

"NO! She hasn't. Why would he give her that?"

The smirk is fading and Chris is starting to look uncomfortable. Tom pushes him in the chest. "Chris gives out ecstasy to all the girls he tries to get off with. That right Chris? He's so effing impotent it's the only way he can pull."

"Fuck off Tom."

"No you fuck off."

They're prodding each other in the chest now. Oh man, don't start a punch up. What if security calls the police? I need to put a stop to this, like NOW. So I burrow between them and shove them apart. "SHUT THE HELL UP," I scream. "She could be dying."

Tom backs away, mumbling some sort of apology and kneels down beside Amy. I scooch down next to him.

"Well, what do you think?" he says. "Has she overdosed?"

How am I meant to know? Oh – of course, I'm a nurse. I feel her forehead; she's burning hot and dripping with sweat.

"She needs water," I say, managing to dredge from some dark recess of my mind that the biggest risk from Ecstasy is dehydration. So I send Tom off for water and get Chris to help me stand Amy up. We grab an arm each and drape them round our shoulders, then we pretty much carry her into the corridor – her feet aren't working at all.

We prop her in a corner and wait for Tom to return with the water. At one point a barman walks past clutching a huge tower of empty glasses. He lingers in front of Amy frowning. "She OK?"

"Um, yeah," I say, "bit too much to drink."

He looks doubtful then he spots Chris and glares. This Chris bloke clearly has a reputation. I pull out my NHS badge. "I'm a nurse," I say, "I can handle things. I'll let you know if I can't."

Well I'm clearly sober and responsible, so he nods and wanders off. But what if he alerts security? It's obvious Amy's on drugs. Come on, Tom, hurry up. I want to get the hell out of here.

"Oh here you are!" It's Tom, clutching two full pints of

water. I grab one and hold it to Amy's lips.

"Amy, you've got to drink this." There's no response and I'm really starting to panic. I sling half the water in her face and she seems to come round a bit, or at least she mumbles and groans.

"AMY. Listen to me. If you do not drink this you will overheat and die." I tip back her head, prise open her mouth and begin to drizzle in water. Half of it dribbles back out again and some goes down the wrong way because she starts to cough and splutter, but I'm watching her neck and she's definitely downing something. Well, best not to drown her so I stop for a bit and dunk a tissue in water, which I dab at her face and chest. Her skin's looking less red and sweaty. She's beginning to cool down.

"Amy can you hear me?"

"Y… yes… sick… feel sick." She heaves but I don't mind, at least she's conscious. Puke away Amy; just don't bloody die. I look up at Tom and Chris.

"Help me get her outside."

They nod, their faces white with worry. They heave her up, one on either side and drag her up the stairs. When we get to the top I jump in front and order them to stop. "You can't leave like this. It looks well dodgy; like two firemen and a corpse. Chris – hold her by the waist again."

Chris groans. "She's so heavy. It's hard to walk like that."

"Well, if the doorman calls the police I'll be happy to tell them where she got the drugs." Gosh, I like being Sam – Jess would never be this assertive.

Suddenly Chris is ever so compliant. His arm shoots round Amy's waist and her head flops onto his shoulder. He shuffles them out the building, looking like a loving boyfriend supporting his tipsy lady. Tom and I follow and I'm relieved to see Amy's feet start to move on their own, instead of just being dragged across the floor.

When we're well clear of the doors, Chris deposits Amy on the bonnet of a car and doubles up, hands on knees, huffing and puffing. I think he's just having a rest, but no, it's actually his car. He produces a set of keys and we all help bundle Amy in the back.

"Wait," says Tom, staring at Chris with suspicion, "are you fit to drive? What have you taken?"

"Nothing!" Chris has the cheek to look outraged. "What do you take me for?"

"Why's she on 'E' then? Oh wait, I don't want to know…" Disgusted, Tom clambers in beside Amy and I get in the front.

"Here, put your postcode in this." Chris hands me a TomTom and I punch in my address. He's awfully well equipped for a student. Rich parents or a lucrative business? Actually, I don't care. I'll let him drop us home but after that I never want to see his sleazy face again. I mean, what possessed Amy even to dance with him? It's not that he's ugly, just that he looks like such a dickhead. He has this curly blonde hair that you can tell would be frizzy if he didn't spend hours in front of the mirror, teasing it into little corkscrew curls. His eyes are on the small side and he has this arrogance about him, like he's better than all us oiks. His lips are a bit too big and when they aren't smirking they seem to be sneering. He reminds me of a Gestapo guard from some old war film and that's never a good sign, is it?

The roads are quiet so it doesn't take long to get to my house. We pull up in front and Chris suddenly looks shifty and scared. "Eh… you still live with your parents?"

"Me? No."

"Wow." He stares at the house. "Maybe I should go into

nursing. Didn't know it was so well paid."

"It's not," I snarl, "it was my mum's house, but... she's not with us anymore."

"Oh. That's tough. Sorry." He doesn't look sorry. In fact he looks really quite cheerful. He gets out the car and slams shut the door.

"Sssh." I hiss. "The neighbours are old and really very nosy."

He mimes zipping shut his mouth and does this exaggerated tiptoe round to Amy's door, like he's a character from Scooby Doo. We haul Amy out and she manages to stagger up the path, using Tom and me as crutches. I stare at old Clarkey's window, waiting for the curtain twitch, but there's nothing. The old bat must be asleep.

So I get Amy into Ollie's bed and spoon feed her milky tea. Tom stays by me, fiddling with my hair and gently rubbing my back. It's lovely. "Whose room is this?" he asks, staring doubtfully at the Airfix models dangling from the ceiling.

I look up and smile. "Oh those, yeah, they're my brother's. His flat at uni is full of super cool arty bits, but here... he likes to stay little."

"I've still got a few planes," grins Tom, "though they're at the back of a cupboard now. For some reason girls don't seem to dig them."

I wince at the thought of Tom with 'girls', but manage to muster a normal voice to say, "Ollie's never brought a girl back here. I wonder why not. Weird."

"S... not... weird... he's gorgeous..." Lust for my brother is bringing Amy back to life.

"Oh it can speak then. Jesus Christ, Amy, what the hell were you thinking?"

She groans and flips over, burying her face in the pillow. I turn to Tom. "Can I have a few minutes with my friend, please?"

He stands up. "Sure, I'll make some tea."

"See if you can find some grub as well, would you?" He nods and goes. "Amy. AMY! Turn over would you?" She doesn't move, so I grab her shoulder and yank her round so she's facing me.

"Ow." Her eyes fill with tears.

"Jeez Amy, don't start blubbing. My sympathy's wearing thin. Seriously, I'm this away from calling your dad." I hold up thumb and finger about a millimetre apart. "So either pull yourself together or I phone the parents – which is it to be?"

Amy struggles to sit up, groaning and clutching her head. She looks terrible, but at least she's conscious.

"My head hurts," she whimpers.

"Good."

"What? Oh... yeah, you're right, I deserve that. Look, I'm sorry, Jess." Her voice is so small and scared that I start to melt. I'm such a sap, I really am.

"I know you're sorry. But how could you take that muck without warning me? Don't you think I had a right to know you were getting completely off your face? Actually it was more than that. You almost died, Amy."

"I know," she sniffs, "you saved my life. You really did. I didn't mean to... I didn't really know what I was doing..."

"He spiked you?" I'll throttle that Chris.

"No. Not exactly. He had this little bit of paper with a strawberry on it. It looked like a sweet. He said to open my mouth and I did and he popped it in."

"You thought he was giving you a sweet?" I may sound a tad sceptical.

Amy buries her face in her hands. "Yes. No. Oh, I don't know. I just opened my mouth. I didn't think. I was so stupid. At first it felt brilliant too, but then it was horrible and I really panicked and I honestly thought I was a goner. You've no idea how fast my heart was going, Jess..."

"Oh don't go getting upset. You're alive and that's all that matters." I stroke her hair. "Get some sleep, eh? You'll feel better in the morning." I stand up and she grabs my hand.

"Your man seems lovely, Jess. At least you picked a good 'un, eh?"

"Yeah. But I don't get to keep him, do I?"

"Why not?"

"Because Amy, he thinks I'm a nurse called Sam. He's a second year student, so he won't want to be seen with a schoolgirl. Actually, what did you tell Chris?" I have a sudden flash of hope that Chris knows Amy's age and isn't bothered.

"We didn't do much talking. Just dancing and snogging."

"Did you at least swap names before swapping saliva?"

Amy shakes her head. "I didn't even know he was called Chris."

"Oh my god! What are you like?" We both burst out laughing. "Right, I am going down to make the most of my night with Tom cos tomorrow I gotta give him back."

11

RUMBLED

I'm going to have a big mug of tea – I reckon I deserve it – then I'll snog the face off that Tom. Or have a 'lumber' as my gran would say. Yeeeuch. Some old Scots words are so weird. I mean a 'lumber'? Seriously? About as romantic as a date night down the pit. Even 'snogging' sounds crude. See, when my mouth meets Tom's something magical happens and 'kissing' doesn't cover it either. There should be more words for lip-to-lip contact in the English language – nice ones – not ones like lumber.

I can hear Tom clattering about in the kitchen. Isn't he great? Gorgeous and good at tea. I wonder if that pig Chris is still here? I stick my head through the kitchen door. Tom's peering into a smoky grill. He's making cheesy toast, but the grill pan's so filthy the whole kitchen reeks of cremated crumbs.

"Where's Chris?" I ask and Tom jumps back from the cooker with a guilty look.

"Sorry, I…" He bats at the smoke with a tea towel.

"S'okay. Not your fault. Has Chris gone?"

"Nah, he's in the living room I think."

"Ah, right. I'll try and get rid of him then." Tom nods distractedly.

Okay, I can do this. Sam can do this. Be polite but assertive. Just make it clear you want him gone. He's not going to argue, is he? I mean, I could report him to the police. He should be grateful he's not facing a manslaughter charge.

I open the living room door and there he is, lounging on the sofa, feet on the coffee table, smoking a spliff. What the…? How dare he smoke drugs in my house, after what he just did to Amy! Okay, calm down Jess, don't start an argument. Just send him packing then you get Tom to yourself. So I say, "Thanks for dropping us back, Chris, Amy seems okay now – you can go."

He examines the end of his spliff, then takes a drag, "Actually, SAM, I thought I might stay the night."

"What? No you can't…"

"Yes, SAM, I can…"

Okay, so he's putting a really weird emphasis on the word Sam. The question is why? Oh no. He's seen something with my name on, hasn't he? But what? There's nothing lying about – no homework in the holidays and I don't get mail. Has he been nosing through my things? That dirty, rotten, scumbag. I'll… oh, crap, my eyes are filling up. Don't cry, Jess. Don't let him see you cry.

"Oh, you're upset, Jess… oops, I mean SAM… don't worry, I won't tell." He holds up my school tie and gives it a jaunty wave. Has he been in my room?

I lunge and snatch it off him. Then I realise I'm holding a school tie and my eyes dart towards the door in case Tom comes strolling in. Oh god, what do I do with it? My head's like mince, I can't think straight. There. Down the back of the sofa. "You've been in my bedroom!"

"Well, yes, I wanted to get to know you and now I do. But dear oh dear, if only Tom knew he was about to do the dirty with an underage schoolgirl."

"Shut up."

"Where did you get the NHS ID by the way? It's really rather good. I could be doing with one of those."

"Why?"

He shrugs. "Dunno. Maybe get me access to some interesting pharmaceuticals."

"Well, I'm not telling you."

He stares at me for a moment then bursts out laughing. "Oh that's priceless. You nicked it didn't you?" It's like he can see right through me. Takes one lying scumbag to know another.

"Tea's up." I spin round and there's Tom clutching a tray of steaming tea and cheesy toast. I must look seriously freaked out, cos his jaw drops and he goes, "Are you okay? Is it Amy? Has something happened?"

"No. No, she's fine. It's just…"

Tom glances towards Chris. "Oh the drugs… Chris, man, put that out. Nurses don't like that sort of thing…"

I feel sick. Is Chris going to blab? I stare at him. He says nothing for what feels like ages then he sits up and stubs out the spliff. "Sure, I'll put it out. Though I heard that nurses were wild. They like to partaaay."

"Not this one," I snap.

So Tom dishes up the tea and we sit on the rug by the coffee table, munching our cheesy toast. It was what I was dreaming of upstairs but the reality isn't in the least bit cosy or romantic because Chris is still sat there on the couch, smirking down at us.

"So where do you work?" he asks, looking all innocent and interested.

I flap a hand. "Oh you don't want to hear about that."

"I do," says Tom. "You were amazing tonight. It's lucky you're a nurse – I mean, who knows what would have happened without your training..."

"Yeah," smirks Chris.

I splutter, spraying tea across the table. "Er thanks. But I'm not actually that medical. I'm a psychiatric nurse. It's really boring." I need to change the subject, pronto. I know, I'll ask Chris what he studies.

"Law," he says. "But that is boring and I'd much rather hear about your patients." He folds his arms and leans back. He clearly thinks he's caught me out – that I can't be convincing about life on a psychiatric ward. But of course I'm rapidly becoming an expert. So I tell them all about my patients – the one with the God complex, the one that strips naked and the one who believes the devil's inside her.

Tom shakes his head. "That's really heavy. I don't know how you can do that day after day."

Chris, though, is looking thoughtful, then he pipes up, "What did you say your mum died of?"

Damn, he's worked out where Mum is. "Cancer," I growl.

"Jeez!" cries Tom. "Way to go with the tact, Chris."

I've had enough; I want that pig gone even if it means Tom leaving too. I can't take the stress any more. I'm holding my breath every time he opens his mouth. "Look, I'm tired," I say. "You should go now. Both of you." Tom says nothing, just stares at his shoes, looking miserable. But Chris jumps up and I can't believe he's leaving without a fight. And sure enough he isn't.

"Actually, I'm too stoned to drive. I'll crash in the spare room, yeah? Leave you lovebirds to it."

Well what can I say? Insist he gets in the car despite smoking drugs? I can't do that, though I bet he does it all the time. Still, at least he'll be out my face and for that I'm pitifully grateful. "Fine," I sigh.

"Nighty-night then," he disappears out the living room. He'd better not go near Amy. I listen as he plods upstairs and pads into the room overhead – Mum's room – which is on the other side of the landing from drugged up sleeping girls. Phew.

Tom's on his feet now, pulling on his leather jacket.

"Oh, you're going?"

"Yeah, I can get a bus. Or hitch..."

"Oh."

"Isn't that what you want?"

"No! No, it's not what I want at all. I was just desperate to get rid of him and I thought he wouldn't go without you. Sorry. He was just..."

Tom smiles and shrugs his jacket back off. It slides to the floor as he bends down and reaches for my hand. "Shall we go upstairs then?"

My face must be a picture of panic cos Tom's smile disappears and suddenly he's rambling, "I... I... don't mean for," he swallows, "you know... that... I just meant... I mean..."

Poor boy, he's as flustered as me. But I couldn't take him to my room even if I wanted to – there's school books piled on the floor.

"I'm not... ready," I whisper, thinking crap that sounds so immature – he's bound to go bolting for the door. But he doesn't. In fact, if anything he looks relieved.

"Oh. I know!" he springs to his feet and starts hauling cushions off the couch. "We could make a little nest down here."

I'm so happy I almost cry. Yes, that sounds perfect. So I help him lay the cushions on the floor then we grab some throws and snuggle down under them. He leans over and kisses me then, but it isn't like before; I'm too stressed to really get into it. His hand's resting on my hip and I keep wondering if it's going to wander and what will I do if it does? I feel so warm and tingly down there that part of me longs for his fingers to stray, but I know I'll have a heart attack if they actually do.

We don't kiss for long, just wrap ourselves round each other and soon my eyes feel heavy. Mmmmm. Cosy-comfy, it doesn't get better than this.

* * *

Jeeez. What's with all the banging? Where am I? Oh, yeah, on the living room floor with some bloke I pulled in the pub last night. Eeeek. I struggle out from under Tom's arm. He groans and flops over, mumbling in his sleep. Then the banging starts again. Someone's at the front door. Who the hell could that be at this time on a Sunday?

I stumble into the hall, pulling down my skirt and pausing at the mirror to have a quick squiz at my face. Red raw mouth and panda eyes; check the nick of me. I give the wandering eyeliner a quick dab with my sleeve and call out, "Who's there?"

"It's Angela, dear. Is Amy ready for church?"

Church? Church! Amy didn't say anything about going to church.

"Gosh sorry Mrs Duncan, I don't think she's up yet. I'll go check."

"Goodness, that girl! If you let me in, Jess, I'd like to thank Ollie for last night."

Bloooody hell! What to do? "Oh... man... where can those keys be?" Stalling for time, I sound like the world's most hammy actress. "I just need to find my keys, Mrs D. Won't be a mo..." Aaaaaaagh. I race upstairs two at a time and charge into Ollie's room. The bed's empty, so Amy's already up. But the toilet door's wide open. Where can she be? Oh no. She wouldn't have, would she? I ease open the door to Mum's room and sure enough, there's Amy fast asleep with scumbag Chris and utterly starkers by the looks of it.

"Your mum's here to take you to church," I hiss in her ear.

"Mmmmm?" she rolls over, the picture of sleepy contentment and one bikini-striped breast flops out from under the duvet. I really didn't need to see that.

"GET UP!"

Well that wakes her. She flails around. "Mmmh... wha... Jess?"

"Yes, it's Jess. Your mum's at the door! Are you ready for church? And she's asking to speak to Ollie too. What the hell am I supposed to do?"

Amy attempts to sit up but Chris rolls on top of her, nuzzling her neck, making disgusting horny noises. "Church? Why, you can't go to church you filthy little strumpet. Stay here and service me..." Amy giggles and I feel like slapping her.

"Amy. This is serious. If your mum twigs Ollie isn't here, I'm done for. Remember..." I kneel down to whisper cos I don't want Scumbag to hear, "... they'll put me in care."

"Oh. Yeah. Gerroff Chris." Amy shoves him and he sits up, revealing a rug of blonde chest hair in all its glory. Honestly, it's gross – like anaemic pubes. He regards me with interest.

"In care, eh?"

Dammit, he heard. Next thing, he's striding towards the window. "What are you doing? Why you opening the curtains?" I try to grab him but all that white flesh is making my skin crawl and I don't know where to put my hands. Now he's opening the window. "Stop!" Too late.

"Morning Mrs Duncan," he says. Well at least he knows Amy's surname; that's a step forward.

"Oh, morning Ollie!" I peep out the window and see Mrs D squinting up; the sun's in her face so she's using a hand to shield her eyes. "I hope Amy was okay last night. Not too giggly gone midnight."

Chris smirks. "Actually, she was a right handful. A naughty, naughty girl." Oh my god! I kick his bare butt and he grabs my foot, making me fall over. "I'm just jesting with you, Mrs D. Good as gold they were. Watched a film and went to sleep. A bit late, but that's sleepovers, eh? Sorry, I would come down, but I'm not decent."

"Oh that's okay dear. I know you students like a long lie. You get yourself back to bed. And I like the hair by the way; I'd no idea perms were back in fashion."

I'm still on the floor when Chris closes the curtains and clambers back into Mum's bed. "What the hell did you think you were doing?" I hiss. "If she wasn't half blind with the sun, you would have landed me right in it. In fact, you would have landed yourself right in it. She'd have marched you down the police station for having sex with her underage daughter and then what'd become of your law career?"

"Amy's sixteen, she's perfectly legal. Besides, it all turned out fine. I saved your neck and now you owe me."

Oh yes, Amy's a few months older than me. "But..." I'm no longer angry, just intrigued. How can he have known that Mrs D would think he was Ollie? Or is he so mental he just doesn't care? "You're an absolute idiot. What if it'd been raining? Eh? You're lucky my brother has blonde hair..."

"No Jess. Not luck. I'd done my research," he points to a heap of photograph albums piled on Mum's bedside table. "Your brother's colouring is the same as mine, so I knew from a distance if Amy's mum was expecting to see Ollie then Ollie was what she'd see. Simple."

"Where did you get those photos?" Bored now, he shrugs and lights a spliff. Fine. Whatever. Where's Amy? I scramble off the floor and go running for the bathroom. She's in there putting on her Sunday best – a demure little frock, all flowers and butterflies. Her hair, though, is completely ratty from being soaked in beer and stinks like a brewery. I spray it with deodorant and order her to pin it up. Then I go dashing back downstairs to deal with Mrs D. But what am I supposed to do? I can't possibly let her inside. The whole house smells of drugs, but the lost key excuse is wearing pretty thin. I'll have to face her outside, so I open the door and there on the step stands Mrs D chatting away to Tom.

Oh. My. God. It isn't even ten o'clock and I'm about to have a heart attack.

"Oh, there you are," beams Amy's mum. "Ollie's friend here was just telling me about his university course. It does sound interesting. I always wanted to study literature, but my father made me do secretarial. Shorthand, typing – terribly dull."

"They do part-time courses at uni. You could go to night school," suggests Tom.

"Oh that would be lovely," laughs Mrs D. "But I think Aberdeen is a bit far for me to travel..." Aberdeen is where my brother goes. Tom looks totally confused.

"Aberdeen? But I go to..."

"TEA! I'd love a cup of tea, Tom, if you're making one."

He looks at me, perplexed, then obediently trots back indoors. Phew. I smile at Mrs D. "Amy won't be a minute. She's just doing her hair. Sorry, I'd have got her up if I'd known she was going to church."

"Don't you worry yourself, Jess. You've enough on your

plate without mothering my daughter. At her age she should be able to get herself up and dressed. Honestly, sometimes I think we've been too soft on her; she's absolutely no idea... oh, speak of the devil. Here she comes. Gosh, you look tired, darling. What time did you go to sleep?"

Amy scowls. "It's the lack of make up mother, I've not had time to put it on."

"Oh. Yes. That must be it..." Mrs D, though, does not look convinced and keeps glancing at Amy as they walk down the drive to the car.

"Cheerio then." I give them a wave and slam shut the door, relieved to be shot of my friend. Now all I have to do is oust the junkie, then I can take myself back to bed and never get up again.

I stand at the bottom of the stairs and screech, "CHRIS! I need to go to work, so get up and disappear." I wait. No response, which means I have to drag my weary ass back upstairs where I find him still in bed, reading Mum's diary. Even I've never done that.

"For Christ's sake!" I snatch it off him and hug it to my chest. "What is with you? Have you no concept of boundaries?"

"I'm a people person. I like to get to know them."

"But... but you can't just go raking through people's stuff. Do you do this everywhere you go?"

"Pretty much."

"How've you not had your head kicked in?"

"Because if you scratch beneath the surface, Jess, even just a teensy bit, there's always a secret. And I collect secrets; that's how I keep my teeth."

I perch on the edge of the bed, both fascinated and repulsed. He's perhaps the most odious person I've ever met, but he's really smart. He's what... only eighteen? And yet he's incredibly perceptive. I can't resist. "So, go on, what's Tom's secret then?"

Chris looks me straight in the eye and smirks. "You must know?"

"Me? No. I've no idea."

He snorts. "It's you. You're Tom's secret." My mind goes blank. How can I be Tom's secret? Chris rolls his eyes. "Don't you get it?"

"No. Oh..." Now I do. "But we didn't have sex. I can prove it."

"Doesn't matter. Nice guy like Tom. If it gets round uni he's been fucking a fifteen-year-old... well, he'll die of shame. Me on the other hand? I'd wear it like a badge of honour."

I jump up. "You are the most..." I'm so angry I can't even begin. "If you dare say a word... I'll... I'll..."

He laughs. "Calm down. I've no intention of splurging. As I said, I collect secrets. If I have to share one, well... it's because a relationship's failed and I don't want that. And nor should you." Am I being blackmailed? Seriously, is he blackmailing me? Great. I flounce out the room, absolutely seething, but then halfway down the stairs my mood switches to sadness cos I know I can never see Tom again. I can't keep lying to him, but how do you dump someone you desperately want to be with?

I find him in the kitchen, buttering toast, looking all dishevelled and delicious. "Sam!" His face lights up and he holds the buttery knife above his head as he leans in to kiss me. I can't let him, not now, so I duck out the way, causing his nose to clash awkwardly against my cheek. He backs off, looking hurt and confused, rubbing his injured nose. "I guess I have my answer then," he says.

To what question? Give us your phone number? Can

I see you again? Will you be my girlfriend? Yes, yes and double yes. Instead I say, "I'm sorry. I'm so busy right now…"

"It's okay. Please… just leave it." He can't look at me so pretends to be engrossed in slopping jam on toast. But then neither of us can actually eat it. And so there's silence. I mean, what do you say to a guy you've spent the night with but have no intention of seeing again? Awkward. In fact, so awkward we're even pleased to see Chris. He comes sauntering in, still zipping up his flies, looking mighty pleased with himself.

"Chris! You're up…"

"Can we go now?" Tom grabs Chris's jacket and thrusts it at him.

"Hold your horses man. What's the rush? I need a bit of brekkie first. No one eating this toast?" He picks up a slice, looking first at Tom then at me and he's clearly caught the vibe. "Oh dear," he makes a sad face, "who did the dumping?"

To think I was relieved to see him. "Chris, can you please just shut up and go. I have to get ready for work."

"No worries. I can drop you there. Give you more time to get ready. Go get your uniform on."

"We don't wear uniform these days. Makes it less institutional."

"Shame. I like a woman in uniform, don't you, Tom?" Tom just scowls.

"Look, thanks for the offer, but I'd really rather get the train."

"Nonsense. I'll take you."

Well, it's not like I have a choice, is it? So I go up and rummage through my wardrobe, searching for something respectable to wear. Sam usually wears plain blue trousers and a white blouse to work but I don't have anything smarter than jeans. Actually, sod this! Why on earth am I colluding with Chris? Why not just tell Tom the truth? Okay, he might be angry, but at least he won't be hurt anymore and I can quit lying. But then... I can't bear the thought of him hating me. And I can't cope with a whole load of conflict right now. In truth, I'm scared to come clean. Cos I almost tricked him into doing something illegal and he'll be really bloody raging about that.

So I go to Mum's wardrobe and find a pair of grey checked trousers and a white frilly blouse. Wow. I look like an office worker. I pin on the NHS badge and patter downstairs, anxious to usher us all out the door. Chris, though, is in no hurry; he's happily raking through my kitchen cupboards. "You do realise at least half this food is out of date?"

"Yup. Can we go now?"

"Who's the veggie?"

"For Christ's sake, Chris, could you give it a rest? I really need to go."

He pulls his head out the cupboard. "Okay, okay."

So we all troop to the car, Tom and I in awkward silence, but Chris is blethering away about god knows what. I get in the front passenger seat and as Chris climbs into the driver's side I catch a whiff of stale spliff off his clothes. "Actually, wait a minute, Chris, you can't drive. You've had a joint already."

"Sam dear, that was just my morning constitutional. I am in no way stoned. Now if I hadn't had a joint – then you'd need to worry."

I don't have the energy to argue, so wearing my stolen ID badge, I allow a drug-addled dealer to drive me to my bogus job. Really, is it possible to sink any lower?

12

BARS AND BRAS

This is like the most uncomfortable car trip ever. I mean, how long does it take to get to Carthill? I thought Chris would be some sort of speed freak, but he's driving like a geriatric. Come on; put your foot down, man. I can feel Tom's eyes on the back of my neck – waves of injured silence striking me from behind. Honestly, it's giving me the creeps. Chris, though, is babbling away about his charity work with disabled children. Seriously? Charity work? He's such a weirdo. I can't suss him out.

Oh, thank god, there's the big blue sign at last. Chris pulls into the car park and yanks off my NHS badge. "I'll have this," he laughs. "I think I'd make a great nurse, don't you? What with my bedside manner. Fnar, fnar." I snatch it back and bury it in my bag, well out of reach. Chris winks at me. Yuk. Who winks these days? Sleazy old men and embarrassing dads. And why the wink? Oh, was he doing me a favour? Whatever. I'm just glad not to be wearing the badge as I step out the car. What if Sam had seen? I slam shut the door and glance at Tom sitting huddled in the back. He doesn't look at me, just gives a floppy half-wave as they drive off. Oh, thank god, I can breathe at last. I never want to be that stressed again, EVER!

Sam lets me in. She isn't chatty; in fact she's a bit cold. Is it cos I was rude to her yesterday or has she sussed it was me who nicked her badge? Maybe she's preoccupied because she's about to get the sack. Oh man... I'm back to not breathing again. Every time Sam looks my way I think she's about to call the police. I'm now officially the most paranoid person on this ward and that's really saying something.

Mum, though, is having one of her good days. She spots I'm wearing her clothes, which I think is a huge step forward. I tell her there was nothing else clean and she seems satisfied with that, but then she says, "You look really tired," and I could jump for joy cos that's such an ordinary thing to say.

"Uh. Amy kept me up half the night talking. You know what she's like." I roll my eyes and make a blah, blah, blah gesture with my hand.

"She slept over, did she?"

"Um, no... I'm staying at hers."

"Oh." Mum suddenly looks really sad. "Had enough of Ollie, have you? You two been fighting?"

Eh? What's she on about? Surely she knows he's in Europe? I did tell her. Perhaps she was too drugged up to take it in. I give a non-committal shrug and try to change the subject, but she isn't so easy to distract.

"Jess... you can tell me the truth. Is he mad at me?" For the first time in ages she looks me in the eye and I'm appalled to see hers are shining with tears. Her bottom lip trembles as she fights to go on, "Only... he's not been in for a while..." She pulls a tissue from her pocket and dabs at her nose. "He's every right to be angry. Every right. I don't blame him. I'm the worst mum..."

"NO! No, you're not! You're ill. That's all." She tries to smile, but she can't. And suddenly she's crying, loudly. Big, heaving, gulping sobs. It's awful, but also rather wonderful as well, because crying is what normal people do, isn't it? But I have no idea how to handle it. I've grown so used to her just staring into space that I can't think what to do. I jump up and pat her shoulder, shuffling awkwardly from foot to foot – there, there now, pat, pat, pat – you'll be okay. God, I'm acting like my brother. What she really needs is a big sodding hug. So I drop back down on the bed and reach out my arms, but in the end I can't. She's become such a stranger to me that the thought of putting my arms round her makes me want to cringe with awkwardness and shame. It should be the most natural thing in the world, shouldn't it? Giving your mum a hug? But I just sit there, arms outstretched like a rigid Zombie, unable to actually make contact.

I can't let her cry like this. I must tell her Ollie's away, but that he calls every day to hear how she's doing and the second he gets back he will be straight in to see her. But then what about me? Will she call Dad or even social services if she knows I'm on my own? I have to protect myself too. Oh, but look at her wretched, tear-sodden face. She looks so frail and vulnerable, I can't leave her like that. I have to make it better, even if it means being shipped off to Dubai.

"Mum, Ollie's not mad at you. He's not even..."

"Helen! Are you okay?" A breathless Sam comes dashing in, precisely at the wrong bloody moment. I leap to my feet, feeling vaguely guilty, as if I'm to blame for all of mum's misery. Sam glances at Mum and then up at me.

"What...?" I shrug and wander over to the window, where I linger for a bit, glad of a bit of a breather. When I find the strength to turn back round, Mum's much quieter. Her head's on Sam's shoulder and her hand is also clutching one of Sam's. I feel like yelling 'get your hands off my mum, she's mine!' Of course I don't. What right have I to feel possessive?

"I've lost my son," Mum sobs quietly into Sam's neck. "It's all my fault, but I've lost him."

"Oh, Helen, I'm sure that's not true," says Sam, her voice so soothing and calm. "Boys that age are useless. They can't handle anything emotional. As soon as you're out of here, he'll turn up with a sack full of washing, looking for his dinner. Acting like nothing's happened. You'll see."

Mum's head snaps up and her swollen eyes peer into Sam's, scouring for sincerity. She nods slowly, satisfied that Sam isn't bullshitting. "Yes. Yes. You might be right. He's quite uptight is our Ollie. Oh but then, he'll be so embarrassed by all of this, he won't want to come near me. I'm the mother from hell..."

"No you're not!" I cry. She ain't great, I'll give you that, but there's far worse out there, I'm sure.

Mum stares at me, surprised. Then she actually smiles. "Who's that on your bag?" she asks, nodding towards the floor by her locker, where I dumped it when I came in.

"Eh?" I can't actually remember which bag it is, so I have to walk round Ann's bed to take a look. "Oh, that's my Kurt Cobain bag. You know, lead singer of Nirvana."

Mum smiles again. "I was so in love with Kurt Cobain," she says, sounding all wistful. "I hated Courtney Love. I mean how did that witch get to marry him?"

"You're joking! I had no idea..."

"Oh yes," she says, "I was quite the grunge groupie. Your

dad too. He had piercings, all up his ears. And his nose."
How did I not know that? I want Sam to go now, so I can
talk to my mum. Ask her about the bands she liked, who
she saw in the 90s. Then I'll tell her about Ollie and we'll
hug and talk and...

"Ollie was so shocked when he saw photos of us at uni,"
says Mum, turning to Sam. "He looks like me, but he's so
clean cut and proper. I don't know where he gets it from.
I know he's always wanted me to be a bit less hippy and a
bit more 'mum' and I tried. I really, really did. But he has
such high standards. I think he'll only be satisfied with a
twin set and pearls. And now look at me. The final straw,
I think..." She stares down at her hands, tears once again
sliding down her cheeks.

Please go, Sam, I can make this right, but not in front of
you. I need to talk to my mum. I'll tell her everything and
she'll understand, cos we're the same, we are. Now I see it.
I might not look like her, but underneath we're the same.
Just two lost souls struggling with our roles.

But it's too late; the moment's slipping away. Mum's
getting more and more upset. Less lucid. The mantras of
psychosis are flitting back through. She's harping back to
that bloody ceiling – saying how things with Ollie would
be fine if she hadn't fallen through it. And I feel like
screaming, 'I am here you know!'

Now Sam's muttering about getting something to settle
her and I feel like a complete bitch, cos I know all it would
take to calm her is a few words about Ollie. But not in
front of Sam. So instead I do what I'm best at, produce a
steaming great pile of bullshit. "Ollie can't come to see you
because he's working day and night." I blurt it out before I
fully think it through.

"What's that?"

"Ollie. He's had to take a job in the supermarket because we're so sodding skint. So he's never free at visiting hours, otherwise he'd be up here."

"Really?" Mum sniffs, "you're not just saying that?"

"Uh-huh." I don't sound too convincing and Sam gives me a really strange look, but if Mum suspects she's being lied to, she doesn't seem to care. She grabs hold of my words like a life ring.

"Oh Jess, you don't know how much better that makes me feel. Why didn't you say so? It's because of the money, isn't it? Because I was so awful last time you brought it up. Oh, Ollie. Bless him. Having to work so hard."

Yeah, good old Ollie, what a star.

"You know, Jess," says Sam, grinning now too. "We can make arrangements for Ollie to come visit; it would mean such a lot to your mum. Even if it's really late I can still sneak him in. I'll give you my number, then he can text to see what shift I'm on."

Oh for god's sake. Just piss right off, Sam, and take your do-gooding meddling elsewhere. I try a smile, but I suspect it's not terribly successful. "Thanks Sam. I'll let him know."

"So when do you think he'll come?" asks Mum, her eyes shining like a kid on Christmas morning.

"Soon Mum, I'm sure." Well, I can't take much more of this. Time to skedaddle, I think. The second I get outside I call Ollie. Sod the phone bill. Sod the cost. I need to talk to him now.

"Jess?" he answers in a panic. "What's up? Is it Mum?"

"No. Yes. Sort of." I start to cry. "Oh Ollie, she thinks you hate her. She can't understand why you haven't been in. She thinks you've disowned her cos she doesn't own a twin set and I was about to tell her the truth, I was. But

Sam wouldn't leave us alone, so I said you're working in the supermarket – day and night to make ends meet – and she seemed so overjoyed that now I can't possibly burst that bubble. And I feel like a shit and I don't know what to do."

There's silence on the other end and I feel like killing him until I realise he's crying too. He's trying his best to hide it, but I can tell by the snuffles he's struggling to breathe through his nose.

"Oh Jess," he says at last, "I'm sorry. I should never have left. It was stupid and selfish and I regret it every day."

"S'okay," I squeak. "I did kind of force you. But yeah, it was a really dumb idea. Are you at least having fun?"

"Um, it's all right. But Jack and Tim want to spend the whole day getting wasted. And if they aren't drunk, they're copping off with girls. I'm finding it all a bit... samey. And I'm worried about you and Mum and money and... everything really."

"Well, aren't you copping off with girls too? I thought that was the whole point."

He doesn't say anything for ages then he says, "I don't know how into girls I am, Jess."

"Oh."

There's an awkward silence, then he goes, "I mean, I'd rather see some sights – you know, other than bars and bras."

"Oh... cos for a second there I thought you might be... you know... coming out to me. Haha." It isn't a real laugh, more like a nervous hiccup, but I snap shut my mouth the second it escapes.

"God no!" He says it so fast, like it's the most ludicrous thing imaginable. He hangs up pretty quick after that; says he's desperate to phone Mum and once again I feel awful. For the second time today I've missed the chance to share something meaningful with my family. I've lied to Mum and upset Ollie. I wonder if he's really gay? Or am I reading way too much into one off the cuff remark? But it would explain a lot, wouldn't it? I mean, really, what teenage boy gets fed up looking at bras?

What a day. My head's killing me. I just want to go home and flop into bed. So I get the train back to town, stopping off at the supermarket for a few treats, then walk the mile or so home.

The smell hits me as soon as I open the front door. Spliff smoke. I step inside, dropping my bag to the floor and look around. The hall is cloudy with smoke. Could it have lingered since this morning? Nah, it's way too strong. There's someone in my house. Must be. Oh hell. My heart is racing like I've just run a marathon. What should I do? Slink away or stand my ground? At any rate I should probably call the police. Oh, but what if they ask where my parents are? Shit.

I'm frozen. Police or no police? Make a decision, Jess, before someone gallops out and plunges a knife in your neck.

"Welcome!" a cheery voice wafts through from the living room, followed by snorts of poorly suppressed laughter. My heart sinks. Chris! How the hell did he get in? Know something? Right now I am too damned weary to care. I'm off to bed.

I creep up to my room and slide between the covers. There's a right old racket coming up from below – crashing and bashing and boisterous banter. I sling a pillow over my head and close my eyes. It does nothing to muffle the noise, but I'm so worn out I could sleep through a tornado. It'll take more than a few dopeheads to keep me awake, I can tell you.

13

WEARING SOUP

Six in the morning. I slept right through – that was like, fourteen, maybe fifteen hours sleep. A new record. I think it's all quiet downstairs – at least there's no loud voices still seeping through the ceiling. I wonder if they've left, or if they're all conked out on my living room floor. I really hope they've gone; I could do without the drama today.

I've got this big ball of dread in the pit of my stomach. First day of the new term, you see. Total nightmare. Everyone will know about Mum and Hannah will be out for revenge. I'm about to become the class punch-bag.

Right. On with the uniform. I'm going for sensible shirt and tie up top; frayed denim mini and chunky boots below. Mussed up hair and lots of eyeliner – I hope Ollie's right about the whole grunge vibe acting as armour. But it's hard to see how ripped tights and smoky eyes will fend off Hannah's army.

Okay. Here goes. What's the damage downstairs? I tiptoe into the living room to find three stoned blokes snoring on the floor. Hmmmph. I bet Amy's tucking into a boiled egg right now, while her mum packs her lunch and polishes her shoes. No wading through empty Carlsberg cans for her. I peer at the faces passed out on the floor, gagging at the scent of stale smoke and beer breath. No Chris. I bet I know where he'll be though. Sure enough, back upstairs I find him snoring away in Mum's bed. I poke him on the shoulder.

"Mmmm? Wha... what time is it?"

"I dunno, about seven."

He snaps straight up and throws back the duvet. "Jeez, I've missed my tutorial. Why didn't you wake me?"

"Eh, because you've broken into my house and I'm not your mum. Anyway, how do you have a tutorial at 7am in the holidays?"

"Seven in the morning!" He looks at me like I've gone mental. "I thought it was seven at night. What the hell you doing waking me at this time?"

"Eh, cos some of us have school to go to."

He coories back in and smirks. "Oh yes. Loving the uniform, by the way. Not quite what old Tom expected, but still HOT, like a naughty Britney Spears." He stares at my skirt. "You allowed to wear denim?"

No I am not, but I am now officially a rebel. "Oi! Eyes to the face perv. Don't you dare look at my legs like that! Anyway, how d'ye get into my house? If you've broken a window you'd better fix it."

He looks horrified. "What do you take me for? I'm not a burglar. I used a key like any other civilised human being."

"A key? Where d'ye get a key from?"

"Kitchen drawer."

I'm lost for words, I really am. This guy's so amoral he seems to think swiping a key from someone's private drawer is perfectly reasonable behaviour. I think hard for a moment and then say, "I'm not going to waste my breath asking for it back, Chris, because I know you won't give it. But you listen here, if you make that kind of racket again, old Ma Clarkey next door will call the police and this arrangement will be over. If you want to hang out here, you need to be sensible or you'll land up in jail. Now personally I think that's the best place for you, but we both know I have my own reasons for avoiding the law right now. So just reign it in, okay?"

His eyes haven't moved from mine throughout this little speech and I glance away, uncomfortable. When I look back up he's still regarding me with interest. He scoops up a half-smoked spliff from a plate beside the bed and lights it.

"You know something, Jess?" he says, blowing out smoke. "I like you. We're on the same wavelength, you and me. And yes, you're absolutely right. I got carried away last night and it won't happen again."

Stunned, I nod. "Um... okay."

"But did you see I left my car at home?" He looks like he's expecting a round of applause.

"Yeah. So what?"

"Well. It's all part of my plan to become your brother. See, I've found myself touched by your predicament and I was wondering how to help you. And I thought, I know, I'll drive your mother's car then everyone will think Ollie's home and not off sunning himself in the Med."

I'm too weary to ask how he knows Ollie's in Europe; no doubt it involves rummaging about in my brother's bedroom. But I'm totally sure of one thing. "You are not driving my mum's car! You're permanently stoned and I doubt you're even insured. Just drive your own and park round the corner."

He looks hurt. Honestly, I don't think he's faking. He actually thinks I'd want him joyriding about in my mum's motor.

"Well, I need to drive it today," he says, all huffy like. "I've got a few things to do and out of the goodness of my heart I left mine at home."

"You are not! I'm not giving you the..." I spot the grin. "You've got the keys already, haven't you?" He nods, proud as punch. "Oh for god's sake. Right, whatever. Just this once though. And please, make sure those inebriates are gone by the time I get back."

He gives me a salute, stubs out the spliff and slides back under the covers. As I stand to leave, he says, "I could bring you a present, you know. Tonight. Starts with a T ends with an M..."

Oh, how I long to say yes. Tom's just the kind of carrot I need to get me through the day. But I shake my head. I can't go through all that lying again and it'd just give Chris more of a hold over me. "Don't ever, ever, do that," I say. "I never want to see him again." And as I exit he mutters something I don't quite catch, though I think it might be,

"Now both of us know that's just not true..."

* * *

Since I can't stand being at home, I get to school super early then hover round the corner till the bell goes. I keep my head down during registration. There's no one too obnoxious in my form class, but I can't face talking to anyone. And I need to psych myself up for first period. Higher maths. Hannah Walters is in my maths class. In fact, she's in most of my classes – registration and art are the only ones Hannah-free.

The bell rings for first period and Mr Somerville yells, "Straight to class people. No dawdling. And for Pete's sake, keep the noise down." I get up to go and he steps in front of me. "Not you, Miss Brody. A word, please?"

I was expecting this and I'm not really that bothered. At least it means missing a bit of maths. Somerville waits till the class clears, then sits behind his desk, linking his hands behind his head.

"So," he says, staring up at me. "You going to tell me what this is about?"

"Don't know what you mean, sir."

"Oh for goodness sake, Jess. First day back and I'm depressed already. Don't you think there's enough numpties round here, without you rolling up dressed as Siouxsie Sioux?"

"Who?"

"Oh never mind. The point is, I count on you to be sensible. My space-cadet quota is already full. I do not need another one. So go to the toilets, scrub off the eyeliner and tomorrow wear a skirt."

"I am wearing a skirt."

"That..." he jabs a finger in the direction of my legs then averts his eyes, embarrassed, "is not a skirt. It's a pelmet. You know you're not allowed anything that short. If Mr Tenant spots it he'll send you home." I shrug, making him tut in disgust. "Thanks a bunch for ruining my day. Go on. Disappear." I slink from the room, feeling slightly guilty. Mr Somerville's really nice; I didn't mean to ruin his day.

By the time I make my way to the other side of the school, maths has already started. I quietly open the door and scan the room for a spare seat. Get this. The only free one is next to Hannah Walters. She smirks and mouths, "I saved it for you." Well, what can I do; I have to sit beside her. As I park my bum, a murmur goes round the class, prompting crabbit Miss Bowie to glare.

"Silence!" she growls, turning her evil eye on me. "Don't get comfy, Miss Brody. You are not welcome in my classroom dressed like a tramp. Kindly take yourself off to Mr Tenant."

Well, banished from the class by five-past-nine, I reckon it must be some kind of record. I'm not sure though – I've never actually been sent to the Head before. And look how calm I am. Last term I'd have been quaking at the thought; now it just seems like kids' stuff.

I have to cross the playground to get back to the main building and there in a corner is school Goth, Meredith Baker, huddled over a cigarette. She raises her eyebrows when she sees me and sorrowfully shakes her head.

"How sad," she says, "when a good girl goes bad. Fag?" She thrusts a red and white pack at me and I think, why not? So I slip one out and light up. Eeeugh. It tastes no better, but I persevere. We smoke in silence for a bit then she says, "You been sent to the Head?" I nod. "Me too," she says. "Same old, same old."

"Oh. You've been before, have you?"

She snorts, "Yeah. Like only every day. Sometimes twice."

"Ah. What's it like?"

She thinks for a moment. "It's not so bad. Me and Old Tenant have an understanding. He knows about my… issues… and I don't cause him any real trouble. Short skirt and smoking. It's not like I'm beating folk up."

I stare at Meredith as she speaks and for the first time notice how pretty she is. I've always avoided her, assumed she was ugly cos of all the hissing, snarling attitude, but actually her features are really rather delicate. She wears her hair cropped into the scalp and dyes it different colours, depending on her mood, I guess. Today it's black and she has these little pointy bits pulled down under her cheekbones, making them seem razor sharp. Her eyes are big, but somehow all the eyeliner makes them look smaller. I imagine that scraped clean, Meredith looks all wide eyed and innocent – like a little pixie. I don't say that, though; instead I ask what Tenant's likely to do to me.

"He'll come down on you like a ton of bricks," she says, drawing her hand across her throat.

"Why?"

"Oh come on, Jess. You're one of his top pupils, he's not going to risk you going off the rails. Me? I'm a lost cause. But you need to get your shit together and get your arse back into class. Only way you'll escape this dump for good." Meredith drops her fag butt and grinds it out with the toe of her Doc Marten boot.

"You're really bright!" I cry. "You can do anything you want. What makes you think you're stuck round here?" Meredith opens her mouth as if to say something then closes it again, leaving the thought hanging. I have this weird feeling it's important, though, so I try to nudge it out of her. "What? You were about to say something, what was it?"

She shakes her head. "Nothin."

"No, go on. Tell me."

She sighs. "Look, how many GCSE's did you get, Jess? Thirteen?"

"Yeah, more or less."

She looks annoyed. "Well either you did or you didn't."

"Yeah. I got thirteen."

"So why not just say so?" She sighs again and stares off over my shoulder and I think she's had enough of me, but then she says, "Guess how many I got?"

I don't have a clue. Meredith is clever, but she's rarely in class. "Eight? Ten?" I guess.

"Try zero."

"Zero! Nah. You're joking."

"Do I look as if I'm joking?" No she does not; she looks like she might thump me.

"Why? Did you not bother sitting them?"

"I'm not that much of a rebel, Jess." She gives this little laugh that's completely devoid of joy. "Nope, I sat a few and screwed them up. Then the pressure got too much and I wound up back in the bin."

She stares me straight in the eye, all defiant like and it takes a few moments for her words to sink in. 'Back in the bin?' Does that mean...? "NO! You've been in Carthill?"

She nods. "Say a word to anyone and I'll kill you."

"As if! God no. I take it you've heard about my mum?"

She raises a sardonic eyebrow. "Duh! Why do you think I'm telling you?" She says 'you' with such scorn that I feel my hackles start to rise – just when I was warming to her as well.

"So... like... what's wrong with you?"

The sleeves of her blazer are partially rolled up and the arms beneath are covered in bangles and studded strips of leather. She unbuckles the largest of these to reveal the skin underneath. Oh my god, you should see her arm! New scars, old scars, vivid scars, fading scars, even oozing scars – her skin is a patchwork of pain. I stumble backwards, slapping my hand to my mouth in horror.

"Christ, Meredith! What have you done to yourself?"

She doesn't look at me; she's trying to get her studded cuff back on, without much success, and I can tell she's starting to panic in case someone passes by and sees. "Here let me help." I snatch it off her and have it secure in seconds. Distraction over, she has no choice now but to look me in the eye and she doesn't much like what she sees.

"Don't you dare look at me like that," she hisses. "You

can't fix me and I don't want your pity. So fuck off." Jeez, she's a hard girl to like. She starts stomping off and I grab her by the shoulder and I'm shocked by how bony she feels; there isn't an ounce of flesh on her.

"Oh don't go," I beg. "You've got it all wrong. I don't pity you. I pity myself. In fact, I'm so immersed in self-pity it's a wonder I don't dissolve. I'm out of my depth, Meredith. Help me, please!" She stops then and turns around, her face still hostile and suspicious.

"I'm not your friend," she says, "and I don't want to be. I've no desire to start bonding about the loony bin. But I'll give you a bit of advice. One," she holds up a finger, "don't give Tenant attitude. Tell him the truth and you'll be surprised by how much slack he cuts you. Two," another finger shoots up, "don't trust Amy. Popularity's too important to her; she will betray you – it's only a question of when." I start to protest, but she cuts me off with a bad tempered "Sssh. And three – don't let Hannah Walters sabotage your potential. By all means indulge your little Goth phase at school, but at home you hit those books. Got it?"

Wow. I mean, WOW! Standing there with her black lipstick and bovver boots, she is actually telling me to knuckle down and study! She is perhaps the most sensible pupil in my year.

"So go," she says. "You see Tenant first. I'll have another fag while I'm waiting."

"Okay. But first, can you just tell me this? Was it your mum's mental health problems that drove you to… you know… that…" I can't think of a word to describe what is on her arm.

Meredith bursts out laughing, this time for real. "My mum's the most well balanced woman you'll ever meet in your life. She doesn't have mental health problems. She said it to protect me when we were spotted up there."

"Oh! Cos I heard..."

"... She's a drug addict?"

I feel my face going red. "Yeah."

Meredith snorts. "It's amazing how these tales develop a life of their own."

So I go to the Headmaster's office and I follow Meredith's advice. I almost don't. He's such a conservative looking man – grey hair, grey skin, grey suit – how can he possibly understand why I need to wear so much eyeliner? But he does. Cuts me a deal. No more denim and he'll turn a blind eye to mussed up hair and big black boots. He asks if there's anything he can do. Will it help if he speaks to Hannah Walters? Nah, I say, being branded a clipe will only make things worse.

So I toddle on back to maths and Miss Bowie is real surprised to see me; she does a double take as I slink inside the door. "What on earth are you doing here?" she barks. "Have you actually been to the Headmaster?"

"Uh-huh."

"Well, didn't he send you home?"

"Nope."

Miss Bowie looks completely enraged. "I don't believe you," she says. "Class. Finish that page on Functions and I will return in just a moment." She drapes a drab tweed jacket over her ancient shoulders and marches out the door. Poor Mr Tenant is about to get an earful. Of course, the minute she leaves all thoughts of Functions go with her. In fact, everyone's attention immediately turns to me.

"What's with the makeover, Jess?" Scott Johnstone sidles over and stares down at me, looking amused. "You've gone a bit... grubby."

"Um." My face has gone red, I can feel it. What am I supposed to say? "Um…"

"Who cares?" laughs Craig Collins, reaching from the desk behind to give my shoulder a friendly pat. "It's wound up old Bowie. So keep it up, Jess, go as manky as you like."

I smile, mortified to be under such scrutiny but also half-enjoying the banter. The boys in my year are really nice. They're completely clueless when it comes to gossip; I bet they don't even know about Mum. Judging by Hannah's face, though, they're about to get the full sordid story. She turns in her seat and announces in this silly, simpering voice, "Haven't you heard boys? Jess's mum's gone mental. And now Jess has morphed into Meredith Baker. What is it with crazy parents that turns their kids into complete and utter freaks?"

I drop my head in shame, tears stinging the back of my eyes. I will not cry, I must not cry. Then there's a hand on my shoulder again and this time it's a squeeze, not a playful pat. "Oh man, Jess, are you okay?" I manage to glance up and Craig's freckled face is all worried. I've known him since I was five years old. If Hannah thinks he's about to turn against me just cos my mum's gone mental, she's got another thing coming. In fact, Hannah's bitchiness seems to have backfired cos none of the boys are laughing. There's this awful silence, then Craig says, "You're a complete cow, Walters."

Hannah's face turns scarlet. "Yeah? Well at least my mum's not a paedo," she hisses. "Jess Brody's mum has traumatised my little brother."

Oh. The whole paedo thing. Yeah that should do it. The boys might be nice, but no one likes a paedo. I hold my breath, bracing myself for the onslaught of abuse. But it doesn't come. Craig says, "You're so full of shit, Walters –

just a vindictive wee lassie that nobody actually likes. So keep the poison to yourself, cos no one wants to hear it."

I could kiss that boy, really I could. He doesn't believe her. I look up. None of them do. No one's looking at me with revulsion, they're all either glaring at Hannah or gazing awkwardly out the window.

The girls, though, are rallying round poor, humiliated Hannah. "You're well out of order," screeches Courtney James – she's like this plump clone of Hannah who hangs off her every word. She pokes a chubby finger at Craig's chest. "I've a good mind to report you to Mr Tenant. Intimidating a girl like that. You'll be expelled." Craig just shakes his head and stares at her with contempt.

"Quick, Bowie's here!" comes a screech from the back and there's a mad scramble for seats like it's a really urgent game of musical chairs. Bowie's face is like fizz. She scowls at me aggrieved and out for revenge. "So Miss Brody," she says, draping her moth eaten jacket back over her seat. "It seems Mr Tenant can bend the rules for certain pupils." She sniffs in disgust. "But I can assure you that I do not. If you ever turn up to my class looking like that again, you will be out of Higher maths. Understood?"

"Yes, Miss Bowie." Jeez, I don't want to get chucked out of maths. If I lose the denim mini will that be enough? Or will she only be satisfied with me scrubbed clean and respectable. Actually maybe it doesn't matter, cos at this rate I'm gonna fail anyway. I can't concentrate on a word the old bat is saying. It's like there's no space in my head for anything but Hannah Walters and her sordid slurs. I've copied down all I'm supposed to off the whiteboard, but looking at my jotter it's just like this random jumble of numbers and symbols. It's completely meaningless to me. How am I ever going to get through this year?

Oh, the bell for first break, thank Christ for that. I am so outta here. I snatch up my bag and go barging past everyone, like a rugby player charging for the line. I desperately need a drink. Honestly, my mouth is like sandpaper, so I go hurtling down the empty corridors in the direction of the vending machines. If I get there before the hordes descend, I can scuttle off to the loo with my bottle of water and hide out there till break's over. That way, no more ugly scenes. Almost there, just under the mezzanine now. Oooh. What's that? Something just plopped on my head. Can't be bird poo indoors, can it? I touch my hair. Ooh. Gross. Something sticky and warm. I force myself to look at my fingers – yuk – it's dark, it's green, it's phlegm all right. Someone's gobbed on me! I glance up and catch a flash of departing black tights. Hannah's harpies. Should I chase after them? Catch up and give them a doing? Who am I kidding? Hiding in the toilets will take all the strength I can muster. Pathetic or what?

* * *

Physics, yawn. English, now, which I usually love but I just can't concentrate. My head's all over the place. I keep forcing myself to listen, but then my mind goes toddling off again on it's own wee journey. Know something? I'm worried I'm turning into Mum. This is how it started with her. She'd sit down with a book, but never turn a page. Or ask me umpteen times what was happening in Eastenders. Could madness be contagious? Have I caught it off her? Ah well, at least it's lunch soon. I'm absolutely starving. As my old Gramps used to say, I could eat a scabby heided dug. I'll get a proper cooked meal too, my first in weeks. Mmmmm. I wonder what's on the menu.

Eh? What's going on? Everyone's staring at me. Oh crap, I'm in trouble, aren't I. Mr Liddell's striding over, shouting that I have to start reading from where Lena Wilson stopped, only he knows fine well I have no clue where that is.

"We're waiting..." he says, drumming his fingers on my desk. I've not even opened the book. I reach for Macbeth and flip the pages, but Liddell snatches it off me.

"We're not reading Macbeth, Ms Brody. We moved on to another text ten minutes ago. Here's a thought. Why don't you tell me which one it is?"

"Eh..." I have no idea. My mind is a blank. A complete and utter thought-free zone. Liddell is furious and he's usually so easy-going.

"This one!" he slams down a copy of Janice Galloway's, 'The Trick is to Keep Breathing.' I stare at it, then I stare at him. I can tell I'm looking gormless – I've got a look on my face that any teacher'd want to slap, but I can't seem to stop gawping or shut my gaping mouth. We're reading that book? I can't read from that book. I know what it's about. I twist round and look at Hannah Walters, who smirks and twirls a finger by her ear – you know – universal sign for crazy person. I stand up.

"Sorry, sir. I have a migraine." And with that I wander out the class. Mr Liddell's yelling something, but I'm way past caring. Now what? I look at my watch. Just ten minutes till lunchtime. I might as well be first in the queue.

"You're keen! We're no open yet." The dinner ladies look amused as I poke my head round the canteen door.

"I know. I thought I would just get in first, for once."

"Och, in ye come then." A middle-aged lady, as wide as she is tall, yanks open the door and ushers me inside. "It's nice tae see a lassie hungry for some dinner. Yer aw too thin these days. See how thin she is," the dinner lady yells at her colleagues. "There's no a pick on her. No a pick." They all nod, looking me up and down with solemn faces. "Yer awffy pale as well, hen. You get in there and get yerself some meat. Ye'll be needin the iron. Haw, Marie. Can ye load up this lassie's plate wae some o that moussaka. Double helpin." She turns back to me. "You make sure you eat it all now. Every last bit of it."

I nod, and pick up a tray. For some weird reason I have this awful urge to fling my arms round this enormous woman and sob into her heaving bosom. No one could get to me in there. If I cooried in deep, I wouldn't hear their taunts there either. I look at her chest with longing, but manage to resist. Just.

Plate piled high with a moussaka that looks suspiciously like mince and tatties, it's time to find a seat. As the first person in, I feel really exposed, so I sit near the back, head down, and wait for Amy. She'd better get here quick. I'm so anxious I can hardly swallow. The moussaka's tasty, but it's not going down well. Hurry up Amy. My throat will clear once she's here. I know it. God, imagine needing moral support to manage a bit of lunch.

The tables are filling up now, and still no sign of Amy. Where can she be? She should be here by now – everyone else is. Oh Christ and here comes Courtney James. What's she smirking about? I expect a smart-assed comment as she walks on past, but she just keeps sniggering. Ow! What the...? My back, my bloody back! It's on fire. I leap out my seat and spin round to find Courtney clutching a half empty soup plate. The rest of it's down my shirt. Lucky the school soup's never actually boiling. But look at the state of my shirt! Tomato soup on a white blouse – I look like I've been stabbed.

"You cow," I hiss.

Courtney raises a hand to her mouth, trying to look all wide-eyed and innocent. "Oops, clumsy me," she titters and walks off, shoulders shaking with laughter.

I sink back into my seat, dabbing at the soup with a crumpled tissue.

"Had an accident, Jess?" I look up to find Hannah Walters gazing down at me, top lip curled in disgust. "Oh dear," she says. "At your age you really must learn how to feed yourself." She picks up a spoon and mimes eating soup. "See! You put the spoon to your mouth, you don't let it dribble down your front." Her groupies find this hilarious and Hannah looks triumphant, basking in their admiration. "Anyway, enjoy your lunch," she says, starting to walk away.

But as she goes, her hand catches the side of my tray and swipes it off the table. My lunch! Custard and moussaka rain down onto the filthy floor, while the whole canteen explodes into a cacophony of foot stamping and applause. Why does everyone get so excited when a lunch tray gets dropped? My face burns with shame, embarrassment – anger. I turn to Hannah and she leans in close, hissing, "Now you can eat your dinner like the dog you are, Jess Brody. Go on, lick it up."

I wanna give that spiteful face of hers a good slap – scratch her eyes out, slam her nose into the custard-moussaka mash. But I don't. The whole canteen is staring – the last thing I need is for the, "Fight, fight, fight!" chant to erupt. Besides, I can't be getting hauled off to the headmaster for a second time on my first day back. Jeez, this is a disaster.

A sour faced dinner lady appears with a mop. "You should be more careful," she chides. "Honestly, we're up to our necks in it here. The last thing we need is to mop up your mess."

"Sorry," I mumble. Maybe I'll go home, give up on school. It's just not worth it. I'm still starving too, and I've no bloody money left.

"Here." A banana and a roll suddenly materialise in front of me. Who…? Oh, it's Craig. He pulls out the chair next to mine and sits down. "Eat up," he says.

"Aw. Thanks, that's so… that's just so…. so…" I'm starting to blub. Great. I managed to survive the bitchiness, but now a random act of kindness has pushed me over the edge. A stray tear slips down my cheek and my face starts to crumple.

"OOOOooow!" My foot. Meredith Baker has just stomped on my foot with her clumpy steel-toed boot. "What d'ye do that for?"

She kicks back the seat opposite and flops down into it, waving a warning finger at me. "Don't," she says. "Just don't. The minute you start weeping and wailing, you let the bastards win. Take that pain and hold onto it. Focus. Go on…"

I do. I focus on my throbbing toes and the urge to cry evaporates. Is this why she cuts herself? "Thanks," I say.

"Anytime," she shrugs. "So," she says, biting into a baguette, "where's your little friend today? Thought you two were joined at the hip."

"Who? Oh, Amy. Dunno." I look around. She's still nowhere to be seen.

"Dumped you has she?"

"NO! No. Amy would never do that. We've been friends for like, a gazillion years."

"Oh yeah? She likes to be liked though, doesn't she? Bit of a princess…"

"Don't. Please…"

"OK. Fair enough. Anyway, you'll see her after lunch. Art, next period."

Oh, yes, art. Thank god. No Hannah Walters and it's the only class I get to see Amy. I can relax a bit, even if just for an hour.

Meredith munches her baguette and swills down a coke while I nibble on my banana. Craig's talking to some pals from the football team on the table behind. I tap him on the shoulder and wave the yellow, spotty skin at him. "I'll pay you back tomorrow," I say.

"Don't be daft," he says and again I feel like crying. Oh no, this time the tears are going to win. Except Meredith is on her feet and pointing to the gleaming tip of her boot.

"Do I really have to... again?" she asks and I shake my head.

"No. No. I'm calm. Honest I am." Those boots must be magic, cos the tears have gone again.

"Good. So, come on, get up then. I'll chum you to art."

"What...? Oh. Yeah..." Walk with Meredith to art? Really? But what if someone sees us? I don't mean to be mean, but I'm kinda fighting for my reputation here and Meredith's like social vermin. If I get lumped in with her, there's no going back. That's it; I'm unpopular forever. Oh, god. Just listen to me. What am I like! I sound like such a shallow cow, don't I? The only girl that's been kind to me all day and I don't want to be seen with her cos bitch-face Hannah might not approve. Of course I'll walk with her to art. Except I've blown it now, cos she's stalking off, incensed by my indecision. Way to go Jess, you're really on a roll today.

"Wait!" I stumble over my bag and almost fall in my hurry to catch up. "Wait! You don't understand."

Furious, Meredith spins round, "Oh, but I do! I really, really do."

"No you don't. I was just being stupid. Of course I'll chum you to art."

"Oh thank you! Thank you!" she exclaims, clasping her hands under her chin. "You are such a special person to do that for me."

Eh? She's being sarcastic, right?

"Fuck you," she snarls and stalks off.

Yeah, I guess she was being sarcastic.

* * *

I'm a bit late for art. Truth is, I'm trying to avoid another confrontation with Meredith; I've had all the aggro I can handle for one day. I'm not that late though. Not late enough to justify my so-called best friend pairing up with someone else. What the hell is Amy doing with Paige Armstrong? She sees me and mouths, "Sorry," and I give a little shrug to show I'm not bothered when really I am bothered – very bothered indeed. I know I said she should keep her distance, but I never thought she'd do it. Not in a million years.

So now I've no partner. And that's for the rest of term too, cos Mrs Carroll won't let you chop and change. The teacher stares at me over the top of her half-moon specs. "Come on Jess, take a seat, please. I'd like to get started."

Where though? Oh. One chair left and guess who it's next to – Meredith Baker, of course. Is this like destiny or what?

"Mind if I...?"

Meredith shrugs and looks away. "It's a free country..."

"Look Meredith, I'm sorry if I..."

"COULD YOU GIRLS AT THE BACK PLEASE SETTLE DOWN! I would like to begin this class before it's time to go home."

I swear, I have been in more trouble today than in all my years of school put together. Still, the rest of art is nice and peaceful – practising landscapes with pretty watercolours. I do a sort of Monet like piece, full of spring green trees and water-lilies, while Meredith dobs a sludgy brown hill in the rain. I point out that it looks like the Somme and she chuckles, thawing a bit. I try to catch Amy's eye, but she won't look at me. I'm ready to pounce at the end of the period.

"Amy! Wait."

"Jess! How are you?" She tries to smile, but her eyes are zipping all over the place and she's already inching forward.

"I've been better." I point to my shirt.

"Gosh! Are you all right? That's not blood is it?"

"Soup. It's soup. That Courtney is a right..."

She looks at her watch. "I'm sorry Jess, I really can't stop. I need to talk to the netball coach before English. I'll hear about it later, okay?"

"Eh... um..." She's walking to the door. I need to stop her, so I grab her arm and yank her back.

"What are you doing?" she yelps, shaking off my hand and smoothing down the sleeve of her blazer.

"Just... meet us in the toilets at break then, yeah?" I whisper out of the side of my mouth. "We can huddle in a cubicle so you won't be seen. It will be like a secret tryst." I do this manic grin, trying to convey that I understand it's hard for her too.

"Oh Jess, I would if I could, but I can't." She cocks her head to one side, trying to look sincere. "Sorry. I'll call you tonight though, yeah?"

"Yeah, okay." I feel so sad, but not only that, I feel humiliated – like I just plucked up the courage to ask out a boy and he sniggered in my face. She'll call later, I know she will, all gushing apologies, but that's no help now, is it? How am I supposed to get through this on my own?

Meredith Baker sidles on past. "Told you so," she says.

14

PIZZA PERFECTION

Amy's not at the gates at home time, so for the first time ever I have to walk home alone. It takes twice as long as well. Or at least it feels like it does. Usually it passes so quickly and we're still gossiping away at the end of my drive. But on my own, each dismal step seems to take forever.

I let myself in and find Chris lounging on the sofa, watching kids' TV and smoking a spliff. He has on this pastel Ralph Lauren shirt and expensive jeans that have clearly been ironed – who by? Mummy? Housekeeper? Himself? He looks up and drawls, "Hi Honey. How was your day?" like a 1950s housewife from a clapboard suburb.

"Well, since you ask – I've been spat on, dipped in soup and my best mate don't wanna know me. So why don't you just…"

"All right. Keep your shirt on, I was only asking." He cranes his head to one side. "Move, would you. I can't see the telly."

I flop down on the sofa and we both stare at a lurid cartoon for a bit, then I point to his spliff and say, "Give us a hit then." I reach out to take it and he snatches it away, holding his hand high above his head. Of all the selfish...! "Give us a bit! I only want to try it. After the day I've had..."

He shakes his head. "No. I'm not giving you doobs." "Why the hell not? Give it here." I get up on my knees and grab his wrist but he simply transfers the spliff to his other hand and chucks it in a half-drunk cup of coffee. "What d'ye do that for?" I lean over and stare into the mug, there's no rescuing it now.

"So," says Chris, as though nothing's happened. "You don't strike me as the type to get tortured at school. You're not ugly. Not a geek. Is there a body odour problem?"

I laugh, though I'm still raging. "No! I'm not normally this unpopular. It's all to do with... my mother's... er... cancer."

"Ah... the old cancer. Tough one that. I can see folk might find that freaky round here. Was the cancer very public? Like drooling, ranting and full frontal nudity?"

I laugh again, "Yup."

"And this friend that's dumped you – would that be Amy?"

"Yup again."

"That's a real shame." He looks gutted and I'm surprised by his empathy until he says, "Cos I was hoping she might be up for some afternoon rumpy pumpy."

"Right. Silly me. For a second there I thought you might actually be human. You are absolutely unbelievable."

"Oh don't get a strop on. I'm only joking. I..." His phone buzzes and he answers it, holding up a hand for silence. He's got the latest iPhone – five hundred quids worth at least. "Yep... uh-huh... yes, I'll be here all evening. And don't forget the cash this time. No more freebies." The person on the other end must make a joke cos Chris roars with laughter before hanging up. "So where were we?" he says.

"Who was that?"

He gazes down at the phone. "Um… no one important, just a friend."

"A friend that won't get 'freebies'? A friend that pays in cash? Are you dealing drugs from my home?"

"Look Jess, I'm not a drug dealer. Tom gave you completely the wrong idea about me. I merely supply to a few close and trusted friends. They do, however, occasionally take the piss and try not to pay me. But that's all. Nothing major. Nothing big league."

"I don't believe you. Those guys on my floor this morning? They weren't students. They looked like right raj bastards."

"Ah now, but I wasn't supplying to them though, was I? We were just having a smoke."

Why though? Why would a well-off law student choose to hang out here with dole scrounging dopeheads, when he could be partying in the halls with hot student tottie? I'm about to ask when my phone rings. I fumble in my bag, find it and stare at the screen; it's Amy. I have a good mind not to answer – that would show her. Or would it? Why would she even care? I try not to press that little green button but in the end can't stop myself.

"Hello."

"Oh Jess, there you are. I'm so sorry about today. I know it looks like I was avoiding you, but I've just been incredibly busy. You know how it is at the start of term with all my sports and clubs. Anyway, how was it? Really rotten? That was so awful about the soup. You poor thing."

"Where were you at lunch?"

"Oh… well… I took in some sandwiches and a few of us ate in the park. I would have asked you along… but it was all us netball girls. Planning the season ahead. You'd have been bored senseless." Yeah, but at least I wouldn't be wearing a plate of tomato soup. And Hannah Walters plays netball too. Was she at this little picnic?

Chris leans against me, trying to eavesdrop, so I shove him off and scooch to the opposite end of the couch. Undeterred, he shuffles along too till I'm jammed against the armrest with him almost in my lap. I have no idea what to say to Amy. I know if I open my mouth I'm going to sound like some needy wife hassling a no good, cheating husband. So I say nothing and for the first time ever there's this really awkward silence between us. Of course Chris soon fills it by yelling down the phone, "Amy, you saucy little minx. Come to me babe and I'll make you come..."

"Oooh. Is that Chris?" she screeches.

"Yeah," I sigh, holding the phone away from my ear.

"Oh Jess. Tell you what, why don't I come over? I'll bring the chocolate and you can tell me about your day. I'll just grab a bite to eat first – I should be round in about half an hour. Okay?" Grab a bite to eat, my ass – go wax your lady bits, you mean.

As soon as she hangs up I wallop Chris on the shoulder. "How could you?" I yell.

"What? What did I do?"

"I won't know now, will I?"

"What? Know what?"

"Whether she wants to see me! Or if she's just coming round to get jiggy with you."

"Get jiggy?" Chris bursts out laughing. "Where did you get that from?" I have absolutely no idea, but that is entirely beside the point. My phone's going again; this time it's Ollie.

"Hey, Jess." He's calling from a bar and is having to

shout above the thumping music. "I just wanted to know how you got on today. Was it as bad as you thought?"

"Worse," I say mournfully.

"What's that? I can't hear."

"WORSE!"

"Hold on a sec, I'll just go outside." Well, why not do that in the first place? Grrr. I listen with growing impatience as he squeezes through the crowded bar, apologising profusely in Franglais. "Right, I'm out. Sorry. Bit loud in there. So how was it?"

"Bloody awful. And the grunge gear didn't work either. Got me into a whole heap of trouble, but none of Hannah's henchmen found me scary."

"Well, maybe you need to beat one up? Then the rest will leave you alone."

God, girly catfights – when was the last time I had one of those? "And what if I lose? Then I'll have a daily drubbing to look forward to..."

"Oh yeah, fair point. Listen, let me have a think. I'll call you back later. Okay?"

"Yeah fine. Wait Ollie...?" But he's already rung off, so I put down the phone and use both hands to shove Chris off. "Could you get out my face! What is with you? You are constantly invading my personal space."

"Jess! I'm hurt. Look, if someone's giving you hassle, I do know people..."

"Don't!" I stick my fingers in my ears. "I do not want to hear about the kind of dodgy types you know." Although, in truth I am a little intrigued – what kind of contacts does he have? Gangsters? Hitmen? Actually, best not to go there; might prove way too tempting.

"I was only trying to help."

"Well don't."

"Fine. Oh! Before I forget. There was a phone call for your Ollie earlier, so as his stand-in, I dealt with it on your behalf." He looks at me expectantly, "You may thank me."

Really? Thank him? Okay. "Thank you Chris for committing fraud. You're going to make such a fine lawyer."

"I detect a hint of sarcasm, but I'll let it go. Anyway, it was the hospital about your gran. They're transferring her to Carthill tonight, wanted to know if I would go with her. I said I was working but that you probably would. I think they said to get there for 4.30."

"What? Since when are they moving Gran? And why wasn't I told?" I look at my watch. "It's ten past four, I'll never get to the General in time."

"It's not far."

"It is when you need to take two bloody buses."

"I can drive you."

"Really? What about Amy?"

"Text her. Leave the back door open and tell her to wait."

Okay, that could work. We get in the car and I point Chris in the direction of The General. It's in the opposite direction to Carthill, which is why I haven't been to see Gran in weeks. I suppose I could have skipped a visit with Mum, but if I'm honest I didn't have the headspace to worry about Gran when Mum's been in such a state. She kinda creeps me out too – with her whiskery chin and old lady skin. And half the time she doesn't even know me, so what's the point? But still... I feel kinda awful. She won't have had a single visitor. Not a one. See, we've no family round here. All Gran's sisters and cousins are in Ireland and are now way too fragile to travel. What must the nurses think? A poor old lady, abandoned by her rotten, selfish granddaughter.

Chris keeps glancing at me. "You OK?"

"Yeah, keep your eyes on the road!"

"I could... come in with you, if you like? Just for a minute."

"Would you! Really? Oh that would be great." Why did I say that? What is wrong with me? Who takes a blackmailing, drug dealer in to see their granny? Well, clearly me for one. I'm so scared of getting chewed out by the nurses that I cling to Chris as he swaggers in, all big, greasy grin and charm. Of course the nurses love him. He even signs some transfer forms before they lead us through to Gran's room.

She's sitting on a chair by her bed and oh my god, she's gone downhill. It's like looking at a breathing cadaver. She's lost so much weight that you can see the skeleton beneath her skin. Her hair hasn't been set and the old lady perm is sticking up, un-brushed and frizzy. She has this manic look about her too. "Where's Helen?" she gasps, as soon as we step through the door.

The nurse sighs. "That's all she says, all day long. She's been quite distressed since she got here. It'll be such a blessing for her to be beside her daughter."

Oh my poor wee gran. I hang back, tears spilling down my cheeks. Chris, though, perches on the bit of bed beside her chair and takes her Skeletor hand in his. "Ollie!" she beams at him. "Ollie, where's Helen? I can't find her, where's Helen?"

"You'll see her soon," he says in such a kind and gentle voice that for a moment I almost believe he's Ollie too. "We'll take you to her in just a little while." She nods and lets her head rest on the back of the chair. After a moment her eyes start to close.

"Oh he's so good with her," coos the nurse, squeezing

past to get on with her rounds. "I haven't seen her this calm since she arrived."

Chris looks at his watch and makes a face. "I need to go."

"S'fine," I sniff. "I can take it from here."

"You sure? Cos I can always…"

"Yeah, I'm sure. You go and do whatever… and thanks." I mean it too.

"Listen, I'll pick you up, okay? Just text me when you're done."

Oh, yes, getting home. How's that going to work? The thought of hanging round that deserted train station at dusk gives me the shivers, but I don't want to accept anything more from Chris. Not when I can't figure out what's in it for him. "Nah. I'll be okay," I murmur, though none too convincingly.

"No you won't. It's awful up there in the dark. I'll come get you. Really. No more arguments."

"No!"

"Why not?"

I look at his face and for a second I can't think of a reason. He just looks kind and concerned and I desperately want his support. But then, hold on a minute! Rewind there, Jess Brody. Kind looking? Am I really so desperate I can delude myself that Chris is just being kind? I think back to the first time I saw him, how he reminded me of a Gestapo guard with his big, mean mouth and shifty eyes. So why does he look so different now? His mouth doesn't look mean at all, it's just kinda pouty. And when he sat with my granny, his eyes were ever so gentle. Well… no matter how he looks, this is still the guy that fed my friend drugs and screwed her despite her being barely legal. So get a grip, Jess, and tell him where to go.

"Listen," I begin, "I do not know who you are and I've no

idea what you're doing in my life. But I do know this – you deal drugs, you snoop around, you blackmail people, you sleep with drugged up schoolgirls. You have dodgy mates, a dodgy haircut and you wear jeans with a crease down the front. So tell me this, why would I trust you? Frankly, I'd rather take my chances with the madmen of Carthill."

He stares down at his shoes and when he looks up I expect the trademark sneer, but he just looks hurt.

"You're right," he says. "You don't know me and I've not made a good first impression. But have you ever wondered why I smoke so much weed? Is it because I'm such a well-rounded, happy human being? Or is it because I'm so utterly miserable that I'd rather spend my days in a coma than face up to my life?"

What the heck does he have to be miserable about? "And what's wrong with your life? Has daddy cut off your allowance? Mummy cancel a trip to the Caribbean?" God that came out so sneery – I'm as bad as him, I really am. "Sorry. That was out of order. I know nothing about your life. I'm..."

"No." He shakes his head. "You're absolutely correct. I'm rich and privileged, so I don't have feelings. Know something Jess, I thought you were different, but just forget it. I'll go." He turns to leave but I grab his arm.

"No wait. I'm sorry. Really, I am. Please, tell me."

He sighs. "Well, you make such a big deal about Amy and me, but I'm only a year or so older than her – I'm not yet 18 – I'm hardly Jimmy Saville. I'm going into my second year of a law degree, which I despise – but everyone in my family is a lawyer, so apparently I have to be one too. I'm homesick. Everyone at uni hates me..."

"Well do you blame them? The way you act..."

"Chicken and egg, Jess, which came first? I'm dim, okay?

All my mates went to Oxford or St Andrews, but despite my ridiculously expensive education, I've ended up at a second rate university where everyone hates the rich kids. I don't fit in. They loathed me the moment I walked through that door. So why not misbehave? Mmmh? Why not be the clichéd bastard they think I am?"

"Oh." I think back to Saturday night. How much of my initial revulsion was based on the way he dressed and spoke?

"I've no hidden agenda, Jess," he says sadly, "I just like hanging out at yours cos it's quiet and it reminds me of home. If I want to give you some help in return, is that such a bad thing?"

Really, is he telling the truth? Or am I being scammed again? Is this an elaborate ruse to gain my trust then... then what? Steal my money? All sixty quid of it, ha! Get into my knickers? Nah, he has Amy for that doesn't he? But wait, what if he's using me for cover? Maybe it's safer to deal drugs from my house – less chance of getting caught. Hiding out from the police in my leafy suburb.

I look into his eyes. Heroes in books can always tell when someone's lying by gazing deep into the windows of the soul, but I never can. His eyes are unusual – such a pale, icy blue – is that why I thought they looked cruel? Baddies always have icy eyes, don't they? But right now he looks like a kitten that's just been kicked.

"I can't make you out, Chris," I say. "You're one of the oddest people I've ever met. And I don't trust you. How can I?"

Suddenly his demeanour flips. The kind, sad look vanishes and the arrogant git returns. It's like two separate people sharing one face; how different his features are when the top lip curls into a sneer. "Your loss," he shrugs.

Maybe, but for now I have to focus on Gran. The paramedics have arrived, bustling through the door full of cheerful banter and Chris disappears without a word. I hover about, feeling useless, while they strap Gran into a gurney and tuck a white, waffle blanket round her legs. She glances at me for reassurance. I don't think she's 100% sure who I am, but I'm familiar enough to bring her comfort, so perhaps I'm some use after all.

They get her into the ambulance, no bother, and we set off for Carthill, one paramedic driving, the other in the back beside Gran. "RIGHT MARGARET DEAR. WE'RE TAKING YOU TO CARTHILL NOW TO BE WITH YOUR DAUGHTER. ISN'T THAT NICE?" booms the green clad medic, in that voice they reserve for old folk and the disabled.

The look on her face! Talk about horror. This wee wummin is about to go mental. "My daughter is not in Carthill. What on earth are you talking about?" She is so indignant.

Confused, the paramedic frowns at his clipboard. "Yes. Yes she is, that's why you're being moved there."

"MY DAUGHTER IS NOT IN CARTHILL. WHY ARE YOU SAYING THAT, YOU VICIOUS LITTLE MAN?" She stretches out a trembling, transparent hand and tries to slap him. What is it with my family and paramedics? I intercept the hand before it makes contact and hold it tight in mine. It's so cold I start to give it a rub, but the skin's so thin I'm worried it might tear. I tuck it between mine and lay them on her lap like a hand sandwich.

Fearing we might face a lifetime ambulance ban, I smile at the paramedic, eager to placate him. "Eh, maybe just leave her to me?"

"Gladly." He scowls and goes to sit up front.

"It's all right, Gran. He got muddled up, that's all. Mum's not in Carthill. It's just easier for her to visit you there." More lies.

She nods. "Bloody fool. Imagine saying that!"

"I know." We sit saying nothing for the rest of the journey. I warm up one hand, then the other and she seems quite content. If she's bothered about going to Carthill herself she doesn't show it. Perhaps it never really sunk in.

The geriatric wing of Carthill is in one of the older buildings, just two blocks over from Mum's. A harassed looking nurse opens the door and directs us to the women's ward on the right. The paramedics push Gran through and we linger by reception, waiting for someone to check her in. I look up and down the ward. It's painted a palette of cheery colours, but there's no disguising death's waiting room. Rows of wizened old folk lie propped up on pillows or dozing in chairs by the side of their beds. They all look so shrunken and colourless – like they've been boil-washed in bleach. Near the end of the ward a splash of yellow hair stands out amongst the grey and I realise Mum and Sam are waiting by Gran's bed. I grab the gurney and start to jog towards them.

"Oi! You can't do that. You need to..."

Yeah? Just try stopping me. Mum's spotted us and she's hurrying our way. It's like one of those movie scenes where the lovers run towards each other on a windswept beach – only this is a depressing hospital ward that stinks of pee. Still, Mum couldn't look more gooey-eyed if she had been hurtling towards a hunk at sunset.

"Mother!"

"Helen!"

Mum kneels down in front of Gran and they hug and

laugh and both of them are crying and I look at Sam and I can see she's about crying too. It's a lovely moment, though I do feel a twinge of envy. Why's Mum never that pleased to see me?

While Mum bustles about getting Gran's clothes unpacked, the wee wummin from the next bed along comes over and takes my hand. "Come get a sweetie dear," she says, tugging me towards her locker.

"Eh, OK, thanks." I take a treacle toffee and sit down beside her. She seems desperate for some company, but I can't really think what to say. "Um... so you been in here long then?" is the best I can come up with.

She nods and says, "All my life."

Her big moon face is remarkably smooth for a woman of her age – there's barely a wrinkle. And she has this strange expression about her as well – almost childlike. She must have dementia. I say, "You can't have been here all your life. This is a geriatric ward."

And she laughs and says, "Oh, not on this ward, dear. This hospital. I've been in this hospital since I was a girl."

She must be getting muddled. What do I do? Are you meant to just agree with them or try to bring them back to reality? I look over at Sam and mouth, "HELP."

Sam leans across Gran's bed and says, "Bella's right, Jess, she's been in here for sixty-odd years."

"WHAT?" I look at Bella and she's smiling, nodding with satisfaction at being proved right. "Why would anyone be in here sixty years?"

"I was a bad girl," says Bella, "so they took away part of my brain."

"NO waaay!"

"Ssssh," says Sam, though most of the other patients are far too deaf to notice.

"But... but... she's not serious, is she? How could they take her brain?"

"Do you want me to explain, Bella?" Sam asks. Bella nods again, still smiling away. Sam leans towards me, her voice low with conspiracy. "Bella was caught, how shall I say? Um... touching herself as a young girl. In those days that was seen as a disease – nymphomania – and one of the ways to 'cure' it was a lobotomy. Cutting away part of the brain. Of course, once they did that she was no longer fit to take care of herself, so she's been in here ever since, in a variety of different wards."

"But why on earth wouldn't her parents stop them?"

Sam's big, brown eyes are full of sorrow. "It was her parents that asked for it, Jess. It was a different world back then." Back then? Sixty years isn't so long ago.

Well, that is possibly the most depressing story I have ever heard – a complete waste of a life and for what? I need to get the hell out of here. The heat, the pee, the pickled looking people – I am about to freak out, big time. I say my goodbyes and hurry outside to suck in the fresh, cool air. Oh, that's better. The air's so clear after that stuffy ward, though there's definitely a hint of autumn. And something else too. I sniff; is that weed?

"Jess!"

Jeez, I almost jump out of my skin. It's Chris, of course, skulking in the bushes smoking a spliff.

"What the hell are you doing here? For god's sake put that out! " He grins and throws his roach on the grass, evidently enjoying winding me up.

"I came to take you home. Pleased to see me?"

"Eh. NO! What happened to your hot date?"

His face goes blank. "Hot date? Um... oh, you mean Amy. Well... I dipped my pen and now I'm done."

"How romantic. She's a very lucky girl."

He smirks. "Do you want a lift or not?"

"Of course I want a lift. Where you parked?" He points towards the car park by Mum's ward and we start to make our way over. Why's he here? I wonder if he's still mad at me. I glance at his face, but there's no trace of either the sneer or sadness from earlier; in fact he seems really perky. Too perky. "You seem happy?"

"Yep."

"What have you taken? Cos if you've had anything stronger than weed I'm not getting in that car with you."

He stops dead. "Why do you always do this, Jess? You're like such an uptight killjoy. I do something nice for you and what do I get in return? Insults."

"Well, have you?"

"No! I don't do anything stronger than weed. Well, except a few mushrooms and a bit of speed..."

"Right that's it." I start stalking off towards the train station.

"JOKE! For god's sake, I was joking. I've done nothing more hardcore than hash. Cross my heart and hope to die."

"Chris, you do realise that your jokes aren't funny. In fact, I'd like you a whole lot better if you didn't joke. At all."

"Aw, you're just saying that."

"No, I'm not. Ditch the cocky bullshit, lose the drugs and we might actually be friends."

"Who says I want to be your friend?"

"Oh Christ, I give up. What are you doing here if you don't want to be my friend?"

"I just don't want your murder on my conscience that's all."

"You have a conscience?" I've so had it with him and his

stupid, mind-games. He is such exhausting company, he really is; I never know where I stand.

"Sure I have a conscience. I just hide it well. Now are you getting in the car, or what?"

"Hmmmph." Well, it's either that or get the train, so I start marching to the motor while Chris saunters after. I yank open the passenger door and I'm suddenly hit by this hot bready smell. What else? Big sniff. Mmmmm, oregano and grilled, gooey cheese. There, on the passenger seat, sits the most enormous pizza box I've ever seen. It must be at least sixteen inches. I've barely had a bite since breakfast and the smell's making me drool like Homer Simpson. Bet the box is empty though – Chris probably scoffed it already and now I'll be tortured by the aroma all the way home. I lift the box to chuck it in the back, but it doesn't feel empty; in fact, it feels decidedly heavy and deliciously warm. I open it up and there before me glows this pristine pizza. I swear the grease on that cheese looks like pure edible gold. I turn to Chris. "For me?"

He nods, smiling, and I tear off a slice and stuff it in my mouth. Nothing, I tell you nothing, has ever tasted this good.

15

THREE WEEKS ON

Don't you think it's incredible how fast the bizarre becomes mundane? Mum's been in hospital three weeks now and it's starting to feel, well, normal, I suppose. Routine, even. She's improving as well. I think it helps having Gran beside her and now she's no longer a risk to herself she's allowed to visit Gran on her own. There's even talk of letting Mum out on weekend leave. I've tried to look enthusiastic, but all I can think of is the state of the house and where to hide Chris for forty-eight hours.

Oh yeah, talking of Chris, it's amazing how normal it feels to have him around too. A month ago I didn't even know the bloke. Now we share a bathroom and bicker over who gets the last of the milk. He's not so bad, really. Don't get me wrong, he drives me round the bend, but with things so awful at school, it's good to have someone to slump in front of the telly with.

Hannah's still being a complete and utter cow and Amy still gives me the old body swerve in class. But that doesn't stop her coming round most nights to slurp on Chris's face. I keep thinking I should tell her to get lost. If she can't support me at school, why let her lodge on my sofa? But I can't do it. She's always so sympathetic when she comes round. I don't think she's putting it on. I think she's genuinely upset by the whole situation; she just doesn't have the guts to stick her neck out at school.

Ollie continues to phone. He's not having a great time either. He keeps saying he'll scrounge money off Dad to come home early, but I've said not to bother and I mean it. My worst problem is school and he can't do anything about that. Dad calls sometimes too. I haven't told him Mum's in hospital, but I managed to cadge some cash on the basis that she's too depressed to work. He transferred five-hundred quid into Mum's account, which takes the pressure off a bit.

So with all that going on at home, it's hard to sit here in Chemistry and act like I'm just another pupil. Cos I'm not. I'm this weird hybrid – half adult, half kid. Trying to pay the bills and care for my mum, while wrestling raging hormones and keeping up with homework. The kids in my class feel like a whole different species, larking about like they haven't a care in world. Oh, I know they've all got their problems – everyone has – but at the end of the day, they're all just still kids and I'm not. So how am I supposed to relate to them?

Oh god, Mr Thompson's popping out. He'd better come back quick, or Hannah's gonna start. I slump down deep in my chair and bury my nose in my book. I glue my eyes to the text, willing her not to notice me. And it seems to be working, cos I've now read the same sentence thirteen times and still no hassle from Hannah.

God, they're getting rowdy though. I don't want to risk raising my eyes from my book, but it sounds like the class is having a full on riot. If they're not careful, Tenant's gonna march in here and give us all detention. There's a funny smell too. Ugh. What is it? Someone's yelling 'FIRE!'. Shit.

"JESS! YOUR BLAZER! JESS!"

What...? I jump to my feet and that's when I spot the black piece of fabric burning in a fume tank. Is that really my blazer? It can't be! Mine was on the back of my... oh... what d'ya know, the back of my chair is bare.

"OUT OF MY WAY! OUT OF MY WAY!" Mr Thompson's barging past, clutching a massive, foil, fire blanket. He drops it into the fume tank and swaddles the blazer till he's confident the fire is out. Then he holds up the scorched, black rag that used to be my blazer and stares round the room accusingly.

"Who. Does. This. Belong to?" he asks, over-enunciating every word.

I raise my hand warily. "I think it might be mine, sir."

"YOU! Of all the stupid, dangerous stunts. Well, Missy. Your rebellious phase is officially over. I'm having you expelled. Do you hear me?"

What? I can't believe I'm hearing this. "You seriously think I would set fire to my own blazer? You must be mad..."

"Don't you dare talk to me like that!"

"Well, don't you dare accuse me of setting fire to my own blazer!" I can't believe I'm giving him backchat, but right now I'm so bloody angry I don't care. "It's easy to blame me, isn't it? Then you won't have to punish the real culprit. The one with the mouthy, governor parents who could have your job in an instant."

Thompson's face has gone scarlet. His mouth is moving but there's no words coming out. He looks at Hannah. Yeah, he knows who I'm talking about all right. Hannah flashes him a dazzling smile, full of sweet, good nature and sympathy. The two-faced bitch. I have had it. I have had it!

I lunge for her, hands outstretched. I'm gonna lock my fingers round that scrawny throat and throttle. That'll wipe the smile off her smarmy face. Hannah's eyes go wide – she can tell I mean business. Ducking under a desk, she starts to crawl towards the door, so I get down on my knees and follow.

"Come here, bitch. I'll have you. I will!"

She scurries along on all fours, pert little bottom wiggling in the air. Even her arse is taking the piss, so I crane my neck forward and sink in my teeth. "OW!" she screams, bashing her bonce off the desk up above. "Jess bit me! That mad bitch bit me." She slithers out from under the desk, rubbing her injured derriere. I'm after her; I am so ready to finish this. As she tries to scrabble up, I grab her by the tie and yank her back down to the floor. She wriggles and squirms like a worm on a hook, but I hold firm. If I can get her on her back then I'll sit on her. Refuse to move till she takes it all back – every rotten, last word of it. I let go of the tie to get a grip of her shoulders and someone takes advantage to grab me under the oxters and yank me backwards.

"Hoi!" I twist round, expecting to find Mr Thompson, but it's Craig Collins. Traitor! He bends down, grabs me by the waist and heaves me over his shoulder in a fireman's lift. I pummel on his back. "Lemme down!" But he trots out the classroom and deposits me in the corridor. I make a lunge for the door but he yanks me back by the arm.

"No!" he says firmly and starts dragging me hissing and spitting across the playground towards the canteen.

"My blazer! My effing blazer. I'll have her, I will. I'll take her anytime, just you see. She'll regret ever messing with me. Just when she thinks she's safe, BOOM! I'll jump her from behind, I'll..." I look at Craig's face, "What's so funny?"

"Sorry. Just, gives a whole new meaning to the word blazer, doesn't it? You know, blaze-er."

"What?" I'm so confused. "Oh," I groan. God Craig, that's lame even for you."

He grins. "Yeah. But at least you've stopped ranting."

Oh. Yes. The Hulk has gone and all I feel now is shame and embarrassment – particularly since my skirt's hitched up, which must have given an excellent view of my arse as I departed the class on Craig's back. At least I'm wearing tights.

I adjust the skirt and slink inside the canteen. There's still a few minutes till break, but the big-bosomed dinner lady lets us in and Craig fetches a couple of teas, while I find a seat.

"Here," he says, setting down the drinks and dropping a packet of bourbon creams on the table. "Cathy thought you could do with some biscuits."

"Thanks," I say, turning to give her a grateful wave. I wonder if she'd adopt me? She could feed me up till I'm the size of a cow then we'd live a roly-poly life together. I put my hands round the polystyrene cup. "You're so nice, Craig and I know you mean well, but you shouldn't have stopped me. They won't let up till I do something drastic..."

"Yeah, but getting expelled isn't gonna help. Is it?"

"Ach, I suppose you're right. Though I might be expelled anyway. What d'ye think Thompson's going to do?"

Craig shrugs and stares into his tea. "He knows what's going on, Jess. They all do. They're not blind. I reckon you'll be OK, so long as you're prepared to grovel."

Yeah, I can grovel.

Craig leans back and sighs. "Hannah Walters is such a cow, but why didn't you stop her? She was dancing about with your blazer for ages. When that didn't wind you up, she held it over the Bunsen Burner by your bench. I think she thought you'd grab the blazer before anything drastic happened. But then it caught light and she threw it in the fume tank."

"Did she? I didn't even notice. I thought if I kept my head in a book it would keep me out of trouble."

Craig snorts tea across the table. "Yeah, great plan."

I can't win, can I? "So what do I do? If keeping my head down ends in a riot, what other options are there?"

Craig's thinking so hard it looks like his head might explode. I wait patiently, expecting some pronouncement of wisdom, but in the end he just shrugs and says, "I dunno."

I tut. "Well, that's helpful isn't it?"

"You're asking me about girls and I don't have a clue. But I do know that Hannah's parents have a lot of clout round here and you do not want this going to the governors. Can't you try getting on her good side?"

"How?"

Again with the shrugs. Hmmmph. He mumbles something with a mouthful of bourbon cream, then we chat away about other stuff – UCAS applications and telly. We're still there when the bell rings for break and the hordes descend for their bacon rolls. Meredith's one of the first through the door, though as a veggie it's not meat she's after. She grabs an apple and slides in beside us. Craig looks at her shyly, though he doesn't run away. I feel like telling him he can go now but don't quite know how. Then Amy comes in. She's on her own for once and she stands in the doorway, head going from side to side like she's searching for someone. She spots me and I expect her to scurry off, but she marches right up to the table like it's actually me she's after.

"Jess, I've been looking everywhere for you. I heard what happened! Are you okay?" She pulls out a chair to sit down, but then she sees Meredith and freezes. Meredith takes a big bite of apple and gives Amy a 'what you gonna do now,' kind of look. I hold my breath because if Amy turns round and leaves – well that's it for us. I can't keep ignoring how rotten she's treating me at school.

There's a moment's silence, then Amy says coldly, "Hello Meredith," and dips her head like a Queen addressing a flea-ridden subject. My eyes meet Meredith's and we both burst out laughing. Bewildered, Amy sits down, glancing between us and blushing. "What? What is it?"

"Nothing," splutters Meredith, slinging an arm round Amy's shoulder. "I'm just so honoured to have you sitting next to me, I think I might... might faint." Meredith presses her free hand to her forehead as if coming over all dizzy.

"Shut up, Baker." Amy angrily shrugs her off. "What you doing here anyway?"

"Don't you know, Amy? Jess and I are now BFFs? She's kinda needed one ever since you dumped her."

"Are we?" I look at Meredith with interest. Is she only saying that to wind Amy up or does she actually see us as friends? It's true we've been spending time together – our paths often collide in shadowy corners as we try to avoid the Coven. But every time I thought we were getting close, she'd back off, snarling with a bitchy comment.

Like now, for instance. Her face clouds over with a deep, dark frown. "Why? Do you have a problem being my friend?"

What is she like? "No. I would love to be your friend,

Meredith. It's just... you're a bit, prickly at times."

"Who moi?" she presses a hand to her chest and grins. "Tell you what. I'll forgive you for blanking me for four years, if you put up with my prickles."

"Deal." I stick out my hand and we shake on it.

"Just as long as you realise I don't do girly chats, manicures, pedicures, sparkly stuff, boy talk, sleepovers, giggling or celebrity gossip."

Amy's eyes go wide. "Whatever will you talk about?"

Meredith stares at her with obvious distaste. "Well, you, for one. And what a shallow little bitch you are for dumping your best friend at the first sign of trouble."

"Er," Craig scrapes his chair back. "Think I'll um... get going."

I squeeze his arm and mouth thanks, but Meredith's eyes don't leave Amy's for a second. "So, Amy," she says, "it's make or break time. Have you the balls to stand by your very best friend, or are you going to prove to us all what a vacuous little twerp you are?"

Amy's mouth opens and closes but nothing comes out. Then she turns to me and says, "Are you going to let her speak to me like that?"

I shrug.

"Seriously, Jess. I came to find you cos I had an idea, but if you're going to hang out with Meredith then there's nothing I can do to help you." She turns to Meredith. "I'm sorry to be so blunt, but I can't work miracles. You really don't help yourself, Meredith Baker. If you could try being even a little bit nice then I could maybe do something. But it's like you're asking to be hated. And if you really want to help Jess then you'll back the hell off. The last thing she needs right now is to be seen hanging out with you."

"Amy. Don't." I shake my head at her. "You know nothing

about Meredith, so just leave it, yeah?"

Meredith plants an elbow on the table, props her chin in her hand and gazes at Amy intently. "No, go on, Amy. I'm desperate to hear it. How would you help me? Oh I know..." She clasps her hands together and bounces up and down, all faux girly excitement. "Oh, oh, oh. Do you think a makeover would make them like me? Do you?"

"Yes! Exactly! If you tried to fit in a bit more. I could help with that, we could do a..."

This is way too painful. I have to stop it. "She's taking the piss, Amy."

"Oh." Amy looks so deflated that I immediately feel sorry for her. Sometimes she seems like such an innocent. I know she has her faults, but I really don't think there's a bad bone in her body; she honestly does want to help. But Meredith throws her a look of utter contempt.

"I would rather be beat up and spat on than moulded into a bitch troll like you."

"And what about you Jess?" Amy looks at me in panic. "Are you really going to follow her advice?" She jerks a thumb in Meredith's direction. "Oh, promise me you won't get all bitter and twisted like her. I've got this great idea, but it will only work if you ditch the weirdo. Listen to this. It's genius..."

"Wait. Amy. Stop." I mime zipping my lips together and she pauses. I nod at the door and Amy twists round to look. Hannah Walters is walking in, flanked by her devoted clones.

"Oh!" Amy jerks back round, face deadly pale – she'd slide under the table if she could.

"It's okay," I say. "She hasn't seen you – go now and there's no harm done."

Amy begins to wriggle in her seat, eyes darting between Meredith beside her and Hannah, who's approaching fast.

"We could just go now, you and me, Jess," begs Amy, her eyes pleading. "We'll work this out together. In private."

How tempting it is to take Amy's hand and scurry off together, best mates once more. I could become popular again – not that I was ever that popular to begin with, but at least I'd get back up off the bottom rung. I can't cope with being the saddo who gets tortured every day.

Then again, is it really that tempting? Okay, so it's not nice being gobbed on, and having my blazer set on fire is certainly a new low. But dumping Meredith is no longer an option – not just because it would make me a two-faced hypocrite, but because I genuinely like her. She's fun and feisty. She makes me laugh and keeps me on my toes. But more than that, she's been there for me since day one of this nightmare. So I say to Amy, "Sorry. I know how uncomfortable this is for you, but me and Meredith come as a package. Buy one, get one free. So honestly, go if you like. I will understand. It's just... we won't be friends anymore."

Her eyes fill with tears and I honestly think she'll run, but she stays where she is, even when Hannah Walters stops by our table and asks why she's hanging out with the freaks.

"Um... I was just having a quick chat with my friend," mumbles Amy.

"Friend?" spits Hannah. "Which friend? Freak one or freak two?"

"Um." Poor Amy looks completely confused, clearly trying to work out which Freak is which. Meredith stands up and scrapes back her chair, letting it clatter to the floor with a clang.

"Come on, Jess," she says, "I told you we wouldn't be welcome here. You're a complete bitch, Amy Duncan.

How you can treat Jess like this, I don't know! She's not a skank or a whore."

I stand too, my brain struggling to catch up. Ah, I see what she's up to. Amy, though, has no idea. "But… but… I didn't…"

"Shut up and don't deny it!" snaps Meredith, before adding, "Cow!" as a parting shot. All eyes follow us as we leave the dining hall, but know something weird? I really don't care.

"What'd you do that for?" I ask when we're safely in the corridor, "I thought you'd enjoy watching her squirm."

Meredith shakes her head. "I must be going soft, but it was like watching this ickle, fluffy lamb being lined up for the slaughter. I dunno. Call it a reward for showing some backbone. She can thank me later. Look…" Meredith points though the porthole to the canteen and laughs. "Hannah's sat down next to her, so she must think Amy called you a skank."

I elbow her aside to take a look. "Yeah. Thanks for that, by the way. Skank? Real nice."

"Pleasure."

"Oh wait. Amy's getting up. She's walking towards us. Eeek. What do we do? Hide?"

"Why on earth would we hide? Jeez, sometimes you're as bad as her. Wait, move…" We both step back as Amy comes slamming through the double doors. Her face is red and she looks like she's hyperventilating.

"Oh god, were they awful to you?" This is all my fault for making her sit next to Meredith Baker. But Amy's eyes are shining and not with tears. She looks excited; in fact she's grinning now.

"I did it, Jess!"

"Did what?"

"I've put the plan in motion."

"What plan?" I suddenly feel sick. What's she up to? "Shouldn't we have discussed it first?"

"Nah. Chris said not to."

"Chris! You've concocted a plan with Chris and expect me to like it?"

Meredith looks intrigued. "Eh, dish the dirt. Who's Chris?"

"Who's Chris? I'll tell you who Chris is!" I'm so outraged I can barely get the words out. "Chris is my… lodger and her lover." I point at Amy, who looks ashamed and proud in equal measures.

Meredith's eyebrows shoot up. "You have a lodger? And she has a…" She makes a vomit face like the word's too revolting to think of, let alone say. "…a lover? Yeeuuch." She shudders.

"Well, he's more of a bonkbuddy really," says Amy, like it's the most normal thing in the world. "It's not like we're going out."

Meredith clutches my arm and yelps. "Whoa! Barbie's full of surprises today. Bonkbuddy!" she chuckles, "Classic."

"He's an absolute idiot, that's what he is. What have you done, Amy? You'd better tell me now or I'll…" Meredith and I stare at her, expectantly.

"Let's just say I think I have the answer to your problems. I am a genius and so is Chris. So there." She sticks out her tongue and walks off.

"Can you believe that?"

Meredith shakes her head. "No. But I'm starting to warm to that chick. I really am."

16

THE PARTAAAAY

Days go by and nothing much happens. Same old, same old, yawn, yawn, yawn. And then just when I'm least expecting it – boom – something weird goes down. And do you know what's so weird today? My house. It's clean. I mean, how the heck did that happen?

I can tell there's something up as soon as I get back from visiting Mum. It's the smell – like mouldy vacuum cleaner mixed with Mr Sheen. I dump my bag on the kitchen floor and stare. The worktops are gleaming, the sink is sparkling and the dining table's laid with napkins and fresh flowers. Eh? Is this even my house? Oh my god, you don't think Dad and Pippa have turned up? Actually, Pippa doesn't clean her own house, never mind mine.

"Hello…?" I call warily.

"Oh Jess, in here…" It's Amy – in the hall by the sounds of it. I kick off my shoes and wander through to find her squirting green stuff on the mirror. She turns and gives me a dazzling smile. "Like it?" she beams.

"Uh-huh. But since when do you clean?"

She stands back to examine her work, then rubs away a smear. "Oh, I only ever clean on special occasions. I'm really rather good at it but I don't want Mum to know."

"Okay. And how exactly is this a special occasion?"

She drops duster and spray into the cleaning caddy and beckons me through to the living room. "Have a seat," she says, as if it's a job interview, and gestures to the couch. I do as she asks, but she doesn't sit, just hovers by the fireplace. I look around. There's something weird in here as well and no, it's not just the absence of dust. Now what is it that's different?

"OH!" I cry. "My couch is empty! Have you murdered Chris? Cos I gotta say I'm fine with that. But you'll need something stronger than Mr Muscle to fool forensics."

Amy smiles. "You'd be well sad if I murdered Chris."

"I would not!"

"Yes, you would. You're like an old married couple, bickering away in front of the telly. Half the time you don't even notice I'm here."

"Rubbish!"

"If you say so. Anyway, the reason Chris isn't on the couch is because he's gone back to halls..."

"He's gone back to uni? Does that mean he's moving out?"

"If you'd let me finish. He's gone back to halls to round up a few pals for our dinner party this evening."

"Dinner party? What dinner party?"

Amy perches on the footstool opposite. "Now, just listen, Jess and try to stay calm..." Uh-oh, that does not sound good. "I had this idea the other day... See, Hannah Walters kept complaining about the boys at school – how spotty and stupid they are. How they're so puny and short – and I happened to mention that I was kind of dating a student. Well, you should have seen her. Demanded to know where I met him, if he had any gorgeous mates, etcetera, etcetera.

Anyway, I was being a bit secretive about the whole thing cos I was trying to keep your name out of it. Sorry."

"S'fine."

"But then I thought. Actually. Why not tell Hannah it was you that introduced us? That you're the one with the empty house, that you could be useful. Then she would have to be nice to you, wouldn't she? So I told her you had a student boyfriend and you introduced me to mine. I said that you have these awesome parties with lots of gorgeous guys and if she could only be a bit nicer to you then perhaps you would invite her to one. I kinda made out that was the only reason I was being nice to you. Sorry."

"S'fine."

"So, er, Hannah's coming tonight."

"What? You have got to be joking!" Is she serious? "I'm not having her in my house. What do you expect? Chitchat over canapés? After what she said about my mum?"

"You don't have to be nice to her. Just... don't be nasty. Keep it together, let her cop off with a student then she'll lay off you at school. I'm sure of it."

I have no time to argue, cos tyres on gravel signals Chris is back. Amy rushes to the window and slaps a hand over her mouth. "Oh, Jess!" she yelps, "You're never going to believe this."

"What? What is it?"

"He's brought your man."

My man? "Not Tom?"

Amy nods. "Maybe it's a good thing..." A good thing! Is she crazy? Has she not seen the state of me? Jeans so dirty they're stiff with grime. Greasy hair, no make up, eye-bags the size of sacks. And what if my homework's lying in the hall? I start darting about in a panic, first to the mirror, then to the cupboard under the stairs, where I bury my schoolbag beneath a mound of jackets. Now what? "Up to your room," yells Amy, taking control and grabbing my hand. "We need to fix that hair."

So side-by-side we go racing upstairs. Amy giggles as she stumbles into my room and slams shut the door, though I'm finding it far from funny. "Did you know he was coming?" I demand.

"No! I swear."

I turn to my mirror. "Oh, you can't fix this," I wail, trying to run fingers through my lank, knotty mane.

"Sure I can." Amy lifts a brush and begins to backcomb the ends while I slap on some make up.

"I don't want him here, Amy. I really, really don't. And what if Hannah starts talking about school?"

"Oh shush. Hannah's been warned. She's coming with her own set of fibs. And you know you want him. Just relax. Enjoy. Stop worrying about everything."

Okay, maybe she's right. I have become a worrier; old before my time, I am. I stare at my hair in the mirror. Greasy at the roots, wild at the ends – doesn't look too bad – and the make up has covered my bags. I smear on some vampy red lipstick, then shimmy into a tiny tartan skirt and some ratty black tights. "He'll love it," Amy smiles.

"Okay," I take a deep breath. "Let's do this!"

So we clatter downstairs to find Chris in the kitchen, dishing out beers. Sure enough, he's brought Tom and two other blokes as well. Tom dips his head at me, looking really uncomfortable, then acts like he's engrossed in the conversation. I say conversation, but actually it's more of a monologue – some nerdy bloke holding forth about 'Derrida's deconstructionism,' whatever that is. Tom's nodding away, trying to look interested. But Chris has on this goofy grin and is pretending to blow his own brains out. I know, I know, all very immature, but you should hear this bloke and his pretentious twaddle. I can't help myself, I start to giggle. Chris catches my eye and grins. Then he starts gargling beer. Nerdy bloke glares at him, "I'm sorry. Is it all too intelligent for you?" Chris swallows, chokes a bit, then says,

"Intelligent, no, pompous, yes. And rude. You haven't even noticed that these fabulous ladies have arrived. Justin, allow me to present the gorgeous Sam Brody and Amy Duncan. Ladies – this is Justin and Alex. Twats from the halls."

We say our hellos, then Amy bustles me into the dining room.

"They're hideous," she cries in a frantic whisper. "I mean ugly doesn't even cover it. Do you see the nose on that Justin? And the plukes! Hannah will never go for him. And the other one's not much better. What's his name?"

"Alex."

"Oh yes, Alex. What do you think? I mean, he's not as bad as Justin, but still..." I glance over, trying to be subtle, but accidentally catch his eye and have to look away.

"I don't know, Amy." He has mousy looking hair – blonde turning brown – that just looks dirty and skin tone of much the same hue. None of his features are actually that bad, but taken together they do not add up to handsome. "He's hardly a looker, but he's not exactly ugly."

"This isn't good enough." Amy beckons frantically to Chris, who manages to tear himself away from the riveting conversation.

"Whassup?" He's grinning, obviously proud of himself.

"Whassup? I'll tell you whassup," says Amy, slapping him on the arm, "You've brought us the wrong blokes, that's whassup."

Chris looks confused. "The wrong blokes. What you on about?"

"They're ugly. We need gorgeous. So take them back and get us some more. "

Chris stares over at them, his eyes narrowed as if appraising a painting. "I can't take them back. It's not a shop. Anyway, I don't know what you mean. Strapping lads, they are." I snort a giggle and this time Amy glares at me.

"They're the opposite of strapping," she hisses. "So take them away. Now."

"I can't," he says and struts off, leaving Amy fuming in the corner. She throws her hands in the air. "It's ruined! All ruined. What are we going to do?"

"Oh Amy, take a chill pill, eh? Weren't you the one who said to stop worrying?"

"I know, I know," she suddenly looks upset. "But I so wanted this to work out for you. To make it all... better."

"Aaaaw." I'm really touched. "Things are getting better. I've got you back, haven't I? And I've got Meredith. I'm not Jessie No Mates, no more." I notice Amy wince as soon as I mention Meredith and my cynical pal pops into my head. I can imagine what she'd be saying if she were here; that Amy needs this as much as I do, maybe even more so. That she isn't just being kind; she's looking out for herself. I shake my head, trying to drown out the Goth. I want to believe the best in Amy. And maybe it's Amy who's right; maybe Meredith is making me bitter and cynical.

The doorbell rings and Amy gapes at her watch in disbelief. "She's early!" she cries, tapping the watch as if it might somehow spirit Hannah away. "Do something."

"Me?"

"Yes, you. It's your house. Open the bloody door."

"Nuh-huh. No way. This was your idea. See to your own guest."

Amy tuts loudly, then flounces out the room. Honestly I've never seen her in such a strop. But she's regained her veneer by the time she flings open the front door. "Hannah!" I hear her shriek from my hiding spot in the dining room. "You look fabulous." Over in the kitchen Justin must hear too, for he stops droning on and stares towards the door to the hall. Has Chris promised him a hot date? If so, the poor lad's in for a disappointment. Not that Hannah's not hot – she is – it's just she would never in a million years go for the likes of him.

Amy comes back through, a manic smile pasted to her face. Hannah totters behind on the highest pair of heels I have ever seen. She's completely overdressed, but she does look good in an Essex, too-much-make-up sort of way. Justin and Alex both ogle her greedily. How is this going to work? The male to female ratio is completely out of whack. Are they going to start scrapping over her? Imagine nerdy Justin challenging bland Alex to a duel!

"So," says Amy, "this is Hannah. She's a friend of mine from... er... beauty school. And this is Justin, Tom, Alex and Chris." Smiling, Hannah nods at the group, but her gaze lingers on Chris. Amy spots it too and grabs his arm possessively. Hannah takes no notice, just places a manicured hand on his other arm and asks what he's studying. "Law," he replies with a boastful swagger and I realise that none of them know him like I do. Who else has any idea how miserable he is, what he would give to ditch Law and study something else? Hannah, though, is clearly impressed – cha ching – I see the £ signs in her eyes.

"Oh! I forgot. I have some chocolates for Jess," she says suddenly and Amy pokes her in the ribs.

Hannah looks bewildered and Amy says, "Sam! You're at Sam's house. Duh!"

"Oh, yes, of course." Hannah slaps her forehead with the palm of her hand. "I don't know where my head is today. Sam's house. Yes. Of course Where is she?"

Tom points towards the dining room and all eyes turn to me. I feel like an idiot, skulking in the corner like the world's least popular party guest – in my own home too! So I plaster on a smile and walk towards the outstretched chocs.

"Why Hannah, you shouldn't have. How kind." Hannah leans towards me and next thing I know we're kissing the air by each other's cheeks. "Mwaah, mwaaah." When I straighten up Tom's giving me this really weird look and I feel my face go red. This is shaping up to be the most excruciating dinner party in history. Not that I've ever been to a dinner party before.

"So, Amy, what's on the menu?" asks Hannah. Yeah, what is on the menu? I sniff the air. Can't smell anything yummy, just Mr Muscle and bleach.

"Er.." Amy blushes, "I've been so busy cleaning I kinda forgot about the food. But the table looks great, don't you think?" It does indeed. But what's the use of napkins when there's nothing to actually nibble on?

"Never fear," says Chris, pulling a wad of cash out his pocket. "Wonder Chris is here. Curry everyone?"

"No!" protests Amy, "I've got chicken and stuff in the fridge; I just need to cook it." No one looks too confident in Amy's cooking skills, so we all protest that she's gone to enough trouble already and takeaway will be fine. She doesn't take much convincing. "Ah ok," she says, staring again at the hand on Chris's arm.

So Chris phones in the order while the rest of us get

seated at the table. We try for boy, girl, boy, girl, but it doesn't quite work and there's an empty place left at one end. Clearly Hannah was supposed to bring a friend. I end up sandwiched between Tom on one side and Amy on the other. A space is left for Chris at the head of the table and Hannah's in between Justin and Alex, who are both vying for her attention. She looks like she's enjoying herself.

Chris returns, waving a bottle of Champagne. "I have ordered a feast," he says and pops the Champagne cork like he's been doing it all his life. He goes round the table, pouring fizz into Mum's crystal champagne flutes and we all say cheers and clink glasses. I'm starting to get stressed, though. What if Mum's lovely glasses get broken?

"So," says Tom. "How's life on the ward?"

"S'okay." I can't think of anything else to say, partly because the subject makes me extremely uncomfortable, but I'm also a bit distracted by the shenanigans on the other side of the table. Hannah's caused a commotion by swapping seats with Justin so she can sit next to Chris. He's lapping up the attention, but this leaves Justin and Alex sitting side by side, staring at their plates in sulky silence. On our side, Amy's fidgeting about, fuming and ready to explode.

"Just keep calm," I whisper, leaning towards her. "Let me handle this." I stand up. "Chris, a word please." He's so utterly engrossed in flirting with Hannah, he doesn't even hear. So I have to yank him by the arm till he reluctantly follows me into the living room.

"What are you playing at?" I hiss, closing the door so no one can overhear. "Poor Amy. How can you treat her like that?" His eyes are shining – with booze or mischief, I can't quite tell. He folds his arms defiantly.

"I am merely doing what you wanted. I am trying to get

this Hannah strumpet on side so she will leave you alone at school."

"Oh." Is he really flirting for me? "Well, you can't do it like that. Amy will be so upset." Chris shrugs. "What? Don't you even care?"

"Well... no, not really."

"You're an absolute pig, you really are."

"No I'm not. Amy's not interested in me. Okay, she enjoys a quick fumble after dark, but that's as far as it goes. She's never once mentioned being my girlfriend. She just doesn't want to lose face in front of Hannah. So if you think about it, Amy's the selfish one. If she were really thinking of you she'd let me get stuck in."

I'm lost for words. What is it with Chris that he always stuns me into silence? He has this way of twisting things... I tell you, he might not want to be a lawyer, but he'd make a bloody good one. "Fine. Snog the Walters then, be my guest. But just think on this, if you treat her like dirt, it'll only come back to haunt me. So go ahead, have a laugh, but this is not a game. It's my bloody life." I go to strop off but he grabs me by the arm and his eyes aren't shining any more. He looks deadly serious.

"I know it's not a game," he says. "I know how hard your life is and I'm going to do everything in my power to make it better. You have my word."

I shake him off. "Rubbish! You love winding me up. You're always making things worse."

"No. Don't you understand? I'm a changed man. I've not had a spliff in seventy-two hours. Haven't you even noticed?"

No I hadn't, but yeah it's true, I haven't seen him with a spliff in days. And there's been no dodgy mates round either. "You've really given up the weed?"

"And the dealing." He nods proudly.

"I thought you didn't deal."

"Er... I mean distribution to a select group of friends."

"See! More bullshit. How can I believe a word that comes out your mouth?"

He takes a deep breath. "Because I love you, Jess Brody. And I'm going to prove it. I am going to woo you." He actually gets down on one knee and it's all so over the top and cheesy that I have no idea if he's taking the piss or not.

"You're going to woo me? Really? What is this? 1945?"

He grins. "That's right. Good old fashioned wooing. And I'm going to start by snogging the face off that Walters witch – especially for you."

"You're going to woo me by snogging someone I hate? You're completely unbelievable, you really are." I give him a shove before stomping out the room; he wobbles a bit then falls on his side. Ha! Woo me indeed.

There's silence as I enter the dining room. Everyone looks up, clearly hoping I can kick-start the conversation, but I'm all out. So I sink down on my chair and stare at my plate in silence. The doorbell rings then and Chris comes back, brandishing two brown bags bulging with curry. He plonks the cartons in the middle of the table and tells us all to help ourselves. Then he turns his attention back to Hannah – feeding her an onion bhaji like it's the world's most expensive oyster. She slurps away all gooey-eyed and I think I might actually vomit.

I'm not hungry, but the curry smells good so I dish myself up some dhal. I take a bite and suddenly my mouth is on fire. I mean seriously on fire, like if I actually swallow, it will strip the lining of my stomach. I have to rush to the bin to spit it out then down half-a-litre of water.

"What the hell was that?" I demand, returning to the

table. No one else is eating but Chris is happily shovelling it in.

"It's a vindaloo," he says, glancing round the table perplexed. "Come on, tuck in everyone. I can't manage this lot on my own."

"It's too hot Chris! Is it all vindaloo?"

"Pretty much, yeah. What? Is that not what everyone eats?"

"No, you idiot, they do not!" Is this another stupid stunt? I've had it with him, I really have. I scrape back my chair and go storming up to my room and about five minutes later comes this gentle knock on the door. "Come in," I mumble. If it's Chris I'll be kicking him straight back out again. It isn't. It's Tom, clutching a plate of jam sandwiches.

"Join me for dinner?" he says.

"Why yes, kind sir. Thank you ever so much." He looks so sweet standing there with his sandwiches, he reminds me of Paddington, so I take one and shuffle up. He parks his bum beside me and we happily munch away.

"Chris driving you crazy?" he asks when we're done.

"Yeah, big time."

"So why not kick him out? Why you putting up with him? I don't get it."

Er, cos otherwise he would tell the whole uni that you banged a schoolgirl. I can't say that, though, so I have to shrug and mumble something inaudible. Then we get down to snogging. It's different this time. Maybe it's cos we're on the bed, but it's a lot more intense. I want him so badly, my hips are grinding under his and the kissing is hard – violent almost. His hand's creeping up my shirt too and I don't feel panicked. Oh my god, his fingers are on my breast. I have never felt this horny. That is it. I want him. Now! Oh, but wait. He still thinks I'm nineteen. If I let him screw me he'll be breaking the law and he won't even realise. And there was that teacher, wasn't there? Got jailed for fucking a fifteen-year-old. I can't do that to him. I have to come clean.

I turn my mouth from his and try to wriggle out from under his weight. "Noooo," he groans, "don't stop." His eyes are glazed with longing and he buries his face in my hair and begins to nibble my neck – light little kisses that send shivers down my spine. My breathing's getting faster, I'm losing myself again.

"No, stop," I moan. "I need to talk to you. CHRIS! Will you stop?"

The lips freeze on my neck and I feel his body go stiff as he rolls off like a log and lies staring at the ceiling. "What did you just say?" His voice is clear now, passion all gone.

"I said I need to talk to you."

"No, before that."

"I said, oh… wait no… that was just a slip. I didn't mean it. You've got to believe me, Tom, I…"

He sits up, his eyes hard and cold. "Are you screwing that idiot? Is that why he's moved in here? God, that's revolting. The thought of you…" he shudders.

"No I am not screwing him. I wouldn't…"

"But you want to? Hmmmm? Is that it? Why else would you call me Chris?"

"No of course not. I…"

But he won't let me talk, just carries on ranting. Cursing Chris – calling him every single rotten name that he can dredge from the depths of his mind. Okay, get it off your chest then. Maybe I'll zone out for a bit.

Except… what did he just call Chris? No, that is just not on, he can't go round saying stuff like that. It's… it's … slander, is what it is. "YOU TAKE THAT BACK!" I find myself shouting. "Chris is a good person. Okay, he's made some mistakes, but what seventeen-year-old hasn't? I tell you this, Tom, he's been there for me. All the time my mum's been in hospital, Chris has kept me company, bought me pizza, taxied me up and down and up and down that bloody road to Carthill."

Tom's face drains of colour. "I thought your mum was dead," he says.

"Yeah. I mean, well… technically, no…"

"She's in Carthill? But… but… how can you nurse your own mother?"

Oops. Busted. "Look Tom, this is what I was trying to tell you when I accidentally said what I did." I take a deep breath. Okay, here goes. "I'm not really a nurse. I'm still at school. I'm almost sixteen though, I just didn't want to go ahead with you know… without telling you first."

He jumps off the bed, his face all twisted. "I almost fucked a fifteen-year-old," he says, like he's hyperventilating. "You're fifteen! I don't believe this, I don't fucking believe it!"

"But I'm fifteen and three quarters," I say, sounding like a stupid, wee lassie. "We could do other stuff till then. My birthday's not that far off, we could just sort of… date, for now."

He snorts, his face full of contempt. "You really think I'd be seen round uni with a schoolgirl? Christ, Sam, I'd never live it down."

"But if you really liked me, surely…?"

He snorts again. "How would I know if I like you? I don't even know who you are? Is your name even Sam?"

I hang my head, cos I can't begin to answer that.

"Oh, that's just great." Tom's nodding away, like one of those dogs in the back windows of cars. "So go on, what is it? What's your name?"

"Jess," I manage to squeak.

"Well, Jess, I hope you and Chris will be very happy, cos god knows you deserve each other."

"But I'm not interested in Chris..."

He gives a mirthless laugh, "Well I'm not interested in you. Quite aside from the fact that you're a lying little bitch, you're obviously in love with that scumbag downstairs. And there's one thing I don't take and that's Chris Henderson's cast-offs."

What's he on about? "I'm not in love with..."

"Oh but you are. Reject you, did he? Have his wicked way and cast you aside?"

"No! I..."

"Whatever!" And with that he flounces out the door, slamming it shut behind him.

In love with Chris? I'm not in love with Chris! Am I?

I picture his face. Those huge red lips that I'd found so repulsive now seem pouty, sexy, kissable. I think of his eyes – too small, I'd thought – but they're the most amazing colour and intelligent too. His hair – nope, the hair's still awful. Nothing can be done with the hair.

But I thought I hated him. I mean, you see it in the movies, don't you, where they bicker and fight at the start of the film, then fall madly in love. But there's always some attraction to begin with, isn't there? A little spark that gets ignited. But for me there'd been none of that with Chris – I'm talking nil, nada, nothing. I'd found him creepy, scary, infuriating. But he's changed, hasn't he? I've changed him. And now...?

17

NOOKIE, NO, NO

I go downstairs. Chris is on his spot on the sofa watching some Saturday night news quiz. The dinner party's over then. "Where is everyone?" I ask, sinking into Mum's armchair.

"Gone." He doesn't look at me.

"Oh, right. Tom's gone too."

Still he keeps his eyes on the telly. "Yes, I heard the door. But then I also heard the creaking bedsprings and heavy breathing. Like sitting beneath a porno." He looks hurt.

"I didn't sleep with him if that's what you're thinking."

"Who you choose to bone is entirely up to you."

Right, he's really beginning to wind me up now. "Well, why the hell did you bring him here if you didn't want me getting off with him?"

At last he looks at me. "It was a test. You failed."

"Oh for god's sake, you're so weird." He has this amazing capacity to make me so mad. Quick, change the subject. "What happened with Hannah then?"

"Let's just say she won't bother you again."

"Oh yeah? What have you done?"

"Nothing really. Just wound her into a frenzy of desire then scorned her when she tried to kiss me. I got Amy to capture it on my phone. Any more trouble and it's all over Facebook."

"Blackmail! For Christ's sake, Chris. I thought you said you'd changed."

It's his turn to get angry now. "I can't win with you, can I?" he snaps, waving the remote control. "You don't want me snogging her, so I don't. But how else do I stop her being mean to you? By asking her nicely? Believe me, Jess, she ain't that kinda girl. So I'm sorry for looking out for you while you were upstairs, writhing under that lank haired hippy."

He's right. I've done what I fancied all evening. Didn't even think how to seize the opportunity to stop Hannah. It's Amy and Chris who've done all the work. Got their hands dirty so I could sit back and be outraged at the immorality of it all. What a po-faced little twerp I am. "Thanks," I manage to mumble. "So… you love me then?" I ask shyly.

"Yup," he snaps, still angry.

"Er…so do you want to know why Tom left?"

"Cos the impotent jerk couldn't get it up?" Okay, he isn't making this easy. The conversation so far has been the opposite of romantic.

"No. It was up all right."

He glares at me, absolutely boiling with rage. "Christ. I need a spliff. To think I quit for you. That does it, I'm outta here…" He springs off the sofa and stalks towards the door. I have to leap out my seat to block his way.

"Let me past," he demands.

"No." I stretch my arms across the doorframe – he'll need to pick me up or dive under to get out. "Just listen to me, would you? The reason Tom left was because I called him Chris."

"Yeah, so?"

"Well, haven't you heard of a Freudian slip?"

"No. I do Law. Only thickos do Psychology."

Really, this is the guy I've fallen for? I take a deep breath. "I called him Chris because it's you I want to be with. I didn't know it at the time, but now I do..."

"Really?" The thundercloud rolls off his brow and his face lights up. "Freud said that?"

"Yes, Chris. That's exactly what Freud said. So. Are you gonna kiss me or what?"

I stand on tiptoes and touch his lips with mine. We stay like that for a moment, not kissing, just sort of breathing each other in. Then he picks me up and I wrap my legs round his waist and next thing we're devouring each other. Slamming off the wall, we collapse on the floor and I want him then. Want every bit of him inside me. I pull at his belt and he slaps away my hand. I try again and this time he sits up panting.

"No," he says, "no nookie."

"Wha...?" I lunge again for the belt, but he's too quick, drawing his knees up to his chest so I can't get near his nether regions. "Why? You did it with Amy."

"I don't love her. I love you. And we're doing this thing properly. Tomorrow I'm going to meet your mum and I want to be able to look her in the eye and say I'm treating you right."

"You wanna meet my mum. Seriously?"

"Yep. And you're going to tell her the truth. All of it."

Well, that's a right passion-killer, isn't it? My mum's like the anti-aphrodisiac. Besides, I've had enough truth tonight to last me a lifetime. But just look at Chris. Isn't he sweet, sitting there, listing all the ways 'we're going to do this thing right.' Except... what's that he's saying? No nookie, not till I turn sixteen! Jeez it's going to be a loooong few months till my birthday.

18

MUM, MEET MY MAN

We're outside Mum's ward. Got here far too early and we now have to hang about till visiting starts. Chris has cadged a cigarette off some old bloke in a flat cap. He doesn't usually smoke fags, but he's finding the spliff habit hard to quit. He lights the ciggie and draws in a lungful of smoke, then he spits it back out in disgust. He stares at the tip and says, "Rubbish. Absolute rubbish," before throwing it in a bush.

I'm a complete bundle of nerves. I really hope Chris is right about telling Mum the truth. I mean, what if the shock of it all sends her psychotic again? She's just getting her head back together; surely this is cruel? And what if she reports Chris to the police, or calls social services? Chris, though, is really chilled. "Your mum won't call anyone," he says, with absolute certainty.

"How can you be so sure? She might ship me off to Dubai or ban us from seeing each other."

Chris kisses the top of my head. "She won't do that," he mumbles through a mouthful of hair.

I take a step back and stare into his eyes. He isn't bullshitting. He is absolutely sure of himself. "I just don't get how you can be so certain."

"Think about it, Jess. Your mum's all alone, she won't want you thousands of miles away. You're all she's got. And as for me, well, she'll simply be sucked in by my charm."

I whack his arm. "Seriously?"

"Well, that and the fact she'll be so relieved you've got someone looking out for you. Believe me, Jess, she's been imagining all sorts of sordid scenarios – like you getting off with a crack-addled punk or doing your favourite teacher. You might think she doesn't worry, but she does. She'll be so pleased by how normal I am, she'll give us her blessing, you'll see. "

I laugh then and Chris gives me this really quizzical look. "What's so funny?"

"Well… it's just, for someone who says 'Psychology's for thickos,' you're really rather good at it."

"Huh… Yeah, maybe I am." And Chris looks rather pleased at that.

We find Mum sitting at a table in the visitor's area. She doesn't usually sit here. Maybe it's a sign. Cos it's a good place to have this talk – better than perching on her bed or shouting above the din in the day room. She looks at Chris with interest, but I can't read her face.

"Mum. This is my boyfriend, Chris." She stands up and shakes his hand. What a peculiar, formal little scene.

"Pleased to meet you, Mrs Brody. I just want you to know that I love your daughter and I'm being a perfect gent. She's in good hands with me." Chris sounds so posh and old fashioned that Mum looks amused.

"Er… that's good to know," she says.

"Anyway, Jess wants to talk to you. So I'm going to slope off for a bit. See if I can find us a pot of tea, eh?"

"What? You're not going are you?" He didn't mention sloping off to me. I thought he'd be here to hold my hand. Traitor.

"Just for a bit. You two need to be alone."

Mum's looking a bit anxious. She can tell that something's up, so I'd better get stuck in. Put her out her misery. Or not. Cos what I'm about to say might be far worse than what she's imagining.

So I tell her all about Ollie going off. That I've been living alone. I tell her about Hannah Walters and the meeting. I even tell her about Chris's drug habit. I tell her the whole damn lot. By the time I'm done her face and mine are wet with tears and we're clutching hands across the table.

"I think I knew really." She smears snot onto her shoulder and sniffs. "I… I…" She stares at our interlocked fingers, unsure how to go on.

Wait a minute. She knew? What did she know? That I was living alone? But then… why the hell wouldn't she do something about it? She doesn't care, does she? She doesn't give a crap about me. I snatch back my hands and bury them deep between my thighs. She has officially lost the right to hold them. "Do you know something, Mum, I've been absolutely dreading this – the day you found out, because I was terrified the shock of it might make you mental again. I thought you would shout at me, hit me… something, anything. But you don't care, do you? All you care about is Gran. You don't love me."

"Oh Jess," she winces, still staring at her empty palms. "You really think I don't love you?"

"Well you've got a funny way of showing it."

She looks at me. "You've been honest with me Jess and I want to be honest with you. Really, I do. But…" her voice falters.

"But what?" I prompt, getting impatient.

"Well, the truth isn't always easy to hear. Especially for someone so young."

"Well, now you've got me imagining all sorts, so you're going to have to spit it out. If you don't love me, just say so, at least we'll both know where we stand."

She nods. "Okay," She stares off into the distance, trying to collect her thoughts. I know how muddled her brain still is so I try to give her time, when all I really want to do is bang on the table and demand she damn well get on with it. "Right," she begins at last, frowning with concentration. "So I've never found it easy being a mum and that's got nothing to do with you or Ollie, Jess, it's me. I found all the noise and demands… well, draining, if I'm honest. I would look at other mums and wish I could be like them, but I always felt… oh, I don't know, inadequate, I suppose. And restless. So there's been times over the years when I got depressed and then I would go on anti-depressants…"

"Really?" I did not know that.

She nods. "They helped. They made me less sad, less scared. But they numbed me, Jess. I might not have felt depressed anymore, but I didn't feel happy either. I didn't feel anything – no love, no joy, nothing. So I know sometimes I might have seemed cold or uninterested. I could see I was hurting you, but it was like I was looking at you from a distance. Do you understand?" She leans forward, her eyes imploring, scanning mine for a hint of recognition. I don't know what she finds there cos she suddenly flops back in her chair sighing. I can't think what to say, so I just gaze into my lap waiting for her to go on.

She says nothing for a bit and I'm about to get up and go, when she says, "This time I welcomed the numbness,

Jess. In fact I embraced it. You can't imagine the fear, when you think there's evil inside you, because there's no escape. Nowhere to hide. It follows you everywhere. Do you get that?"

"Yes." I think I do.

"I know I didn't want to come here but in the end it was a relief. They pumped me full of so many drugs that though I could still feel him in me, I no longer felt scared. I've been walking round in a daze I didn't want to wake from. And you threatened that, Jess…"

"What?" Of all the cheek. I feel like storming off, I really do. After all I've done for her. I scrape back my chair.

"Oh, don't go twisting things. I can't…" she looks at me helplessly, unable to complete the thought. I get it, though. She can't cope with my moods. I'm not allowed to strop off because that's just the kind of draining, childish behaviour that put her here in the first place. Is this how it's gonna be from now on? Me tiptoeing around her, not permitted to express my feelings? Anyway, I call off the strop and sit quietly.

"Thank you, darling. I know you're upset, but all I'm trying to say is that you've been so good, coming to visit me every day. And I haven't been grateful, not because I don't love you but because every time you walked through that door you brought with you so much baggage I wanted to hide from. Reality – it's been just below the surface here." She raises both hands to the sides of her head and suddenly her face scrunches up in distress. Uh-oh, is she going to lose it? Her hands hover for a moment then drop to the table and her face gets that blank look again. "I pushed away all those worries about what you were eating, what you were living on. Whenever they bubbled up, I just buried them deeper. I'm not fit to be your mother,

Jess, but I do love you. You do believe me don't you?"

I nod cos I'm way too upset to speak. It kinda helps though – having the drugs to blame. I mean, now I can tell myself it's not me that's unlovable; it's just the drugs that stop her loving me. Of course, actually believing it is another thing entirely. But who knows, maybe one day she can come off the pills and we'll have the kind of relationship Amy and her mum have. But then... that won't work now either. I can't go back to being her little girl again. I can't have her telling me to do my homework or be home by ten. It would just be... well, false, I suppose.

"Do you think you can ever forgive me?" she whispers breathlessly, looking absolutely petrified of the answer.

"Yes." I say it before I think it through. But is it true? Can I forgive her? To be honest, I really don't know, but I don't say that, just nod my head and start to cry.

Here comes Chris with a big, goofy grin and an armful of chocolate. He must have emptied that vending machine. He sits down next to me, rips open a packet and pops a Malteser in my mouth. And the look he gives me is so tender and so full of love that I feel the tears start to spill again, not cos I'm unhappy, but because I finally have someone to look at me that way. Mum stares across at us and smiles. "You look good together," she says. "I'm glad she has you, Chris. Just stay off the drugs, okay? Look after my little girl."

"I swear, Mrs Brody. No more spliffs for me. I am a new man. I might take up jogging."

Mum laughs and we sit there sucking on chocolate. We have a long way to go, me and Mum, but it's nice to be free of the lies. It feels like a weight has been lifted and I think she feels it too, that something has shifted. Who knows? Maybe this is our new beginning.

19

HOME SWEET HOME

Mum's home now, just for the weekend, though. She'll go back to hospital on Monday, thank god. It's been nice to have her here, but it will be even nicer to send her back again. She's got on my nerves something chronic and we've argued quite a bit, which we never did before. I guess it'll take time to get used to each other again, but I just keep thinking, what right has she to tell me what to do? I mean she was barely in the door before she was like, "Oh, Ollie's back on Tuesday. Where's Chris going to sleep?" At first I didn't get it, then I realised she thought Chris was sleeping in Ollie's room and I said "Chris sleeps with me." Well, she was all shocked and went, "I don't think that's a good idea, Jess." So I was like, "Well it's a bit bloody late now." Chris had to come calm it all down.

And the talking! She won't bloody shut up. It's like she's making up for all those months of silence by just gibbering on until it feels like my ears are bleeding. On and on and on, talk, talk, talk; I almost wish she were a Zombie again. I think that's the really hard part – that she's bounced from one extreme to the other and neither of those extremes is anything like my mum. I don't recognise her; in fact she's so different, it's freaky. Like a stranger's moved in.

Anyway, I'm whinging on, but actually things are good. Mum's on the mend, I've got Chris, school's okay. Hannah Walters steers well clear. She scowls over every now and then, but for the most part she's gone back to harassing Fat Britney. I know I should defend poor Britney, try to befriend her now I know what it's like on the receiving end. But I'm exhausted; I don't have the energy for any more aggro. I suppose that's how witches like Hannah always get away with it.

And we've put the house on the market. Mum doesn't want to move from the area; we just need somewhere smaller so we can release a bit of cash to live on for a while. And actually most of the neighbours have been okay. A lot of them have popped in. Old Clarkey even sent round a casserole, which I thanked her for, then tossed straight in the bin. Still, if I were Mum I wouldn't want to stay round here, not now everyone knows. But she says she's got nothing to be ashamed of and has no intention of running away. I kinda respect her for that, I think.

Anyway, I gotta go. We're going out for lunch with Meredith and her mum. I've no idea if the two old girls are going to get along, but I think Mrs Baker might be really good for Mum. She's so capable and calm and knows such a lot about mental illness. Amy and her mum are coming too, so Chris isn't invited. It's still a bit awkward there... well, you know.

Oh. There's the door. I peer out my bedroom window and there stands Meredith in her combat jacket and Doc Marten boots. I chap on the window, and she looks up. She sees me and gives this enormous toothy smile. Who knew that face could do anything but snarl? And here comes Amy too, tottering up the drive in a towering pair of wedges. Meredith looks at her and rolls her eyes, but in an indulgent kind of way. "Just a sec," I mouth and grab my coat. Man, I'm starving; I hope we're getting chips.

The End

ACKNOWLEDGEMENTS

Thanks to Alan, for all his enthusiasm and encouragement. And to Kim Honor for her grammatical expertise and proofreading skills. Thanks also to Louise Gillett, for her insight and advice. And to Briony at Goldust Design for the brilliant layout and cover design.